SEA
stacks

SEA *Stacks*

THE COLLECTED STORIES OF

J. L. Hagen

Keypounder Books

2020

Fennville, Michigan

COPYRIGHT

For information, address Keypounder Books, 2127 Lakeshore Drive, Fennville MI 49408.

FIRST EDITION

Library of Congress Cataloging-in-Publication Data has been applied for.

ISBN: 978-1-7363257-0-4

Original Cover Photos: Huron Shores Photography
                          Anatoliy Gleb

DEDICATION

For my father, Warren Hagen, who died Christmas Day thirty-nine years ago, having read only one of my stories.

Dad, here are the best of the rest.

CONTENTS

PREFACE

In the late 1960s, when I started to write in high school and aspired to make a living as a novelist, it never dawned on me that half a century would pass before I could realize a smidgeon of this dream. It seems like only yesterday that I penned my first story, but my hunger has never faded for seeing my name in print, however modest that success might be.

As I worked around the country in a demanding professional career and, with my wife, raised a family, I found time here and there to compose stories, poems, dramas, and songs—usually late at night—but only infrequently was I able to find—or even search for—a creative outlet for my work.

Now that I have retired, I am racing to catch up to my aspirations. The stories that follow span fifty years of labor, starting in 1970 when I first published a story in a student literary journal of the University of Michigan. Ironically, I find that the more I write, the more I learn how little I know about writing. The upside is that my writing has improved more in the past five years than in the previous forty-five. So, perhaps, it's time—if not past time—to let go this volume and move on. I hope you enjoy reading it as much as I enjoyed its creation.

—*J. L. Hagen*
Fennville, Michigan
Thanksgiving (26 November 2020)

ACKNOWLEDGEMENTS

I wish to acknowledge the numerous people who have made this work possible.

First, my creative writing professors at the University of Michigan Residential College and School of Literature, Science, and Arts, Warren Jay Hecht and John W. Aldridge, and my creative writing professor at the University of Chicago, Richard G. Stern, who shaped my early prose and literary aspirations.

More recently, writers' groups in Kalamazoo, Michigan, Grand Rapids, Michigan, Tampa, Florida, and New Port Richey, Florida, have been extremely helpful in critiquing this manuscript and other works in progress.

Dan Maddaj, editor of the RC Alumni Journal, was also supportive, and published two of my stories.

Finally, my family—in particular, my sons, Peter and Andrew—read and commented on several stories. My niece Jennifer McGraw and husband Chris were insightful regarding current Michigan hunting practices. And my wife Joy provided considerable insight into psychology and character development.

Nevertheless, any errors, faults, or lapses within the book are entirely mine alone.

INTRODUCTION

In the beginning it all belonged to the Anishinaabe—the two expansive lakes; the tips of the two peninsulas that almost touched, like the hand of man and the finger of God, separated by a mighty straits which held them apart; the islands sprinkled across them, especially the one that resembled a large turtle; the blackened heavens at night with their blue-white stars and gaseous green northern lights; and, most of all, the sea stacks, pillars formed over eons from crushed and reformed breccia limestone, that jutted from the sandy shores, where the inhabitants could sit and contemplate all that was in their dominion and marvel at its vast verdant forests, crystal cobalt waters, and milky sky above. The greatest of these pillars was the one named for Manabozho—the Great Hare—from which the land derived its unspoken name.

This was the world that Jacques Marquette, Jesuit priest and explorer, encountered as he and his small band of voyageurs paddled up the St. Lawrence river from the frontier town of Montreal in the year 1671. And there he—Père Marquette—established a mission in the name of the founder of his religious order, St. Ignatius de Loyola, to bring enlightenment and the benefits of French civilization to the inhabitants, in exchange for their fealty to Church and Crown and, eventually, the furs that became so highly prized in Paris and other bastions of Europe.

Over time, the mission became a village, whose name was shortened to Loyola. The native people had long held their own name, but if their French visitors wished to translate it into their own tongue, they accepted it in the spirit of mutual respect and comity.

When the British arrived, along with their American

colonists, and thereafter drove out the French, to whom the inhabitants had allied themselves, they bowed to necessity and adapted to a new Monarch. With the British troops, came new traders and residents, but also a new Church, one which could not accept a village in its jurisdiction named for a saint of its chief religious and political rival. So, the inhabitants adapted to a new name for their community—Loyale—as one more alliteration of their underlying reality.

And when the colonists finally tired of the extractions and exacerbations of their British cousins and sent them packing, the inhabitants adjusted once again to the dictates of the times. They swore their allegiance beneath the cannons of a new fort which had been constructed to overlook the Straits. Although some of the more vocal of the new inhabitants were inclined to modernize the appellation of their adopted community, in the end, it remained as it had always been—or not—Loyale.

The stories that follow, though entirely works of fiction born of the author's imagination, pay homage—each in its own way—to the land and the people who have called this place—for a brief time or forever—their own.

SEA *stacks*

JENSEN'S BARN

They built the barn that spring, the year he was born. Soon after, the last snows melted into rivulets and streamed through rivers and creeks into Lake Huron. Only then was the weather fair enough. With conditions right, they could put in full days. His mother told him, so its actual happening seemed part of his own memory, so many years past .

He sat at the table eating the pie she baked, while she shuffled around the kitchen cleaning the stove, muttering and fussing as she often did. She turned and said, "Arley, do you remember the day you were born?"

He looked up, blinking, his face covered with blueberries and bewilderment.

"No, ma'am."

"Well, I do," she stated, looking at him over the blade of a carving knife she held. "It was a warm day, Arley, such a warm day." Her eyes and voice softened. "And the day I brought you home, we bumped along the street in the old Ford, one side of the road to the other, dodging potholes, me trying to keep you from getting jostled—being my first, you know." Her smile grew wider. "Came 'round the corner and beneath the maple tree . . . I saw it." She gazed at the wall behind him. "They finished while I was in the hospital. As we drove closer, I thought, 'what a good day . . . a *very* good day.'"

She gave him one of those big, soft, motherly hugs. He shrugged it off and ran out the screen door to play.

❅ ❅ ❅

Now, sixty years later, his mother had been proven right. It was awe-inspiring, a monument for Ojibwa County and still special to the neighbors and other residents. Made of white pine and oak from the mill, the beams were fitted with a

3

cabinet maker's care, fastened in the old way with wooden pegs, siding laid on with iron spikes and painted a deep cherry red.

If nothing else, his father could rightfully claim his skill as a master carpenter.

Yet when he was a kid not older than twenty, it nearly burned to the stone foundation. A serious blaze set one night in July by an angry farmhand, Vernon Paquette. Paquette worked hard, but any form of alcohol made him a mean drunk. Fired from his job, he blew his top and went on a bender.

A neighbor saw him behind the liquor store in Loyale, staggering toward his pickup, sack in hand with a quart of whiskey. The neighbor told Arley's father that he confronted him.

"Whatcha doing, Vern?" he called out.

"Nothin', nothin' *to* do. Leave me alone."

"Sure you're good to drive? I'll drop you somewhere. I'm going right by Jensen's farm—"

"Look, take care of your own business," Vern snapped. "That's the last goddamn place I'd go—that sonofabitch canned me yesterday."

"Terrible, Vern. What's his beef?"

"Claimed I spilled a bunch of kerosene in the feed. I told him it wasn't me, then he calls me a liar, says he's got a witness."

"A witness? Who?"

"'Never mind, it's confidential,' he says. Confidential, my ass. He didn't even give me my wage for the week. He's gonna pay me, and *then some.*"

Right after that, Vern laid a torch to the barn. The weather was warm, dry—why it almost burned down. The building— everything in the county—was combustible as a box of stove matches. It blazed hot as a pine knot. Without the swift response of good neighbors, it would have collapsed in a mound of smoking cinders and rusty nails.

He himself didn't fight the fire . . . it was Friday. He foolishly paid a visit to a neighbor girl, Vonnie Morris.

Vonnie and he were friends before kindergarten. As little kids, they played together. She was three years younger and always shy. He loved to tease her and incite a response, even if she only yelled at him.

Something happened in high school. He invited her to ride horses. Vonnie declined to go on a regular date—with him or anyone—but during their rides became more amenable to his company, although they didn't talk much. On the first occasion he tried to kiss her, she resisted, but he noticed after that, she wore nicer clothes and make-up whenever they met. He persisted and, in time, she submitted. He began to meet her more often, but never in public circumstances.

On that Friday afternoon, they were away riding horses together. They stopped to water them—it was very warm— and to pick wild strawberries that grew in the high meadow. The berries, red as blood, hung ripe beneath tiny plants, delicate and no larger than a fingertip. They tasted honey-sweet.

He and Vonnie roamed through the tall grass picking them, fragrant juice dripping wet and syrupy from their fingers, lips, and clothes.

Across the elevated pasture, they sauntered . . . separated first, then joining, her hand in his. They gazed down the hill over the little shingled rooftops of a half dozen farms, then out to the limestone sea stack overlooking Lake Huron and from there to the horizon. The land and water formed a continuous flow from where he lay with her on the meadow. It stretched forever.

The evening air felt warm, sweltering—every breath seemed to singe his lungs, making it hard to breathe—her skin glowing

5

with perspiration. They rested there, bodies rosy white, entwined amongst the parched grasses, embracing, gazing at one another and the countryside, desiring to move; daring not. Her breasts were snow white as trillium, tips small and red, like the wild strawberries. Dead still, the air was charged, around them no birds, no breeze, no insects. He sensed a surging electricity, a hundred possibilities primed to explode. Then he saw it.

"Oh, my god." He pointed toward the barn.

Far below, tiny orange lights flickered up the walls. Larger, higher, they grew. He froze, not wanting to go, but knowing he should do more than watch. Then, he heard distant shouting and saw people scramble from every direction. Cars and trucks raced up the road, raising snakes of dust. Neighbors ran toward the fire with buckets and hoses; others jerked screeching animals from the burning building. Into the descending night air and through the hills poured clatter and turmoil with the thick black smoke.

On the meadow, everything remained pastoral, serene. He pulled himself up to stand.

Vonnie touched his arm. "Stay," she whispered.

He lay back beside her, small, soft, tender. He kissed her, then again, deeply, held her close. Their bodies melted into one. Only their eyes showed movement as red and yellow light danced across them.

❋   ❋   ❋

Now, a far cry from that sultry night, decades had passed since he was a foolish boy, since he knew the girl. The air is becoming cooler, days shorter and nights longer, too long. After the chaos, nothing came of it. Everything was changed by it.

He sees the old barn through the kitchen window. It is not so bright anymore, grows ever more silver, sags and bulges, still useful but no longer new, seeming to move in a different direction. Or no direction. The roof leaks in the corner, the timbers grow weak, but will endure a few years more. The chill affects him more, and heat from the range comforts this time of year. Outside, the hardwoods display their last colors; rouges and ochres, burnt oranges, flaming scarlets; brown. Even now the maple leaves break off and tumble.

One or two hit and stick to the pane; In their turn, they will fall too. Autumn has a haunting splendor—a last salute to a veteran lowered to his grave. The flag covering his coffin, presented to his widow. The brass notes that send him on his final journey.

He turns from the window, and a moment later stands beneath the maple. Leaves float around him, confetti in a silent parade. Across the yard, he shuffles through those fallen and unlatches the rusty bolt. It is dark inside, but warm and sheltering from the cutting wind.

The barn is empty except for a few tools, idled for many years, yet the sweet dry smell of hay and fertilizer permeates the air—and leather. He sits on an old white kitchen chair, the back long broken away and trimmed flush with the seat, his eyes soon accustomed to the dim light. He looks around the whitewashed stalls, the half-timbers to the loft, and the rough-sawed lumber that are the sides. Even now he can see the char marks where the fire burned. His father built it rock-solid, an enduring piece of work, still tight, even though . . . He shakes his head. The scars of memory have not waned.

Soon, the leaves will turn. The weather will grow colder, and the trees will lose their leaves. Buried under a yard of snow, they will become part of the earth again. The color will be gone. The last fruit of summer will be taken from the freezer, thawed, and eaten. None left by first snowfall, or Christmas. The ground will turn to ice, harder than these timbers when hewn. Winter will shroud the land in white, lay its mantle over the house, woods, the meadow, the water, and him too. *Perhaps.*

And the barn? It might stand through another winter. And the winter after that. But a day would come when he would fail once more to be there. This time, not his fault. If only he had been less selfish, not so… absorbed in himself. He saw now he desired, but never loved the girl—Vonnie—not as Paquette did. It was no reason to set him up, have him fired. After the barn burned, the judge sent him to prison in Marquette. A few months later, an envelope appeared on the kitchen table—a notice from the draft board. When he returned from the war, she had moved away to the city. Everyone paid a price.

Was that the sum of what he could resolve? Too late to mend. Now the barn was timeworn, derelict. Now they were no longer at the start of matters. Why did everything have to grow old?

He rises stiffly from the backless chair, arranging it in front of the stall, setting it in place. He hobbles to the door, pushes it open. A handful of brown leaves rustle onto the planked floor. He turns, glances at the stalls, up the timbers to the burn-scarred plank siding. He pulls the door shut behind him and refastens the rusty latch. He shuffles to the house through the dead leaves. He shudders; it is icy cold

PINBALL EINSTEIN

M e and Lanny McCall was best friends. We used to call him Peanut, me and Obi. He had this weird-shaped head, like a jumbo beer bottle, only turned upside down. Thinking on it now, it didn't look like no peanut, but back then seemed like it did, so that's what me and Obi called him. After a while, the name stuck.

I first run into him one day in the neighborhood with Obi, or at least that's when I started hanging with him. He was maybe four grades ahead of me. I always saw him around and everything, but Obi knew us both, so that's how we connected. Afterwards, he told me that Peanut loved to play pinball—and owned a monster stack of comics. That caught my attention. I went ape shit for comic books.

A few days later, me and Obi walked over to Peanut's house, which was up the block, one of them two-story, brown, asphalt-shingle houses with a gravel driveway. The front storm door didn't have no bottom glass and always hung open, swinging like a broken gate. We climbed up the cement steps and Obi knocked.

Old Lady McCall never come to the door. She yelled, "Com'on in."

At first, we hesitated. Obi gave a push, and we crept in the darkened room. Old Lady McCall sat on the davenport with her back to us, watching tv. She had scotch-taped a sheet of blue plastic over the screen, which made it like color tv. At least how I thought color tv looked. A hand sticking out of the sleeve of a purple housedress pointed up the stairway through a cloud of cigarette smoke.

"Lanny's upstairs," she said.

Obi wheeled around and I followed him up the worn wooden steps. He opened the bedroom door and the stench of sweat and old laundry filled up my nose. Over in the corner, Peanut stood, lifting weights in a undershirt, the same yellow undershirt he used to wear, I swear, every day I ever seen him. Obi flopped down on the mattress by the door, but I hung in the entry, leaning on the jamb.

Obi propped his self up on his elbow. "Going down to Sherry's to shoot some ball?" he asked.

I didn't know nothing about Sherry's, except that my old lady told me to "stay outta there." I thought they was talking about basketball or something.

"Sure," Peanut said. He lowered the weights and huffed out a long breath. "Gimme a sec." He noticed me peeking around the doorway. "Hey, I seen you before. You're Tommy, ain't ya?"

"Yeah," I muttered, half-startled. "I been around," I added, even though I hadn't.

"Play pinball?"

"Nope, don't care for nothing but hoops."

"Hell, Obi, we gotta show your pal here what he's missing." He jerked the bar up chest-high, sucked in his breath, and crammed the weight over his head. It crashed down on the linoleum.

Old Lady McCall's voice thundered up the stairwell. "Damn it, Lanny, stop dropping them weights. You'll wake your pa up. How many times I have to tell ya!"

"Sorry, Ma!" Peanut shouted. He wiped off his forehead with the side of his undershirt, leaving a streak above his wispy eyebrows. He spat toward the corner. "Com'on, let's go . . ."

We walked down Sea Stack Hill to Sherry's, a coffee shop on the south end of Main across from the Coal Dock. When Obi pushed open the big green front door, the smell of donut grease and Pine-Sol hit us like a wave. Inside, we squeezed between the lunch counter and grill on one wall and four booths along the other, toward a pinball machine in the back. Overhead, a high tin ceiling with a bunch of globe lights hanging from chains cast a dim glow.

Peanut tossed down a buck, and Sherry give him a handful of nickels. He scraped them off the faded red countertop and swaggered over to the machine, the Dancing Dolls model. The cheesy-looking girls on the back glass caught my attention. They was wearing these orange and yellow bathing suits and high heels. They giggled and frolicked back and forth in the spotlights, toying with us.

Peanut reached up and touched the one dressed like a cigarette girl—for luck. He dropped a nickel in the slot. The machine lit up big as a carnival. He spaced his feet just right, pulled his jeans up, wiped his hands along his thighs, and gave the flippers a practice snap. With an open palm, he rammed a ball up from the trough into shooting position. He dragged the plunger past some mark only he could feel and let fly. The chrome ball arced out of the chute to the top of the playfield. He shuddered—it was all action.

The ball hammered back and forth between the bumpers. Peanut bumped on the edge of the machine with his left hand. In a silver streak, it whizzed through a lane down to his right flipper, up to a kick-out hole, back to a flipper, up against targets. *Chunk-chunk-ka-chunk.* Bells rang like fire alarms. The lights pulsed and strobed. The little ball twirled and danced, caught in a web hand-spun by Peanut and the machine.

Time and time again, he flipped it upward in a blur, until the scoreboard rolled all the way around to zero. The lights flashed; the sound blared; the girls on the upright flickered and laughed. *Pop-pop-pop*—the machine showed a bunch of free games. Peanut wiped his forehead. I looked over and Obi's eyes looked big as lightbulbs.

"That's the best you done!"

"Yeah, I think I even surprised *myself*. You gotta treat the machine right, just treat her right." He glanced at me. "Take one?"

"N-no," I stammered. "I only wanna sit here and watch. Besides, I don't feel like it . . . anyway."

Peanut checked the counter, which showed ten free games. He shrugged, pressed the replay button. Obi knew how bad I wanted to be that good, not at pinball, but anything, and mostly basketball. He didn't say nothing. They played darn near all afternoon, and I studied on them. We was all drinking Pepsis. Obi popped a few games, but mainly he gave up the ones that Peanut won.

It was like watching a championship fighter, Sugar Ray or Muhammad Ali. He bobbed and weaved, rolled with the shots, and right when the ball lost its punch, he caught and threw it with a flipper back into play. Him and the ball was the same.

Right there, I turned into his number one fan. I didn't have nothing going that summer, so after breakfast, I shot hoops in the driveway. Peanut got up early to help his old man pick leaches. They had a sweet little fish bait business, and Peanut was regularly carrying money in his pocket. One time he told me he expected to make about six hundred. So, mornings I passed my time shooting around. I was getting so I couldn't miss.

When the noon church bells rang, I would grab me a quick sandwich. Out the back, I'd go before my old lady roped me into some chores. I'd haul ass over to Peanut's house. We would hustle down to Sherry's and run through the nickels and dimes routine. I'd buy me and him a Pepsi each and sit down to see him play. He would take a sip and set the bottle next to him on the table. Throw me a glance with them watery green eyes, then a quick nod. Even though I never played the game once, he always made it seem like me and him was in it together.

He would say, "Tommy, we *got* to get five thousand points on this ball." And sure enough, we would bag them. Over time, he built up a real philosophy, and I caught little snatches.

Peanut's home life, same as me and Obi, weren't much, and I guess his true world was the machine. It was how he escaped from his old lady, who never done nothing but sit in front of her color tv. Peanut's old man slept most days on account of he worked the graveyard on the Soo Line. He weren't generally about, excepting when they picked bait in the summer. So, Peanut wrapped his life around pinball.

Nobody could touch him. He was the greatest pinball player I ever seen, even if he had nothing to show when it come to something else. A hundred times I watched him stand over that machine with his scroungy undershirt on, sweet-talking the ball against one or another of Gottlieb's finest bumpers, working, working for every last point.

More than once, he said, "This here's a machine—like any other. They always work the same, got their own rules." He said, "You gotta play by them rules, roll with the bad balls right down the gobble hole, and make them good balls count. Only thing you can do—stay *loose*."

He'd take a sip on his Pepsi. "If you get mad and act rough, ain't nothing going to happen but a tilt on you. Just a game like anything else. If you work yourself up, the machine's gonna whip you while you're thinking how to get even, instead of how you're gonna whip *the machine*. It don't never vary. Always uses your feelings to beat yourself, so you gotta do the same and keep your cool."

That stuck with me good. I'd sit there listening while them lights flashed and Peanut talked about pinball and gave little extra nudges and bumps here and there—and the score counter spun round and round. I seen plenty of players since that time, but none of them ever gave the game or the machine the same pure love or respect. That was the thing about Peanut. He was some kind of genius—a pinball Einstein.

That's what finally nailed him.

❋ ❋ ❋

One day late in August, me and Obi hiked over to find him and ask if he wanted to walk down to Sherry's. I almost didn't make it. My old lady was dead set against me hanging around him. And like I mentioned, the last place she wanted me was down at Sherry's. But I grabbed Obi, and we snuck over to hunt him up.

The whole day was crazy strange 'cause everything seemed to happen just like that first day I seen him play.

We jumped the porch steps, and the storm door was banging against the shingles, bottom window still out. I thumped on the inside door and waited for Old Lady McCall to yell from the living room.

She glanced over her shoulder as we entered. "He's in his room."

We ran up the same worn stairs and opened the grimy white door. Peanut stood there, pumping the bar. I can't help thinking how little good that weightlifting done. As he huffed and puffed away, me and Obi sacked out on the dingy mattress with a comic book.

He had one of the lousiest builds I ever seen. He looked like them guys you might kick sand in their face. Maybe that's why he worked so hard, to be that Charles Atlas guy in the comics ads. Finally, he stopped lifting and let the weights crash on the linoleum.

He wiped the edge of his undershirt across his forehead. "Where you been lately?"

Obi glanced at me to answer.

"Painting the house with my old man."

"Fun, ain't it?" he said, reading my thoughts. "Whatcha say

we go to Sherry's and shoot a few."

I didn't have no chance to respond before we headed down the stairs. We made a quick ramble, and all the way I could see us there in the corner—just me, Obi, and Peanut, and the machine—winning away and sipping Pepsis. We opened the green door and a couple of flies buzzed off into the sunlight.

"Hey, somebody's playing already," Obi whined.

Me and Peanut turned to where he pointed. Peanut wiped his mouth on the shoulder of his undershirt and stepped over to the flashing machine. Three high school guys was standing next to it, smoking cigarettes. They was watching a fat kid in a leather jacket with long hair combed back in a duck-ass.

As Peanut walked by him, he glanced around. "Fuckin' machine," he swore. "Damn thing's rigged."

Peanut didn't say nothing, just scowled.

I brought over some Pepsis and set them on the table. I peered down past the fat kid's boots right as Obi said, 'Hey, they put ashtrays under the front legs."

"Big deal department, Geronimo," he sneered. "Only way you can beat this fuckin' thing."

"You're cheatin'!" I said. It never struck me someone could do that. He give the machine a kick that would have cracked the leg if it weren't metal.

"Hey, cut it out," Peanut said.

"Fuck off, pal. It's only a shit-ass pinball—and I own it." He gestured with his thumb toward his chest to prove his point. His three sidekicks stood up straight and glared at us.

Peanut's eyes grew more waterier. He wiped his mouth again on his undershirt. The fat kid turned around and gave the machine another kick, only harder. It tilted.

"You goddamn moldy whore!" he screamed.

"Cut that out!" shouted Peanut.

The fat kid grabbed hold of the machine, slammed it down.

Peanut grabbed hold of him.

The kid gritted his teeth. "I said fuck off—jackass!"

Two of his wormy-looking friends jumped Peanut and shoved him towards the table. He tumbled into Obi. I didn't know what to do, excepting duck. Sherry yelled at them. Nobody heard her but me.

Peanut whirled around. Tears rolled down his long, pockmarked face. I wanted him to show them bastards so hard. His chin kind of puckered up. His mouth quivered. He snatched my Pepsi off the table and hurled the bottle straight at the fat kid. They all dodged. The bottle glanced off the kid's head and ricocheted into the scoreboard glass. It exploded, shattering all over the room. The machine started to make a racket. The lights flashed over and over. A stream of blood dripped down the kid's face.

His three pals grabbed Peanut. They commenced to wail on him. Punched and kicked him. The fat kid beat him with an ashtray. Sherry yelled again. They kept hitting him. She picked up the phone and shouted, "Stop it, I'm calling the City Police."

They started running out the back, and Peanut slumped to the floor, pale as moonlight. Blood spilled out his nose. He spat, and a bloody tooth skittered across the floor. Obi started to bawl. I felt queasy and hollow. Cops from all over come flying in the door.

I never did figure why he took them on that way. He could have whipped them any time on the machine. That night when I went to bed, I cried for hours, with a pillow pulled over top of my head, and I hardly never done that.

The next week, the cops nabbed Peanut to go see the judge. My old lady made me promise not to hang around with him no more. Before I realized, school started up, and I was hard on it, so I didn't have no extra time anyway.

One day I managed to sneak over to his house. I scrambled

up the steps and knocked on the door. Old Lady McCall yelled, "Com'on in." When I stepped into the room, she was sitting as usual in front of the tv, smoking.

She turned to look over the couch. "You're too late," she said. "Uncle Sam took him in the army last Tuesday." She twisted back around to her program.

This was just before basketball season, so I fell into the dumps. I wanted to prove to him how good I learned. And I learned darn good. I was JV first string, and after a while, I made it up to varsity. But it would have been a whole lot better if we was hanging together like old times.

❊   ❊   ❊

After high school graduation, I couldn't find no job, so I left town to work construction. If I didn't come home for Christmas two years later and seen the Loyale paper, I might never read what happened to him.

The article said they assigned Peanut to the 101st Airborne Division in Quang Tri Province, Vietnam. It stated they destroyed 1,782 enemy in the operation, but only 386 Americans lost their lives. He was one of the last ones. When I finished reading the story, I tried to hold back, but I couldn't help it, I sobbed like a little baby.

On Saturday, Christmas night, I drove to the Sand-Bar with my cousin Ronnie. When we walked in, Obi was leaning on the bar in a army uniform. With his black hair cropped short and bronze skin, he looked real snappy. I almost didn't recognize him.

"Geez, Obi," I said. "I can't believe it, I ain't seen you since high school. Didn't know you joined up."

"Drafted, Tommy," he stated, drawing on a Lucky Strike. "Pulled a trey. One of the first to go."

"Wow, what a bummer."

"Naah, it's okay. But my old man had a heart attack, so they let me come home over the holidays before I ship out."

"How's he doing? I'll bet he was glad to see you."

"Yeah, damn glad. He's out of the hospital but taking it slow. His drinking days is over, which is a plus for everybody—you still swinging a hammer?"

"Unfortunately. I done lucked out, though. Hired on a project for the Navy, so they deferred me—for now. Hey, you read about Peanut?"

"I saw it, but they left out a bunch."

"What's that?"

"A buddy of mine in the military police told me. He heard me and Peanut was both from Loyale and asked if I knew him. Someone he met in the JAG office said Peanut was sent to a village with a pacification team. He was searching a hut and come on two ARVNs. They was ripping this woman's clothes off, trying to bang her. After My Lai, this was like a 'firing squad' offense.

"Peanut ordered them. 'Cut it out!'

"They pointed at her. 'She Cong, she Cong,' they said, laughing.

"Peanut grabbed one guy to pull him off, but the other one started to pound him. The first guy jumped him too. Peanut threw a hail of punches. He dropped one of 'em to the ground and lunged at the other trying to run away. The one in the dirt pulled a knife, reached up, stuck him in the back, then sliced his neck. Peanut slumped over. They both took off running. The woman yelled for his squad, but he bled out before they could medevac him.

"It depressed me to find out. I couldn't make it to his funeral, so I come in here tonight to get shit-faced in his memory."

Me and Ronnie sat with Obi for a few hours talking high school, and Peanut, and his genius at pinball. It was nice to recollect and all, but dismal knowing he was dead.

It's past fifty years now, but a day don't go by I don't think

18

on him. I can still see him standing there, feet spaced just right for balance, slinging them balls into one of Gottlieb's finest, free games popping like machine-gun fire.

Goddamn War.

THE POLAROIDAL MOMENT

A few months after Bill Carlson started work at City Hall, they hired a new secretary, Carol Wojcik, to handle the phones and do the odd bit of typing and filing. She was such a tiny thing, Bill and his boss Herb Vanderwal wondered how she reached the Selectric. But they noticed right off she was a dynamo. She sat on her swivel chair, Cinderella feet perched on a Grand Rapids phone book, and the keys ricocheted like machine gun fire as she banged out report on top of report. After working awhile, her face flushed—a wisp of hair falling over her gray-green eyes, which she blew into place with a little puff aimed from the corner of her mouth—and a smattering of mascara from her thick eyelashes flaked across the tops of her rosy cheekbones. She reminded Bill of one of his mother's prized antique china dolls.

Herb and Bill agreed there was something fascinating about her. Her gentle sense of humor, warm personality, and down-to-earth intellect captivated them. When she spoke to Bill over top of their cubicles, Herb often cocked an ear to eavesdrop, listening to her voice and faint traces of her European heritage. And when Herb walked her through the office manual, Bill inserted himself into the orientation with comments and practical tips. Bill and she were co-workers—Herb was older and the boss—so they especially hit it off.

At lunchtime, Herb and Bill had a habit of walking to the old Pantlind Hotel, whose basement back in 1977 was an inexpensive cafeteria. But on this day, Bill invited Carol out to lunch, instead, to get to know her better. Shortly after noon, they found a window table at a trendy café on Monroe. After Carol ordered a small chef's salad and Bill a cheeseburger, he jumpstarted the conversation.

"So, Carol, Herb and I have a bet going, and I'm hoping you won't cost me a fiver."

She sat up, blinked. "How's that?"

"Well, since you joined the team, we have been puzzling over how you speak."

She cocked her head.

"You know, your speech patterns, your accent."

"Oh, that." She leaned back, laughing. "What accent?"

"Herb's convinced you were raised in Chicago, but I say, no way. You grew up on the west side of GR, in one of the old neighborhoods."

"Okay, I'll tell you, but whoever is wrong has to buy me lunch."

And that's how Bill learned that Carol hadn't been born in the United States. She was orphaned in Poland during the Cold War.

Later, he filled in Herb. ". . . When she said that, I about fell off my chair. According to her, the Russians held the face cards, and nobody had any money, least of all destitute nuns running an orphanage in the countryside. As she described it, Herb, you wouldn't believe her life, six or seven years old and the smallest kid in such a place."

Herb's eyes widened. "I can't imagine."

"Me either, especially when you hear the details. Oh, yeah, before I forget, she says, we each owe her a lunch."

"Say, what?"

Bill chuckled. "After I mentioned the bet, she wouldn't tell me who won until I promised the loser would buy. I didn't think you'd mind. Since neither of us was right, she nicked us both. Pretty slick, eh?"

Bill related the rest of Carol's story…

She recalled that no one's clothes fit; the older kids handed them down as they grew. They got first choice of shoes to wear, too; the lucky ones a rough felt coat or moth-eaten sweater.

"We ate boiled potatoes," she said. She stuck out her tongue. "I hope I never see a potato again, especially for breakfast. I still have nightmares."

"But the worst was burying the bones. They made the little kids help." The color rose in her cheeks as she shuddered to tell it. "Once in a while, the sisters butchered an animal, a pig, maybe an old milk cow. After the meat was cut from the carcass, they cracked the bones and pushed the marrow out with a knife or the handle of a wooden spoon. The left-over pieces were boiled for broth. Of course, they saved the hide and most of the innards," she noted with a casual flip of her hand.

The older boys dug a deep hole back in the field. The big leg hocks, the skull, the vertebrae began their silent march from the kitchen, out the rear door, down the splintered steps, and across the garden. A grim parade of tiny ragamuffins, each peering over a bundle of greasy, broken animal bones stacked like scavenged firewood, trooped to the edge of the pit, let go an armload, and kicked it into the hole.

Once, Carol had tripped and fallen in headfirst. "I was lucky—the bone shards were jagged and icepick sharp. I lay there, my face covered with guck, arms bloody slimy, hands gummed up with grease. My dress ripped through by a piece of horn." Her voice dropped to a whisper. "I thought they might . . . leave me in the hole." One of the boys jumped down, snagged her out—dragging her up, a sack of rags—and handed her over to the nuns.

The punishment for tearing her clothes? A day with no food.

So, when Carol's mom and dad (good Polish Catholics) adopted her and her brother Stephan and brought them to America—to Logansport, Indiana—she believed everything the sisters had said was true. She had experienced it. First, she had lived in purgatory, and now they had flown her to heaven.

"It wasn't easy, you couldn't just leave the country. My parents made connections through the Church. They sent money overseas to pay the sisters and pay off officials needed to authorize the paperwork. It was hush-hush."

Herb and Bill understood how she would be close to her family who, ten or fifteen years earlier, had been nothing more than well-meaning strangers. They also saw how she might be easy prey for someone taking advantage of her.

When Tug Neely showed up one day, Herb and Bill scrutinized every detail of his demeanor. A burly fellow from Battle Creek with a bushy Fu Manchu mustache and freaked-out shoulder-length hair, Tug worked as a toolmaker. His brain, in Herb's words, had been 'wrenched together from the spare parts in an erector set.' He towered over Carol and was habitually two days behind his razor. But, oddly, they appeared to have chemistry, and Herb and Bill came to accept the notion that any harm resulting from their relationship would more likely stem from foolishness than greed or malice.

For close to a year, this escapade intensified, until Carol wondered if Tug wasn't the one with whom she would like to ride into the sunset. As she confessed to Bill, "Tug's driving me crazy. I lay awake again all night. I don't think I slept two hours."

"That doesn't sound good," Bill replied, his brow furrowed. "What's the crisis?"

She giggled, hand over her mouth. "No crisis—well, not the way you're thinking. It's just I'm sure Tug is set to propose. I'm uncertain why, but I can't get it out of my brain."

As Bill told Herb over lunch, "Carol has convinced herself that on Christmas Eve, Tug will give her an engagement ring."

Herb scowled. "I hope he doesn't disappoint her."

"Yeah, me too. Once Carol makes her mind up, her senses

march in lockstep. All it would take from Tug is an odd remark about Christmas presents or a random glance into a jeweler's window."

＊　＊　＊

The gigantic box that appeared under the tree two weeks before Christmas didn't fool Carol. She relished the image of the ring nested in a box nested in another, etc., like Russian Matryoshka dolls. She was awestruck by the picture of Tug wrapping each box, arranging them in a hierarchy on the kitchen counter, then struggling with his large, awkward fingers to place each inside the next until all were tucked into the largest one, where they and their secret waited to be revealed. *He was cagey, that Tug.*

"Carol, you are just going to love what I bought you for Christmas, I can't believe how cool it is," he taunted. "It's unbelievably cool . . . and," he lowered his voice to a near-whisper, "it set me back a fortune."

She smirked, then spoke in a tone of mock puzzlement. "Why Tug, I simply can't imagine what could be in a box that large."

Tug offered another clue. "Here . . . here, lift it." She could scarcely budge it. She thought, *Oh, he's put a brick in there, too, the big devil.*

This banter persisted for a full three weeks. He hinted, cajoled, and postured. She countered with feigned ignorance, frustration, and tempestuousness.

"Tell me tell me tell me," she yammered, stomping her feet.

"Can't do that, Carol," he replied, palm up, directing verbal traffic. And so it continued until the big day.

In Carol's house, they traditionally opened the presents on Christmas Eve. It always began as a merry affair with the children and the relatives, lots to eat and drink, then off to midnight mass. Upon return, coffee was made and another round of Christmas cookies brought forth to the buffet table.

One at a time, the gifts were unwrapped, so everyone could fuss over them. Then Uncle Stanislaus would snap a Polaroid photo and freeze for posterity the truth and pure rapture of the moment. Uncle Stan had amassed over the years a remarkable collection of joyously contorted faces: Aunt Thelma agog at the keys to a shiny black snowmobile; Cousin Roger sighting into the camera through the scope of a new deer rifle; daughter Marcie hugging her polished white go-go boots. And so on. Family members knew it as the *Polaroidal Moment,* that magical instant forever capturing some momentous event on a small glossy rectangular sheet of photograph paper.

So, when Carol moved into her apartment after Herb hired her, she gravitated toward hosting Christmas at her house. She wanted her parents to see she "had made it" and could live on her own. She wanted to create an opportunity for Tug's mom to spend time with her family. She wanted to avoid a conflict with Tug over where they would celebrate Christmas. And since Tug had gone to so much trouble to surprise her with the ring, she wanted to reciprocate by creating the perfect ambiance for this Polaroidal Moment. That settled it— Christmas Eve at her house, and she would invite Tug's mom, too.

❄ ❄ ❄

The next morning when Carol arrived at work, Bill and Herb were already there, discussing a report at Herb's desk. She knocked on his office door frame and excused herself for the interruption.

"I was wondering if I might take off the Friday before Christmas Eve."

Herb drummed his fingers on the desktop.

"The entire day?" He had previously let Bill go since it took a full day's drive north to his family's house in Loyale. He himself planned to leave at noon to complete his gift shopping.

"Well, yeah," she said. "I'm hosting Christmas Eve for my family—and Tug's."

"What about the December expense reports?" he asked, frowning. "We need them for the Controller."

"No problem, Herb. I stayed late and did them yesterday evening. Missing only last-minute stuff. I can handle that on the 26th."

Herb brushed his hand across his forehead, straightening some imaginary out-of-place hair. "Well, it's time to put the January newsletter to bed."

Carol shot a glance in Bill's direction.

"I have that under control, Herb," Bill chipped in.

Herb stared at Bill. "And I suppose the first quarter grant agreements . . .?"

"I'll work twice as hard when I get back," Carol promised. She looked up with her best "little match girl" expression. "I'll come in on my own time if we fall behind."

What could Herb do? He stood there, arms crossed, brow furrowed, lips pursed, as if deciding to buy his wife a new refrigerator. He groaned in resignation. ". . . Oh, all right." So, Carol won the day, and Herb had to crowd his Christmas shopping into that evening.

❋   ❋   ❋

On Friday, Carol was up at 6 a.m. and by 7:30 pushing a grocery cart through Meijers, piling in groceries, pink champagne; at Gordon Food Service, snapping up napkins, paper plates, plastic glasses; at Cousin Marcie's house, picking up the thirty-cup coffee pot. The rest of that day and the following morning, she cleaned the apartment spic-and-span, shopped for a dress, and wrapped presents to place beneath the tree. Christmas Eve afternoon, she slaved in the kitchen making cocktail frankfurters impaled on toothpicks to heat over a Sterno barbecue and cold sliced ham, beet salad, hard rolls, and a relish tray, plus plenty of Polish specialties—

27

Kapusta z Grzybami and Glabki and Kolaczki.

As Carol worked, she murmured a mantra-refrain . . . *night tonight's the night tonight's the night.* She imagined the Polaroid Uncle Stan would take—she panicked. *How will I feign the right expression of surprise?* She rushed to the mirror, dusted the flour smudge which had found its way to the bridge of her nose. She smiled, frowned, wrinkled her brow, opened eyes wide in mock surprise, covered her mouth with her hand—a dozen different masks—until, at last, she discovered the one: anxiety flashing into joy, warmth radiating like sunrise and a whispered, "Oh Tug, it's so . . . " *Nice*—no, she thought, won't do, not strong enough . . . s*o enchanting*—too affected . . . *wonderful*—not intimate enough . . . *gorgeous*—too exuberant . . . *beaut-i-ful*—that might be *it*. She would confirm it later.

❄ ❄ ❄

The guests were soon to arrive. She put on her new dress, a bright red number that highlighted the cream in her complexion. More like gift-wrap, she reflected. A week's wages, the saleswomen loved it on her, how could she resist? She stopped in front of the mirror for a "dress" rehearsal. ". . . *So beaut-i-ful,"* she whispered. *Beautiful.*

Christmas Eve was set to be a marvelous evening. Pale blue stars washed across the heaven. Little paper Santas hung the length of Carol's walls, and she had strung the tree with tiny, twinkling, colored lights, silvery tinsel, and red and gold ornaments. Marcie stood arm-in=arm with her new companion, Frank. Mom peeled potatoes in the kitchen, corseted into her Christmas apron, hair fluffed as cotton candy. Dad sat in the living room, peering over his bifocals at a glass of Seven-and-Seven and conversing with Tug's mom, small and birdlike. She perched next to Uncle Stan. Stan, resplendent in a green-and-red checked sport coat, loaded a cartridge into his Polaroid camera. Various other relatives and friends draped themselves around the apartment like extras at a high school play.

Two drinks later, the party rolled into second gear and picked up velocity. Frank strapped on a large pearl blue accordion and alternated nimbly between Christmas carols and Beatles tunes. Before long, Marcie convinced Aunt Thelma and Mom to sing their traditional duet of "Holly Jolly Christmas." This led to a round of "Rudolf the Red-Nosed Reindeer" with Marcie joining in (who needed the cover of at least three other vocalists). From there, it was an easy rip through the holiday repertoire with everyone singing raucously. Everyone, except the twins. They were on their hands and knees, peeking into the ends of packages.

"Not that one, boys!" Tug's booming voice stopped the accordion dead. "That's for Carol!" The twins froze, two fawns caught in a headlight. Everyone looked from Tug to the twins to Carol. She stood, a princess framed in the kitchen doorway, white terry cloth apron wrapped around her tiny waist, waffle-holed potato masher upraised in her right hand. She looked at Tug, then at the box. Everyone but the twins followed her gaze.

"Just didn't want to spoil the surprise, Hon," he said. He glanced at her sheepishly, then down at his feet.

Oh, the silly goof, he's so . . . protective, Carol thought. The box's afterimage appeared superimposed—a square green blot—across Tug's barrel chest. "Well, anyway, dinner's ready."

In record time, Frank unstrapped the accordion, and a buffet line formed at the table. "Wait, everybody, let me take a picture," Stan said.

Everyone straightened up, peering up the line toward the camera, hair and smiles lacquered into place, paper plates subtly positioned over this or that wart, bump, scar, or double chin. Twenty minutes later, they reduced Carol's two days of culinary endeavors to gastronomic rubble.

Before they realized the time, Dad ushered the crowd into the hallway where it was on with the coats, mittens, galoshes, and babushkas, then off to the church. Sandwiched in the front seat between Tug and Tug's mom, Carol felt warm and secure, bundled in her thick wool coat. *The evening has passed in a flash,* she reflected, *but it will be eons before we return from mass.* Her mind leaped ahead to the jeweled windows of the church, illuminated by hundreds of candles, the gold in Monsignor's robes. A shiver shot to her toes. *Patience,* she thought. *It won't be long, and we'll be a real family.* In a heartbeat, she knew what she would pray for: healthy, happy children (but not too many) and financial guidance for Tug's mom (who had spent one-third of her estate since her husband's untimely death two years past). Plus, the usual blessings for everyone else. And the kids would go to St. Mary's. *There, that's settled.*

❋ ❋ ❋

Now, an hour later, everyone was back home, rosy-cheeked and re-energized. Marcie had stayed behind to clean up the dishes, put out cookies, coffee, and—to stoke conversation—a bottle of Slivovitz. Everyone settled into place in and around the Christmas tree, cups in hand, saucers bedecked with sweets. The twins were self-appointed gift-passers until they received their own.

Marcie took over. The ritual assumed its characteristic rhythm: shuffle around the boxes, grab a likely package, ship it express to the proper recipient, remove the paper (saving bows and ribbons), pause at the moment of finale for Uncle Stan, followed by a gasp of surprise and the receding echoes of *oohs* and *aahs.*

It demanded artistry, a talent honed by Marcie over years of practice, to ensure the gift passer delivered them in the correct order, from least to most expensive, from youngest to oldest recipient (reversing the age distribution as the gifts moved from mundane to unique). This took a sixth sense, plus knowledge of what everyone was receiving. The point was to eliminate packages one-by-one, creating unbearable suspense and anticipation of the best and last present. When finely orchestrated, the effect was not unlike the climax of an Independence Day fireworks exhibition or, more relevant, the Hallelujah Chorus.

This evening, Marcie was on her mark. And Carol was in gut-wrenching agony. She thought she would die. She was strangling, she couldn't breathe. She had a dozen hallucinations: the kitchen stove catching fire, Uncle Stan dropping over from a heart attack, the twins sticking a hairpin in the electrical socket, Roger dripping with a nosebleed . . . *It was simply awful.* Her make-up felt like brownie mix, her feet were drenched with sweat, and Godfrey, Aunt Thelma's silky terrier, kept trying to lick her toes.

"I'd love to turn that dog into a handbag," she muttered.

Finally, there it was, *The Big Black Box* with silver ribbon, patent-leather shiny, nestled against a fringe of pine needles. Marcie, with surgical precision, had carved out a hollow for it near the tree, isolated from the detritus of cardboard, paper, and chaff spread through the living room. She started for it.

Tug beat her by a step. "This one's mine, Marcie," he intoned. In a solemn ceremony, he lifted the enormous package from its hiding place. "Are you ready, Carol?" he asked, turning to face her. He was hyperventilating. "This is the one you've been waiting for."

The apartment fell silent as a morgue. Carol had placed herself strategically on the couch at the opposite corner from the Christmas tree. Tug approached in measured steps, arms outstretched. A wave of pinpricks danced across Carol's shoulders.

"Oh, look, she's blushing," Aunt Thelma observed. A murmur of approval echoed through the room.

"Steady, Carol, stea . . . dy." Tug peered into her eyes over the top of the package. He dropped to one knee, released his grip, and *there it was,* blump, *in her lap.* The weight of it pressed on her thighs. Her left wrist throbbed against the side. For a moment, she didn't know if she was holding it—or it was holding her.

"It's so heavy, Tug. I-I don't know if I can manage it."

"Open it! Open it!" the twins screamed. They picked up the wrapping paper and hurled it in her direction.

"Stop that right now!" Marcie shouted. She grabbed one in each hand and plopped them side-by-side in an upholstered armchair.

"They're alright," Carol's dad said. "They're just boys." He pushed his bifocals back on the bridge of his nose and motioned to Carol. "Open 'er up, kid."

"I'll hold it, Carol, you pop the top," Tug offered. She looked up. He loomed over her, his dark eyes gleaming. She removed the bow, careful not to destroy, so she could reuse it next year. The room fell to a hush. She slipped the ribbon free, loosened wrapping at each end of the package. The paper was shiny, gorgeous. She lifted it away from the naked box. This was it. Using a fingernail, she cut the tape. The family members pressed forward. Uncle Stan moved around for the shot. Carol's heart was thumping like a tennis shoe in a washing machine. She opened the flap and peered over the edge, expecting to see the next package inside.

Tug jumped to his feet. "Isn't it great? Merry Christmas, Babe! I picked it out myself!" He blurted. Swooping down, he reached into the box. She was showered with a hail of cardboard, Styrofoam peanuts, and tissue paper.

Carol looked up, her eyes and mouth frozen open.

"Watch the birdie," said Uncle Stan. *Pa-poof.* The Polaroidal Moment. GZZZZZZZZT.

"Isn't that THE GREATEST MIXER YOU'VE EVER

SEEN?!" Tug shouted. He held it up. "See, it's got TEN SPEEDS!"

All the air left the room.

". . . It's full metal, belt driven . . . KITCHEN WIZARD, the best!" He knocked on its enameled case with a burly fist. "It's even got A BREAD HOOK." He displayed the steel device so all could see. "Wha'd'ya think . . . cool, huh?"

"GimmeeGimmeeGimmee," said the twins in unison, jumping for it.

Carol looked away from the appliance. "Oh, it's . . . great."

"How sweet," Aunt Thelma purred. "Look, tears of joy."

Stan fumbled to load a new cartridge in his camera.

Pa-poof. GZZZZZZT. Another Polaroidal Moment.

Carol lurched forward, the empty box tumbling to the floor. Her china face was flushed and stained with make-up. Tug looked around, set the mixer on the couch, bewildered.

Carol burst into sobs. She fled from the room. Her mom chased after her down the hall.

Tug's mother glared up at him. "You *lunkhead*, now look what you've done."

"It's okay, Tug," Carol's father said. "She's just a bit overwhelmed by your . . . enthusiasm."

❊　❊　❊

Two days later, when everyone returned to work, Carol walked straight to her desk without speaking. Herb came out of his office for a cup of coffee, and Bill nodded toward Carol's cubicle, pointing to his ring finger. Herb glanced over and saw her left hand was ringless.

"Everyone have a good Christmas?" he asked.

"Yeah, excellent, except for the blizzard we encountered north of Grayling." Bill said. "Spent Christmas Eve in a motel—what a drag. But Christmas day was tremendous. Entire family, cheery fire, lots of presents and plenty of grog. I'm beat—how about you, Herb?"

"All good," Herb said. "I swear I put on five pounds. My mother-in-law makes this lemon meringue pie with a crust of crushed windmill cookies. I take one bite and it's over. I can't help but pig out."

Carol swiveled around from her desk. There was a moment of silence.

"Well, I suppose you're both wondering . . ."

Bill jumped in. "Yeah, how did your big *soiree* go?"

"It-it was great," Carol said. "The whole family was there. Everything came off pretty much as expected."

Herb raised any eyebrow. ". . . what about that bad-boy Tug? Did he behave himself—or do Bill and I need to pay him a visit?"

She smiled. "Oh, he was okay. His mom was there to keep him on his best behavior." She hesitated. "He bought me a really nice . . . mixer."

"A *mixer*?" Herb and Bill said at once.

Carol laughed, then burst into tears. "Yeah, it has ten speeds . . . a dough hook and . . . ev*erything.*"

"Oh, Carol," Bill said. "I guess . . . no ring, eh?"

She shook her head. Her mascara was running. Pulling a tissue from the dispenser on her desk, she blew her nose.

"I'm so sorry, Carol," Herb said.

"Me too," Bill chimed in.

"Thanks, guys, it's okay. I shouldn't have gotten so carried away. I got ahead of myself. It's just that with the new apartment and everything, it seemed . . . it was . . . destined to happen." She started to cry again. "But I've recovered . . . mostly."

She related the complete story. As she told them about opening Tug's present, she reached in her purse and brought out Uncle Stan's Polaroid. At the "Polaroidal Moment," she and Tug stared at a huge white mixer raised in triumph in Tug's beefy fingers. He grinned like a drunken sailor, while she sat wide-eyed, holding her hands to the sides of her face, mouth forming a capital "O."

The three of them couldn't help but laugh.

The rest of the day, everyone kept to themselves. The atmosphere grew more somber as the late afternoon light faded, and Bill and Herb heard quiet weeping from the direction of Carol's cubicle. They left her alone.

Bill offered Herb a wager that the Christmas Eve fiasco would end Carol's relationship with Tug. He didn't bite, even with odds. If asked to guess, they might have predicted she would move back with her parents in Logansport. Or meet someone, say, a shoe salesman, and honeymoon in Branson, Missouri. Or join some religious order and become a nun. But Christmas was not the end—only the beginning.

❋   ❋   ❋

On April 3rd, Carol came to work a few minutes late. She hung her coat in the closet and walked to the coffee machine. Herb and Bill were pouring a cup.

"Me too, please," she said.

They both turned to stare at her—she was a tea drinker. She glowed, her cheeks rosy, nearly flushed; her eyes sparkled. Herb handed her a mug, and she reached for it with her left hand.

"Holy shit!" Bill said. He looked Carol straight in the eye. "He *didn't.*"

"Yeah, he *did*!" she squealed, waving a monster engagement ring and grinning wide. "He did—Saturday night . . . on April Fool's Day!" They broke out laughing.

"Congratulations," Herb said. "I confess, I thought it might not happen. But Carol, what bank did he rob? That rock is enormous—let me see it again."

Carol extended her hand. Herb and Bill bent toward her and studied the fiery diamond-encrusted setting.

"Heck, that thing must go two carats," Bill said.

It was gorgeous. She told them it had been Tug's mom's; she wanted Carol to have it. Tug found a jeweler in Battle Creek and had it reset.

❈ ❈ ❈

In the fall, Tug and Carol held a huge wedding at St. Mary's with six bridesmaids and six groomsmen (including Herb and Bill). They threw an even bigger reception at the Pulaski Club, an eleven-kegger, with lots of food, including the usual Polish specialties—Kapusta z Grzybami and Glabki and Kolaczki. Half of city hall was there. They hired an accordion band called the Sea Stack Ramblers, and everyone danced the polka. There were so many presents that the bridesmaids piled them in a twelve-foot pyramid. They shined a green floodlight, so it resembled an enormous Christmas tree. When she opened the gifts, Carol inventoried twenty-seven Crockpots (they told her it was a church record).

In the next five years, Tug and Carol had three kids: two beautiful girls with wild hair and a little boy with a china face and barrel chest. Tug's employer promoted him twice, and he currently runs a tool and die shop in the Grand Rapids suburb of Wyoming. Carol, whose children are all grown now with children of their own. still works her magic around City Hall.

Herb long ago retired, and Bill moved on to a job with the County but keeps in touch. The other day, Bill and Carol were reminiscing over lunch about her engagement and wedding.

"Hey, whatever happened to all those Crockpots?" Bill asked.

Carol laughed. "After our honeymoon, Tug piled them in the basement. Over the years, I've doled them out as presents to our friends and neighbors." She added that she only had three Crockpots left. "I would have been rid of them long ago, but I refuse to give them to bachelors!"

TWO LITTLE INDIANS

...**O**h, man, he had it so bad for that girl. The first time he saw her, she was seated, legs crossed, at the bar in the Lakeview Hotel. Every few minutes, she glanced away from her cellphone through the windows toward Marine Pier.

"You don't have to watch for the ferry," he said. "They blow their horn when they round the breakwater."

She turned toward him. "Thanks, good to know." She returned to her phone. Thin as a matchstick, she had wrapped herself in a boho-chic, blue batik dress, cinched at the waist with a turquoise and silver belt. The dress set off her long, fiery red hair. It curved around her face, framing her freckle-dusted cheekbones.

He tried again. "I'm Jeff," he said, extending his palm. "You must be visiting the Island?"

She hesitated, threw him a wary look, then reached across the empty seat between them. A tattooed script—*Peace Love Harmony Joy*—encircled her delicate wrist.

"Jenna," she replied. "I just started working here—in Loyale. I've been making my monthly follow-ups with a few of our Island clients." Her voice sounded melodic, like some tropical songbird.

"Business?"

She laughed, her large, hazel eyes sparkling. "Hardly. I've been up in Astoria, in the center of the Island."

Jeff recognized the name. "You mean, Vide Poche."

A puzzled expression crossed her face. "Vee Posh?"

"Yeah, It's French for 'Empty Pockets.' All the locals call it that. Kind of ironic, since it was named after John Jacob Astor, who made a killing here in the 1800s trading furs.

"I get it," she said.

Turns out she was the new children and family social worker for Ojibwa County Social Services, fresh from college. He was a couple of years out of school himself, back in Loyale working for his uncle, Ray. Basically drifting.

"I've been calling on insurance prospects since this morning," he confessed. "It'll be nice to get back on the water for a few minutes."

She smiled. "Yeah . . . it's been a long day—oh, hey, I have to use the ladies' room. I'll catch you later."

She dropped a bill on the bar and scooted off the stool, gripping a large leather purse. As she brushed against him, he caught a faint whiff of something fragrant, citrus. Was it perfume—or her drink? She stepped toward the hotel hallway, bag slung low across her hip, one hand clutching it, the other extended, moving freely, like a supermodel on the runway.

"See you on the boat," he said.

She didn't look back.

Jeff paid for his drink and walked down the street to Marine Pier. A crowd was queuing up to board, eager to get to the mainland and home for dinner or back to their hotels. But he didn't see her in line. The deck hands were hustling the luggage and empty freight containers into the hold, hurrying to make the trip home as well. Once on the ferry, he hung around the steel gangplank until they pulled it across to the deck and cast off the lines. Had she slipped by him?

He took a stroll through both decks and even glanced into the pilot house doorway to see if the captain, spotting an attractive girl, had invited her up for a chat. The crew, from bottom to top, was always on the make, even the female employees. With over ten thousand tourists every day, it was a target-rich environment.

Forty-five minutes later, the boat tied up at the old State Ferry dock. It had been repurposed in the 1960s after completion of the new Bridge across the Straits. He lingered and watched all the passengers disembark, then the crew. No Jenna. She seemed at least mildly interested. Why had she disappeared?

❄ ❄ ❄

A few days later, on Friday, Jeff stopped after work at The Voyageur, a local watering hole on Main Street. Not his regular hangout, but the parking lot looked full, signaling a good crowd, maybe a band playing later. As his eyes adjusted to the darkened room, he noticed several people seated at a large table, more gathered around it. Everyone had a drink in hand and appeared quite animated.

Sharon Wisinski, a neighbor girl who had lived across the street growing up, motioned him over. He grabbed a beer and joined the group, many of whom he recognized as Ojibwa County employees. Just before he moved in next to her to say hello, he saw her turn away and lean toward someone, fingers cupped to her mouth.

". . . really cute, I'll introduce you," she whispered.

He smiled. "You tal—,"

Sharon interrupted. "Hey, Jeff, meet our newest employee."

Jeff turned to where she pointed. One of the people near Sharon stepped away as Jenna turned around. She was radiant, dressed in a gold print top and skin-tight blue jeans.

"Jenna McCauley, this is Jeff Johansen. Jeff . . ."

They burst out laughing. A cloud of confusion crossed Sharon's brow.

"We met a few days ago," Jenna said.

"Waiting for the Island ferry—by the way, where did you go?" Jeff asked. "I looked all over."

"Oh, sorry. Got an emergency call, and by the time it ended, they had pulled away. I took the next one."

"Well, let me buy you a drink."

"No, it was my bad. I'll buy. Besides, I don't let just anyone buy me a drink." She glanced at him with a mischievous smile.

"Me neither," he said.

"For Chris' sakes," Sharon said. "You can both buy *me* one."

That broke the ice. By the end of the evening, they had traded several rounds. Jeff tried to keep one-up, but she insisted on not leaving without evening the score. Finally, he agreed to one last round, but only if he could make sure she made it home safely.

"Great." She ordered a round.

When they finished, he said, "Okay, let me have your keys. I'll drive you home."

Jenna and Sharon both cracked up. Jeff looked from one to the other, clueless.

"I live on Hurley Street—right behind the bar," she said, pointing. "My car's in the driveway." Her eyes flashed that same enticing, naughty look he had witnessed earlier. She stood up abruptly to leave. "Sorry, but I have to be home early tonight."

"Hey, uh, what do you have going tomorrow?" Jeff asked. "Maybe we could do lunch."

"Can't this weekend," she said, glancing over her shoulder. "I'm driving back home to pick up stuff for my apartment. I'm still moving in." She reached into her purse and handed him a card. "Call me next week." He looked down at the card and spotted her cell number.

"Okay, I'll do that."

By then, she was out the door.

❊ ❊ ❊

Saturday morning, Jeff lay in bed, thinking about his two encounters with Jenna. She was so strikingly beautiful, self-assured, yet warm and alluring. The prospect of seeing her again, if only for lunch, excited him. He hated to admit it, but two minutes after they met, he had been hooked and landed.

40

Yet she had thrown him back twice. Was she being coy, or something else?

His last year at college had shaken his confidence. His college girlfriend—Mai Nguyen—had been a major source of friction with his parents. When he brought her home one weekend, they were polite, but noticeably cool.

Later, according to his mom, his dad griped, "Why in hell can't Jeff find an American girl?"

"Mom, she *is* American. She was born in California. Her mother is a pediatrician. Her dad teaches French at Michigan State."

She shook her head. "I understand, but someday your dad wants to have some grandchildren, kids who look like him."

In the end, Mai dumped him, which put out the smoldering family conflict. He didn't blame her. She was brilliant, outgoing, ambitious. His future didn't shine nearly so bright.

Perhaps an "All-American Girl" like Jenna might change that, but he wondered if she, too, was playing in a different league, one in which he could never compete. It was a depressing thought.

He looked at her card again on the table beside his bed. He would wait a day or two, then phone her.

❄   ❄   ❄

The following Wednesday, he rang her up.

"Jeff, so glad you called. Sharon has been telling me stories about growing up with you and your family. We have been laughing all morning."

"Yeah, I suppose she has." He smirked. "Don't believe a word of it."

"Something about falling out of her apple tree—more than once."

"Fall? She and her crazy sister Margaret used to push me out. Constantly. I have the lumps to prove it."

He pointed toward the crescent-shaped mark on his

41

forehead, then realized she couldn't see it over the phone. "So, you still up for lunch?"

"Sure."

They quickly made plans for the next day to meet up at the Railroad Cafe, a waterfront bistro converted from an old caboose overlooking the bay between Loyale's two derelict rail ferry docks.

Jeff arrived a few minutes after noon. Jenna was already seated at an outside table on the adjacent deck. The Island ferries were operating at full capacity and throwing up twenty-foot rooster tails from the powerful twin Caterpillar engines driving their hydrofoil hulls. The breeze off Lake Huron tempered the air, but the overhead sun shone brightly, and she had slipped on a pair of sunglasses. The emerald-colored lenses matched her print top.

He sat down across from her. "Sorry I'm late, got tied up. Been here long?"

"No, they just seated me."

The server brought over two menus.

"So, what's good?" Jenna asked.

"Let me order for you," he said. "When you live at the intersection of Lake Michigan and Lake Huron, there is only one choice. You have to try the fresh whitefish. I guarantee it's the best fish you will ever eat in your life."

"You're quite the salesman," she said, flashing a coquettish smile.

"No, god's truth." He crossed his heart. "My great-grandfather came here as a child from Norway with my great-great-grandfather because he heard of the fabulous fishing grounds around Loyale."

"You're Scandinavian."

He nodded.

"Figures, the blonde hair was a bit of a giveaway—plus, Sharon told me." She laughed. "I actually have a fairly complete biography." She glanced up at him, looking for a reaction.

"Well, now you have me at a disadvantage. So, it's my turn. I'm curious, why Loyale? Of all the places in the state . . ."

"Easy, when I graduated, there were only three jobs in Social Services, two of them in Detroit. I'm the first one in my family to graduate from college, so my parents have a lot of expectations. I wanted to find the right place to 'launch' my career. And we have been renting a vacation place south of here near Nicolet for years."

The server stepped over to bring their drinks and take orders.

"Two planked whitefish dinners," Jeff said.

"Excellent choice." She wrote it down and left for the kitchen.

Jenna squirmed in her seat "Planked? I've never heard..."

"It's the best. Trust me," he said. "I could explain it, but it's better if you let it be a surprise." The sunglasses masked her eyes, but the sun's rays brought out the red-gold highlights in her hair. The blue-green blouse she wore accentuated her fair complexion. She was extraordinarily beautiful. He couldn't believe his luck in meeting her.

"So, are you seeing anyone?" he asked.

"You would ask that," she replied. "It's a sad story. Candidly, I'm doing a lot of soul searching right now. I seem to be strangely attracted to dysfunctional guys. I'm wondering if it's why I decided to be a social worker."

"I don't see . . ."

"Sorry for being obtuse. I was dating this basketball player at Central for three years. I really liked him and the whole sports culture thing. He was good looking, very physical. But the closer I got to him emotionally, the more abusive he became.I woke up one day and realized the increasing humiliation wasn't worth it. I told him I needed some breathing room. Then he threatened to beat me. That ended it."

"Wow, that's heavy. I would never do that," Jeff commented. "In fact, I can't see myself ever physically hurting anyone. It's been a source of friction with my dad. He's ex-military and has pushed me since I was a little kid to join the army. It would be my worst nightmare."

The server brought over their food, wearing thick, padded cloth mitts—a broiled whitefish filet presented on a thick, smoking hot, maple plank with mashed potatoes piped around the edge and dusted with a sprinkle of paprika. On the side, a mix of baby carrots and pearl onions brightened the presentation. She also brought small pots of melted butter and crusty rye bread.

Jenna reached over and placed her hand on his. "Oh my god, Jeff, this is exquisite," she said. "Thanks for inviting me here." She removed her sunglasses and peered into his eyes.

In that instant, he wanted her—more than he had wanted anyone.

"Jenna, I would like to show you a very special place," he said. "I'm not religious, but for me, it's almost sacred. I have been there two or three times now, always alone. For a long time, I have wanted to share it with someone, someone like you."

She squeezed his hand. "Thank you, Jeff. You're very kind. I would love for you to share it with me."

"It's settled then," he said, elated. "It will be my surprise—but now let's eat."

❊ ❊ ❊

On Saturday afternoon, he picked her up at her apartment. He had told her to wear clothes suitable for hiking but revealed nothing else. After a twenty-minute drive north of Loyale, ending on an old gravel road, they parked Jeff's car in a secluded grove of evergreens. To the east, a path led up and out of the thicket.

"We're going to walk up this path to Steeple Rock, one of the area's highest sea stacks," Jeff said.

"Sea stacks?"

"Yeah, it's a unique geological feature of the Straits area. Natural limestone pillars. There are several, many of them hidden away unless you know about them. This is my favorite."

They started up along a wooded ridge leading to a promontory jutting into Lake Huron. Fifty feet below the summit, the incline rose steeply but could be traversed by stepping on the natural outcrops and gripping the crevasses in the limestone column thrust up through the trees below. They crept toward the natural stone platform that capped the formation.

The view from the top for first timers was a visual tidal wave. To the north, the Cedar Islands lay ghostly on the surface of Lake Huron. To the south, the blue tip of Lake Michigan. Between the two Great Lakes, the mighty green and white suspension bridge rose from the Straits, pinning together the Upper and Lower Peninsulas. East of the Bridge and the town of Loyale, lay the Island where they had first met, but from this vantage point, seen in its natural beauty, a giant green turtle wallowing in the inky-blue water. To the west, a vast wilderness of hardwoods and conifers extended beyond the horizon. A few miles away, another limestone pillar rose out of the greenery like a giant castle.

"There's Tower Rock, where endless streams of tourists pay for the same view we get for free," he quipped. "They have been climbing the stairs there for a century."

"Jeff, this is fantastic, almost overwhelming," Jenna said. "The air is so clear you can see everything for miles."

He moved closer to her. "Yeah, it's my absolute favorite. The woods stretching behind us as far as you can imagine, the lake before us, full of possibilities…"

They stood there together, taking in its natural grandeur.

"It's almost a religious experience," she said. "But I don't like looking over the edge, it's as if I'm being pulled into an abyss."

"Kind of a metaphor for life," he joked.

He pointed toward a channel between the Island and a smaller one south of it. "See that lighthouse rising out of the lake. One summer, my grandfather helped build it."

"I noticed it on my way over on the boat—when we first met." She smiled. Her teeth were white as a string of matched pearls. The sunlight caught in her hair, lending her face a radiant, rosy glow. His nose filled with the same citrusy, fragrant scent he had first encountered in the Lakeview.

"We have a photo of him up on a scaffold, painting the sides," Jeff said. "It's black and white, but I imagine he was covered with red paint by the time he finished. The light marks the passage between the two islands. It replaced the old one, which you can still see there on the Block Island shore. It's uninhabited, owned by the State. Imagine, you can sail over from Loyale and anchor, spend the day, and have the whole beach to yourself."

She turned toward him. Her eyes were liquid as the lake below. "Oh, Jeff, thank you so much for taking me here. It's spectacular." He embraced her, and they kissed. Then again, this time deep and long.

He pulled a blanket out of the backpack he had carried up the ridge and spread it on the rock. He opened a bottle of red wine, and they sat together, passing it back and forth, while gazing down the lake.

"I feel like I can almost see Detroit," she said.

He chuckled. "That would be quite a feat. It's three hundred miles south. But I know the feeling. It's almost . . . overwhelming." He turned toward her. "Especially, if you're with someone who enjoys it as much as you do. I've never taken anyone up here before—before you."

The sun's radiance filled the air, enveloping everything it touched. At the horizon, huge billowing clouds floated across the sky. He reached for her now, drew her closer onto the blanket, and she wrapped herself around him. He heard her breathing quicken, felt her breath, moist on his cheek.

"Can anyone see us?" she whispered.

He smiled. "Only the eagles." He pointed toward treetops peaking just above the summit. "From below, the poplars and cedars form a natural curtain. Imagine making love on the top of the world."

Within minutes, they were entwined in a slow, passionate embrace, her sleek, slender body twisting into his own, their clothes strewn on the stone platform around the blanket. The air, cool off the lake, raised the fine hairs on her arms, but the sun's warmth shielded them, a luminous mist bathing them in late afternoon light. Again, and again, they engaged each other, and she pulled him down into the depths of an emotional pool he had never experienced. Into the sweet abyss. It felt so real, he knew it must be a dream.

On the way back down the ridge, the orange ball of the sun dropped over the edge of the lake. She walked ahead on the trail. When they reached the grove where they had parked two hours before, she turned, and they kissed once more in the gathering gloom cast by the surrounding evergreens. The air smelled of juniper berries.

"That was beautiful, Jeff," she whispered.

"Yes, for me too," he said.

Then, she intimated something that caught him by surprise.

"Now that it's over, maybe we can start a real relationship."

❊   ❊   ❊

Within two weeks they were hooking up on a regular basis. Jeff could not stop thinking about her, her laugh, her eyes, her heart-shaped face, and dancer's body. He loved the way she dressed and carried herself. He admired her wit, her energy, her empathy. She wasn't at all like the town girls he had woken up to find in bed after drinking all night in the local bars. They invariably took their cues from too many lurid romance novels or frantic action-movies. With Jenna, it was like drowning. He wanted to absorb her into every pore of his being. She was—no other word could describe it—*intoxicating*. He prayed it would not end—like his relationship with Mai.

So, when Jenna confided that she needed his help, how could he say no? A month after they first met, she hit him up over lunch. He probably should have seen it coming.

"Jeff, I don't know what I'm going to do," she said. "I have this *terrible* family situation on my caseload. I shouldn't even be talking to you about it because of confidentiality."

"Hey, it's a small town. I get it."

She put her hand on his wrist. "Jeff, seriously, you can't tell anyone—not *anyone*."

He crossed his heart and promised.

"Okay. Okay, I have these two Native American kids—more precisely, mixed race. They're living with their mom and grandma, and we're trying to help them and deal with all the problems, but it's not happening. Especially the oldest, Daniel. He hasn't been to school in like six weeks. He just doesn't go."

"That's horrible. Who's their mother and grandmother?"

She swore him to secrecy again, then went on to describe them. Come to find out, he knew of the kids' mother—Leah St. Martin—from high school, three or four years ahead of him.

"I used to see her," he said. "She was always slinking along the hallway, head down, trying to avoid attention, usually on her way to the 'special needs' room. Same clothes every day, a long skirt and blue cardigan, soup-bowl haircut. She had a nickname, 'Pocahontas.' Even some Indian kids called her that.

48

It was pretty cruel, but everyone made jokes about her. Nobody seemed to care, especially the School."

That was probably ten years ago. Jenna caught him up on Leah's current circumstances.

"She's living with her mother, Rachel, who's bedridden with emphysema. There's virtually no treatment. No money. No one else in the house to help."

"So, where's the kids' dad?"

"That's the worst part. Leah's father, Labe Trombley, was Rachel's common-law husband—"

"Oh, god, Labe Trombley?" he interrupted. "The whole town of Loyale knows about him. He's notorious. When he was young, he was a scratch golfer, until he started drinking. He used to cadge shots at the Hemlock Tavern by sticking a kitchen match in a crack in the floor, then lighting it with a nine iron."

Jenna rolled her eyes.

"They say he'd do them one after another in a dead drunk. The tourists lost a lot of money to the locals, betting he couldn't light one more. Finally, drank himself into oblivion. Don't tell me he's the kid's dad, too."

"No, it's just as bad," she replied. "Before he died, he apparently made his twin brother, Jake, promise to take care of Rachel and Leah."

"You mean 'Skunk?'"

"Skunk?"

"Yeah, Skunk Trombley. He's been called that forever. And for good reason."

"Right, Skunk. Seems appropriate since he straightaway impregnated Leah—twice. Social Services finally got the Juvenile Court to throw him out—They should have prosecuted him. Anyway, now, it's just the women—and the two boys."

"That explains a lot. In high school, she was timid, really

skittish."

"Well, unfortunately, neither one of them can handle the kids. Aside from the public health nurse and me, who go check, they're fending for themselves. The youngest, Asher—for whatever reason, they call him Lucky—he's about eight, going to school and, for the moment, holding his own. But Daniel, who's nine, has been AWOL for almost six weeks."

"Six weeks? That's totally unacceptable. Why isn't the School all over it?"

"I've talked to them. They say at this point it's a Juvenile Court issue."

Jenna disclosed to Jeff that the Juvenile Judge was at his wits' end. Social Services had tried all the usual, some more than once. The Judge told her bluntly to recruit someone to get Daniel in school. But she was new, didn't know many people, which was why she was staring at him across the table with those irresistible hazel eyes and a look of intense desperation.

"All you have to do," she said, taking his hand in hers again, "is drive over each morning, roust him out of bed and load him onto the school bus . . . until he makes it a habit. Probably a couple of weeks."

Jeff glanced aside. For an instant, a pinprick of reluctance caught him up. He peered at her, unsure. Her eyes were pleading for his help. "Okay, I'm in," he said.

❊ ❊ ❊

A few days later, Jenna set up a meeting for Jeff with the County Juvenile Officer to establish some ground rules. The Juvenile Court office was in the Ojibwa County Courthouse, a 1930s landmark art deco building constructed by the Works Progress Administration. Jeff had only been there a few times, once in Cub Scouts. As they walked to the main entrance, he pointed out the limestone bas relief sculptures of factory workers and farmers framing the doorway.

"It's a strange image for a place that has, like, no factories and only a handful of farms," he said. "They might have thrown in a few loggers—or a fisherman."

"Believe me, I understand," Jenna said. "Practically everyone on my caseload is making minimum wage as a cook, waitress, or chamber maid—and then only for the tourist season. Or the men, who tend bar or cut pulpwood for the paper companies."

"Been there, done that. I worked summers in a kitchen; later on, the ferries while I was in school."

The Judge's secretary greeted and motioned them toward a conference room which doubled as the county law library. Arthur Belker, the Court Juvenile Officer, met them at the entrance. A small, thickset man, he sported black, horn-rimmed glasses and the carriage of a retired master sergeant. Jeff noted how much Belker resembled his son, Chucky, back in the day, a notorious high school bully. The three of them squeezed around the conference table, surrounded by volumes of the Michigan Statutes.

Belker set the tone. "The Judge wants this rascal back behind a school desk." He pointed directly at Jeff. "He needs structure and discipline. Your job is to do whatever it takes." That was the Judge's way of conveying to Jenna, 'Work something out and don't bring that case back into my Court.'

Belker added, "You can't beat him, tie him up, or lock him in, but anything else is fair game. The Judge will back you up. Make it happen."

The door opened, and a huge, ebullient, overweight, balding man with a bulbous nose and large teeth appeared. His black robes appeared rumpled, and earlier that morning, he had obviously splashed on some bay rum aftershave.

"Sorry I'm late—Judge Deichman." The Judge grinned, shook Jeff's hand, nodded to Jenna, then turned to Belker.

"Art, are we all squared away here? The voters are really depending on us."

"Yes, sir. All firing at the same target."

"Good, good. It's a big challenge." He paused for a moment, apparently thinking. "We're counting on you, Jeff. Are you up for it?" He flashed a broad, toothy smile again, then wheeled abruptly and left the room.

❋ ❋ ❋

Truth was, once he reflected on it, Jeff didn't mind the challenge. It sounded simple. A week or two of effort and some kid might get back on track. It might be long odds, but at least worth a try. Plus, he was ready for *something*.

The previous year, he had arrived at the realization that hanging out in the Loyale bars every night was a dreadful routine, like having a second job. He had stalled completely, no consistent direction—basically drifting—the end of a downhill slide that started, he was forced to admit, before his Senior year.

He had figured out he hated his major, journalism. A summer stint as a stringer on the local weekly forced him to conclude that his ambition of being the next Tom Wolfe, Bob Woodward, or even Hunter S. Thompson was an adolescent fantasy. A reporter was a glorified secretary, attending endless, boring public meetings, most of them at night, then summarizing the proceedings for the reading public. With the recession on, there weren't any newspaper jobs for fresh graduates anyway, so it was moot. He had retreated to Loyale to regroup.

One day, when his father was home for lunch, he came clean about his disillusionment.

"Jesus H Christ," his dad said. "We send you to college for almost five years, and now you decide you don't like the career you chose? Well, you better find something. You can't live *here* forever."

Jeff expected to get a kick in the pants. The Old Man was like that, proud of their Scandinavian heritage and part of a family military tradition going back to World War I. He had his good side too, but he was physically imposing, quick to anger, and invariably focused on results.

"Hey, if you can't figure out what to do, why don't you join the Army?" he said.

"Right, so I can kill a bunch of indigent Muslim peasants to help re-elect the current president, *whoever that* is?"

His dad flashed a menacing scowl. "Well, you could report about it. The Army has people in public relations."

"Oh, so, you want me to *write* about killing a bunch of indigent Muslim peasants to help re-elect some politician?"

His dad grabbed him and pulled him up by his shirt. He jerked back his fist, ready to take a swing. "Watch your mouth!"

"Jack!" his mom shouted.

He hesitated, then gave Jeff a shove that sent him flying to the couch. He stormed out of the house, back to work at the lumberyard, ending another skirmish in their long-running war, the latest of a series of altercations that had started in middle school. They never saw eye-to-eye.

Jeff's dad wore his service as a badge of courage, patriotism, honor. Jeff was physically smaller, more like his mom, who, although reticent about her own achievements, was creative, considerate, with a spiritual view of the world. Like her, he couldn't see how killing someone would be anything but tragic, if not despicable. He hadn't told his parents—or anyone—but he had resolved never to do it—for any reason.

Right after the blow-up, his mom called her sister, Charlotte. Aunt Charlotte spoke to her husband, Ray Nichols, who rescued him with a job. Soon after, he moved out to live on his own.

So, here he was, stuck in Loyale, trying to discover a new arc for his life. He might as well return a little something to the community. 'Bloom where you're planted.' If nothing else, he would be golden with his new girlfriend—Jenna.

❊   ❊   ❊

Tuesday evening, Jeff stood on Leah's porch, anxious about what he would encounter. He had papered over his unease by repeating a mantra his father often preached in relation to confronting a new or contentious situation.

"Seldom right, but never in doubt."

He knocked on the door, primed to lay down the law. The house was a beat-up little bungalow, overlooking the Huron shore. As he waited, he saw the Island just out of reach across the Straits, the Grande Hotel cupolas lit up copper-gold by the cold, fading sun.

No answer.

As he peered through the window, he saw two kids. He rapped again. Harder this time. The one on the couch looked toward the entry, then turned back to the TV. The other slouched in a chair over in the corner and stared at him, then back at his older brother. Jeff burst through the door like J Edgar.

"Hi, I'm Jeff." He grabbed Daniel's hand and gave it a hearty shake. No tactile response, like gripping raw liver. He caught a sideways squint before Daniel turned away.

"And you must be Lucky." He extended his mitt to the kid in the corner. His hand was firm but tender, palms surprisingly large for a small boy. He announced all cheerful, "Hey, guys, Jenna sent me over to lend you a hand getting to school in the morning. I wanted to drop by and make sure everybody understands what they need to do tomorrow."

Lucky looked up at him, a little confused, then peered to his left. He recognized Leah swaying back and forth on a chair at

54

the kitchen table, arms crossed, on a different planet.

Daniel grunted, "Hmph," turned back to the TV.

Jeff checked him out. His hair, jet black, was shoulder-length or would have been if it weren't matted, snarled. A greasy sheen coated his shirt and matched the front of his pants down to the knees. In his lap lay a grimy asthma inhaler. He gave off a pungent, fungal odor. Unfettered as a stray dog.

Jeff sat down beside him, a firm grip on his left shoulder, drilling a stare into the side of his face. He felt him tense up. "Okay, Daniel," he said. "I'll be over about 7:30 tomorrow to help you onto the bus, so you don't miss any more school. Look at me—take a shower. Put on clean clothes—be ready to go. If you want breakfast, you need to start earlier. I'd set the alarm for 6:15—*sharp*."

On the couch to Daniel's right rested a bowl of strawberry Jell-O and a spoon. He scooped up a chunk. He gripped the spoon handle in one hand, cocked it back with the other, and let fly. The red blob splatted on the floor, ten feet away. Across the room, a little orange cat scurried through a bedroom doorway and pounced on it. Daniel peered up at him, eyes narrowed, expression grim. There was his reply.

Then, Jeff saw in the dim light of the bedroom an old woman lying in a yellowed nightgown, her face washed out, hair gray as driftwood, with some tube contraption trailing across her cheek. One eye cracked open, then closed again, a living cadaver. Rachel. He saw now why these kids were on their own.

Next morning, Jenna booted him from the sack, and he was back standing on the porch a little after sunrise. He rapped twice and walked through the doorway. Lucky and Leah had switched seats, and he was eating some cereal. Rachel's door was closed. No Daniel.

He hurried through the kitchen, past Lucky to the back of the house. On the left was a bathroom, on the right a bedroom filled with trash—newspapers, comic books, candy wrappers, soda pop cans, clothes, shoes—and Daniel rolled up in a thin blanket on the stained mattress of a metal-frame bed. The entire room reeked of weeks-old cat litter.

"Daniel, time to wake up!"

He hurried across to the bathroom and began to fill the tub. He glanced over his shoulder. Daniel wasn't stirring. He walked back and jostled him.

"Hey, Daniel, get up and take your bath!"

Daniel groaned and pulled the cover up over his head.

"I ain't going to school. Ain't taking no bath." He rolled away from Jeff to the other edge of the bed, still wrapped in the blanket.

This was going nowhere.

"Of course, you are. You don't have a choice. Now get up!"

"No. I ain't doin' it."

"Okay, we'll do it the hard way." Jeff jerked away the blanket with a mighty tug. Daniel came rolling back toward him to the edge of the bed.

"Aaaawkk!" he screeched. He grabbed for the iron headboard. With the blanket came the empty bowl from last night's Jell-O shot. It clattered across the floor and bumped against the wall.

Jeff pitched the blanket aside. Daniel had slept in last night's outfit. It was putrid, unwearable. He pulled open a laundry bag laying near the bed and grabbed a shirt, underwear, pants, and socks.

"Pull those clothes off," Jeff ordered. "You need a bath before you go to school." he glanced toward the bathroom. The tub was still filling.

"I ain't going to no school, and you ain't gonna make me."

"Okay, we'll see." Jeff grabbed him by his encrusted shirt and ripped it open, buttons flying everywhere. Daniel started writhing about and reached for the other side of the bed. Jeff picked him up by the back of his waistband and toted him flailing across the hall. Into the bathtub he plopped. The water steeped him like a tea bag, instantly turning brown.

Daniel jumped up, hollering, soppy. Jeff shoved him back down in the broth and pressed his head under the streaming faucet to get his hair wet. Something laying on the edge of the tub caught his eye. It was a large, rusty nail. Why it was there, Jeff had no idea. But there was junk strewn from one end of the house to the other. Daniel beat him to it, grabbed it for a shiv and spiked him. It stuck his forearm, making a deep puncture. Biting pain. Then another. Jeff tore it from Daniel's hand and pushed him down into the water. Gasping, wheezing, he clutched at the sides, frantically trying to jack himself up. Blood dripped into the bog of the bathtub. Jeff relented and turned off the faucet. Daniel blubbered quietly, and Jeff handed him a bath towel.

"Wipe yourself off. I'll bring you something clean to wear." Jeff grimaced, walked to the bedroom again, returned with the stack of clothes, then passed into the kitchen to find a paper towel to bandage his arm. Lucky and Leah still sat where he had left them. When he entered the room, they both quickly looked down, avoiding eye contact.

A few minutes later, Daniel appeared from the bathroom, hair dripping, inhaler in hand. A belt cinched tight with six inches extra hanging from the buckle held up a pair of baggy corduroy pants. Tucked into them, a splotchy wet, plaid shirt, undoubtedly from Social Services, clung to his damp torso.

Lucky ate a spoonful of Trix and slurped some milk from the bowl. Jeff told Daniel to get a move on if he planned to eat breakfast.

"I don't want none," he said, sulking.

"Good. Soon as Lucky's done eating, I'm driving you to school."

"Hmph." He eyeballed him, turned to Lucky for support.

Lucky gaped, round-eyed, at Daniel, then Jeff, and went back to eating his cereal.

When they arrived at school, Jeff marched Daniel into the office. He identified himself to the office assistant as a volunteer for Social Services helping him get back in class.

"Yes, we're expecting you," she said. "Jenna McCauley called yesterday and gave us a heads-up."

Jeff nudged him forward. "Well, here's your renegade." He was feeling pumped, like a repo man.

She immediately turned all motherly, making a big fuss over Daniel.

"Don't take the bus tonight, I'll be here to pick you up," Jeff said. This earned another surly stare.

❄ ❄ ❄

The morning's turmoil made Jeff late for work, but his Uncle Ray seemed okay with that.

A couple of doors down from his office, Roger's Barber Shop had opened for the day. Everyone knew Roger Anong, who, typical of many Loyale residents, was at least a quarter American Indian. Fifteen years ago, he had also been a star point guard for the Loyale Warriors. Jeff popped in to schedule a haircut for Daniel.

Roger gave him a knowing glance but stayed cool. "What's the kid's name again?"

He repeated it.

"Oh, yeah, rides his bike past here all the time. A regular junior delinquent. Bring him in—I'll cut it for nothing."

Jeff's phone rang. It was Jenna.

"So, how did it go?" she asked.

"A bit of an adventure." He glanced at Roger. "I had to throw him in the tub. And he stabbed me with a rusty nail,"

"Stabbed you with a nail?" He heard the urgency in her voice.

"Yeah, for some ungodly reason, it was sitting on the ledge of the bathtub. I bled like a stuck pig."

"Jeff, you need to have a tetanus shot."

"Nah, it's okay, I put a bandage on it."

"No, seriously, Jeff. Promise me you'll get a shot today."

"All right," he said. "Probably a good idea."

❆ ❆ ❆

That afternoon, when he arrived at school after getting the shot, Lucky sat waiting, but Daniel was MIA. Jeff walked into the office, shrugged, threw up his hands. "I am supposed to pick up Daniel. His brother says he's not here."

The office assistant glanced up, squirmed in her seat. "He ran away this morning at recess."

"What?" A hot burn flashed up the back of his neck. She turned for support from the principal, who leaned cross-armed in her office doorway.

"Well," she said. "The recess monitor has quite a few kids to watch."

"Seriously? You've got to be kidding—he hasn't been to school for *six weeks*."

"We understand that, but—"

"Don't you think he deserves at least *some* extra attention?"

She glanced at the assistant. "We're doing the best we can."

"Yeah, I can see that," he said. He turned away before she could say anything more and headed for the door, his face flushed with anger.

❆ ❆ ❆

He and Lucky drove the shortest route over to Leah's house, figuring Daniel might turn up somewhere along the way. Sure enough, they spotted him, down on the lakeshore, skipping rocks. When Daniel saw them, he broke into a sly grin.

"Nice to see you so cheery," Jeff said. "Enjoy your little

'holiday' 'cause I'll be back in the morning. I suggest you be ready before I show up, or this morning's episode will seem like a kindergarten picnic."

"You think you can make me." Daniel smirked. "I'll just wait 'til you stop coming."

"Oh, that's mistake number two today." He poked a couple of fingers in Daniel's chest. "I am *never* leaving. I'll be coming to your house every day until you turn eighteen. Even longer— until you graduate from high school."

Daniel gulped. "Really?"

"Yeah, *really*. And tomorrow after school, you're getting a haircut. *Really*."

Lucky and he started back to the car. He turned for a parting shot. "When we go to the barber shop tomorrow, make sure you have your homework, or there'll be hell to pay." He winked at Lucky. Lucky grinned.

❊ ❊ ❊

Next day, Daniel surprised him. He was dressed and ready to go. After school, Jeff arrived a few minutes early.

"How was class?"

"It sucked. Teacher gave me a bunch of make-up work."

"Well, what do you expect? You've been on vacation for six weeks. While you're getting your haircut, I'll check it over, see if I can help you."

Daniel perked up, then quickly pulled back to hide it.

They drove to the barbershop. Roger sat him in the chair, covered him with a gray cape, and picked up a comb. It snagged in the grungy thicket of Daniel's nest of hair. Daniel winced and grimaced but said nothing.

"Little more challenging than I expected," Roger muttered, frowning at Jeff over the top of Daniel's head. Using scissors, he chopped away. Mounds of oily, matted fur tumbled to the floor. A chiseled, black mop began to emerge. Roger combed it out and wheeled Daniel around to face the mirror.

For what must have been a full minute, he peered at the stranger in the glass. His bewilderment melted into a boyish smile. Over his shoulder, Roger's reflection glanced back at Jeff.

"Wow, Daniel, you are wicked handsome," he said. "A regular movie star. In a couple of years, you're gonna be a bona fide lady-killer." Through the mirror, he looked Daniel squarely in the eye. "To mark this occasion, I'm giving you a new name," he intimated. He placed a hand on either side of Daniel's head. "A secret Ojibwa name. *Makoons*—Little Bear." He unfastened the barber's cape and let it fall away. "Go now and wear it in your heart, proudly, Makoons."

Daniel beamed, viewing an unexpected image of himself in the mirror.

❈   ❈   ❈

Every night after work, Jeff and Jenna met, more often than not, for drinks and dinner. When she arrived one evening at their favorite watering hole, the San-Bar, he was cued up and excited.

"You won't believe it. When I got there this morning, I caught Daniel actually standing in front of the mirror, combing his hair. And, he had picked up the mess in the bedroom."

Jenna did a double-take. "That's fantastic—really great, Jeff. Where did he put it all?"

"Well, it was thrown in the closet, but at least he got it off the floor."

"Okay, let's call that progress. I spoke to his teacher today. She says he's mostly completing his assignments."

"Wow, super. You know, given the circumstances, they're actually really good kids," Jeff said. "Daniel pretends to be a little tough guy, but it's really more a game of wits. I have to admit, I'm into the challenge of figuring out the next stunt he'll pull. But, Lucky, he's a pure marshmallow."

She laughed. "Yeah, imagine what would happen . . . if they had a real home."

Jeff looked up, trying to read her face. "That would be a quite a commitment. I thought the plan was to try and keep them in their own house—with Leah."

"It is—for now," she said. "But our fear is that Rachel won't last much longer, and no way will Leah be able to pick up the slack. She's not even handling the minimum, as it is. It's sad, but only a matter of time."

"Hey, I get it. Every morning I see what they're eating for breakfast. A bowl of cereal—at best. Daniel's often standing at the stove, frying bacon. I have the feeling that's all he eats."

"They know how to make mac and cheese. The cupboard's full of it, every time they get their SNAP benefits. And hot dogs. Our home aide takes Leah to shop, but if she encourages her to buy stuff like fresh vegetables, most of it ends up in the trash the next time she visits."

Jeff broached a thought he had been mulling over for a few days. "Since Daniel seems to be responding, it doesn't take me long to put him on the bus. What would you think if I spent a few minutes helping them cook breakfast? I don't think it would take much time to teach them some basic dishes—scrambled eggs, pancakes, biscuits, French toast."

Jenna's face lit up. "That would be so awesome." She reached out and gave him a big hug. "Jeff, you're just the best." Then, she kissed him. She tasted like red wine.

At that moment, he would have done almost anything for her. His aimless path of the last few years had now intersected with a new road. He was hurtling toward some unknown destination, one he embraced but didn't fully comprehend.

❊ ❊ ❊

The next morning, Jeff gave the boys a cooking lesson.

"How about bacon and eggs?" he said. "Daniel, I know you like bacon, but you need to eat other things too, if you want to grow taller and stay healthy. So, let's start with fried eggs. Lucky, you can't just eat cereal all the time. So, what do you say we give it a shot?"

"Okay," Lucky said, nodding.

"All right, Daniel, you cook the bacon."

Daniel set the frying pan on the stove and put in four slices.

"Weren't you gonna have any?"

"Yeah?" Daniel said. He looked up at Jeff, eyes narrowed, a puzzled expression on his face.

"And your mom, did you think about her? Ask her."

Daniel looked toward Leah. "Do you want some?" he asked.

She scrunched up her shoulders, put her hands in her lap, and looked away. "I'll have some," she said just above a whisper.

"Don't worry about me, Daniel," Jeff said. "I already had breakfast."

Daniel glanced up, brow furrowed and a faint smile that suggested he got the message. He added two more slices and turned the burner up to "High."

"Whoa, let me show you something. If you turn the heat down to Medium-Low, it takes a bit longer to cook, but the bacon doesn't shrink as much. You end up with larger slices."

Daniel dialed back the burner.

"Now, when it looks like it's getting a little crispy, you flip it over with a fork. Then when it's done on both sides, place the slices on a paper towel. This absorbs some of the fat. Lucky, find some plates. We'll transfer the bacon to the plates, then use the towel to mop the extra grease from the pan. Okay, now locate the eggs in the fridge. We'll cook them two at a time."

By the time they finished, they had covered the stove with

bacon grease and dripped egg whites, but they ate every bite. After a week or so, they were preparing several dishes in rotation. Jeff was gratified to watch them eat every bite of their own cooking.

Table manners were more challenging, but he made them all sit down together to eat. This encouraged them to be more organized. He wouldn't let them start until all the food was ready. At first, the boys whined, then eventually gave in. Leah never said a word, except "yes" or "no," but she was learning too.

❄ ❄ ❄

For the first time in his life, Jeff felt like he was doing something important. He was all aces with Jenna, and word had spread around town that he was some kind of miracle worker. Roger might have had a hand in that.

Even his job was better. He closed on a couple of big policies, even though he spent more and more time with Daniel and Lucky, especially on weekends. Often, Jenna came along too. They took them to a high school football game. They went for ice cream. They rode the Island ferry, and he arranged with Captain Louis Thibault, one of his Uncle Ray's clients, for each of them to take the helm for a few minutes.

"What do you think?" Jeff said as Daniel stood on a step stool, peering over the binnacle, and steered the hundred-fifty-foot boat across the Straits toward the Island. "Think you'd like to be a captain some day?"

Daniel tried to restrain himself, but grinned and grinned.

Jeff turned to Louis, who was keeping an eye on the helm. "What's the possibility, Cap? Think one of these guys could pilot a ship like this?"

"Well, if they stayed in school," he said, reinforcing Jeff's point. "You have to learn a lot of stuff to get your Captain's License." He glanced at Jeff. "Especially math."

On the drive home, the boys were quiet. Jeff saw through the rear-view mirror they were each deep in thought. He glanced over at Jenna. Her face held an expression that was beautifully serene. She turned to gaze at him, and he was sure she had been imagining a future together. He nodded toward the back seat. She glanced back, then smiled.

"You liked steering the boat, eh, guys?" They both shook their heads and Daniel grinned.

The ferry adventure was a big motivator. Neither one had been offshore before. Daniel could still be stubborn—independent—but as he finished more homework, his grades improved. Lucky had always been quiet, sweet-tempered, baby-faced, but now he had ventured out of his shell and transformed into a little chatterbox. Jeff visualized serious *possibilities*—even *commitments*. Everything was flowing his way. It seemed that his days as a drifter were sure to end—forever.

❋ ❋ ❋

The following Tuesday, Jeff stood on the dock waiting to take the noon ferry to the Island. His phone rang. It was the school secretary.

"Principal Gallagher wanted to let you know that Daniel will be an hour late today."

"Why's that?"

"He has to go to detention."

"Detention? What for?"

"She can explain when you come to pick him up."

"I wasn't planning to pick him up. He's been riding the bus home every day now with no problems."

"Well, someone has to give him a ride. He'll miss the bus today."

Jeff looked at the time on his phone. "All right, I'll be there. I hope this is serious."

"It is," she stated.

He immediately called Jenna.

"I've been expecting it," she said. "With Rachel's situation, and all. Problem is, I'm out in Perkins."

"Perkins? That's west of nowhere, even by Ojibwa County standards."

"Trust me, I get it, I'm on a two-track looking for a trailer full of neglected kids. Plus, I almost hit a skunk th . . . mor—.""

"Jenna, your phone's breaking up. Reception in the woods there is hit and miss. If you can still hear me, don't worry. I told the school I'd pick him up. I am headed to the Island for an appointment, but I'm pretty sure I can get back in time. I'll let you know tonight what the story is."

"Than— . . . —eff, I do— . . . —ow . . . wh— . . . I'd do wi— . . . —ut you."

When Jeff stepped off the return ferry to Loyale, it was three-fifteen, just enough time to make it to the elementary school.

The secretary met him at the door and let him in. "We had about given up," she pronounced.

"I was on the Island. There was a lot of fog and the boats had to slow down a bit."

"Okay, whatever. Daniel's in the detention room and he's not very happy." She pointed to a door next to the Principal's office. "Ms. Gallagher wants to speak with you first." She ushered him in.

"Good afternoon," the Principal said. "Have a seat. I'm sure you're wondering what's up."

"Yeah, I'm supposed to be at work right now."

"During recess today, Daniel hit one of our other students."

"He hit a kid—why did he do that?"

She raised her outstretched palms. "Wait, it's worse. He used a baseball bat."

"What?"

"Fortunately, it was a glancing blow, but it's very serious

behavior. If he hadn't missed so much school already, I would have been forced to expel him, but since you're working with him, he is only getting detention for the rest of the week."

"Who did he hit—and why?"

"I can't divulge that. It's confidential. But it seems to be a typical school yard spat, except for the bat."

"Who started it? Was someone picking on him?"

"Everyone on the playground has a different story, so we don't really know. I informed the other student's parents. They were quite upset, but the boy had on a catcher's mask and chest protector, so he didn't really get hurt. I think they have let it go, rather than tie up the next month in Juvenile Court. They're busy people." Ms. Gallagher looked directly at Jeff. "You need to get control of him. If he repeats this kind of violent behavior, I'll have to hand him over to the juvenile authorities."

"Okay, can I see him now?"

She looked at the clock behind him. "Yeah. His detention time is about up, anyway."

On the way home, Jeff let Daniel stew for a while in silence.

"So, what was that all about?" he finally said.

Daniel looked up at him. "Nothin'."

"Com'on, Daniel, you hit a kid with a baseball bat. That's not *nothin'*."

Daniel scowled. "Well, he started it!"

"Who started what?"

"Mickey Mettner. He kept calling me names when I was batting."

"Everybody does that. He's just trying to distract you from hitting the pitch."

"And he grabbed my ankle when I swung at it."

"Whoa, that's not fair, what did the ump say?"

"Didn't have no ump."

"Okay, the Recess Monitor."

"Nobody was watching. He started making fun of my name."

"Your name? Daniel?"

"No, my real name, my Indian name."

Jeff thought for a moment. *Makoons?* How did he know about that?

"We had to draw a picture and tell about it in class. So, I talked about my haircut and my new name. Mickey started calling me 'Macaroni Head'."

Jeff put his hand on Daniel's shoulder. "Makoons, you can't hit him anymore. He shouldn't do that, but if you hurt him, you'll be in big trouble."

"What about *him* . . . and his *gang*?"

"Gang? A fourth grader with a gang?"

"Yeah, the Zombeez. They keep messing with the other kids, like me and Lucky."

"They better not. I'll talk to the Principal about it." A thought flashed into Jeff's mind. "Does Mickey Mettner and the Zombeez have anything to do with you not going to school?"

Daniel's eyes narrowed. "I'm not afraid of 'em."

"I know, but stay away from them, anyway. And you tell me if they bother you or Lucky again, Okay?"

Daniel stared out the window and didn't respond.

"Look at me. Okay?"

"Okay," he said, a brooding expression on his face.

❄ ❄ ❄

Jeff dropped Daniel off at Leah's house and headed for the San-Bar. Daniel's latest actions threatened to set everything back. He knew what Art Belker would say—or his pop. 'You have to clamp down on him. Hard.'

Twenty minutes later, Jenna slid onto the barstool next to him. She was wearing a dark green dress and leggings that emphasized her red hair and fair complexion. She had splashed on something warm, spicy.

"God, you look great," he said and gave her a hug.

"Thanks, I dropped by the house and changed. You almost have to, after a trip to Perkins . . . so, what happened with Daniel?" she asked.

Jeff related the story. "And the worst thing is, the kid's a Mettner. They're the oil distributor for the whole county. You can't heat your house or run your car or drive your boat without paying them. They're like Loyale Royalty."

"Oh, wow, this is not good, Jeff. I am really concerned. Rachel might go in a matter of days. All it would take is one incident and Belker would come down on those kids and Leah like—"

"A drone strike," Jeff finished the sentence. "What about the Judge?"

"He'll do whatever Belker recommends. His real interest is the probate side of the court—wills, estates, etc. Most counties separate out Juvenile from Probate, but Ojibwa is so small, Deichman does both."

"That's weird, I never thought about it. So, what can we do?"

"To be honest, I don't know. Let's sleep on it tonight. I always think better in the morning."

❆   ❆   ❆

Jenna's cellphone went berserk—ringing, buzzing, flashing—in the dark. Jeff saw her glance at the screen and groan. It was 4:17 a.m.

"Jenna McCauley—what's up, Deputy?"

Jeff hated these late-night calls. They almost always resulted in Jenna meeting a cop to resolve some domestic situation involving children. Many of them came after the bars closed, some while the bars were still open.

"Okay, I'll be there right away." She laid down the phone

and rolled out of bed. Looking back at Jeff, she said, "9-1-1 just dispatched an ambulance to Leah's house. It's Rachel."

"Want me to go with you?"

"It's not necessary. I'm headed over to her house to make sure everyone's all right. I may have to move them to a shelter or foster home. I hope not. We really don't have any good choices right now, especially for Native American kids."

After she left, Jeff couldn't sleep. He made some coffee and sat drinking it at the kitchen table. What would happen to the boys, to Leah, if Rachel died? In a way, she had already passed and was lying in state in the bedroom she and Leah shared. Faintly breathing, rasping through a respirator, her presence was a fig leaf that allowed the Court and Social Services to keep the family together. Her death would destroy everything.

Shortly after five-thirty, Jenna called.

"Is Rachel all right?" he said.

"Actually, no. Rachel is on life support at the med center."

"Damn, I was worried about that. Are you at the hospital?"

"No, the house. You won't need to get Daniel ready for school today," she said. "I'll handle it. Everyone's pretty upset, especially Leah."

"What about the boys?"

"They're taking it hard too. Lucky's can't stop crying, but Daniel's trying to be stoic. He's not saying anything, but I can tell he's really worried."

"You sure you don't want me to come over and help?"

"No, I've got it. I have to figure out what to do."

After she rang off, Jeff continued to mull over the situation. Jenna might be forced to move the family to a shelter or place Leah in adult foster care and the kids with a different family. They might even be sent to another community. She had mentioned the Waucedah Reservation, which was an hour north. Loyale did not have the resources of larger cities. Jenna, Art Belker, Public Health, and a small volunteer network constituted the available bench. Plus, the local police and county sheriff. Could he—he and Jenna—find a third way—together?

❋ ❋ ❋

The next day, Jeff's mom called. They had not spoken since the blow-up with his father.

"I heard from your Aunt Charlotte about your volunteer work," she said. "I want you to know how pleased we are."

"Thanks mom," he replied. "I feel like I'm making a difference. I see their progress every day. But it's touch and go."

"Your dad has been bragging to everyone. He's so proud of you. He would never say it, but he's deeply sorry about the dispute."

"Well, me too. It's just that he's . . . so black and white about everything."

"True, but he wants the best for you, Jeff." She hesitated. "What about Jenna? Charlotte says she's really lovely."

Jeff delayed a moment. This was the actual point of the call.

"Yeah, she's terrific. The County is lucky to have her. And, honestly, me too."

"Sounds pretty serious."

"Yeah, mom, definitely moving in that direction."

"Actually, that's the reason for my call. We wondered what your Christmas plans were. Is Jenna going back home for Christmas, or…?"

"Honestly, we haven't talked about it, with everything that's going on."

"We would love to meet her. Why don't you invite her over for Christmas Eve?"

Since the passing of his grandmother seven years ago, Jeff's parents had inherited the hosting duties of the annual Johansen Christmas party. It had morphed into more than a family affair and included close neighbors and friends.

71

"I'll see what her plans are," he said.

"Promise you'll do that, Jeff. For lots of reasons, we would love to see you . . . and meet her."

❊ ❊ ❊

That evening Jeff related his conversation with his mom to Jenna.

"Of course, I'll come," she said. "I'd love to meet your parents. I was planning to drive back home Christmas morning, then spend the rest of the weekend. My sis has a new baby." She paused a moment. "But what about Daniel? And Lucky?"

"I don't know, Jenna. My gut tells me it would not be a good idea. They'd be the instant center of attention and topic of conversation. They might get peppered with questions from my half-drunk relatives. It might be awkward."

Then Jenna had a bright idea. "Hey, I've got it. Let's invite them over here next weekend for a real family-style holiday dinner. You know, all the trimmings."

"I'm lovin' it!" he said.

❊ ❊ ❊

Jeff was truly jazzed about this. He had financed a good part of his way through college by jobs in restaurants and food service kitchens. Since moving out of his parents' house, he imagined someday cooking a big holiday feast, featuring local game, and inviting all his friends. So, he stepped up, spent most of the following Saturday putting it together. Even bought some small gifts to open.

When Jenna and the boys arrived at his second-story apartment, he had the spread laid out on the kitchen table. It looked and smelled delicious—plum-glazed roast duck, brown rice, butter-sautéed wild mushrooms in a thick red wine sauce, apple-raisin slaw, and a huge blueberry pie. There homemade ice cream in the freezer. When he saw their eyes,

72

round as walnuts, gawking at all the food, he couldn't help but feel energized.

Soon everyone had a heaping plateful. Jenna was practically gushing. "Why this is really quite delightful—isn't it, Lucky?" He looked up, nodded, mouth full of roast duck. She passed the bowl of mushroom sauce. "Here, Daniel, try some of this on your rice. It's yummy."

Daniel made a face, set it aside.

"Oh, Daniel, you don't realize what you're missing."

He put his fork down. "Nah, I don't want none."

"You haven't even tried it," Jeff said. "How do you know?" He spooned some onto Daniel's plate. It sat there, congealing, on his rice and roast duck. He finally nibbled around it. Annoyed, Jeff told him. "Daniel, you try those mushrooms and that sauce. They're wild—I picked them myself."

"No, I hate 'em,"

"Try it, Daniel, it's good," Jenna said.

Jeff chided him. "Don't be impolite, it's bad manners if you won't even taste it."

Daniel froze, apparently trying to wait it out.

Lucky took a couple of bites of rice and sauce.

"See, Lucky likes it, don't you, Lucky?" she asked.

He nodded, looked at Daniel, who was now glaring defiantly.

Jeff stared him down. "If you don't try it, you can forget about the pie."

Daniel threw down his fork, crossed his arms. "I don't want no pie anyhow."

"Suit yourself. But you still need to try a bite."

Around the table, it was hushed. Jenna and Lucky were watching Jeff. He picked up Daniel's fork, loaded on a large, sauce-drenched mushroom, and touched it against his lips. Daniel tried to brush his hand out of the way. It left a deep red smudge. "Open up. You try at least one."

He sneered at the fork, turned away.

"You're holding up everyone else who wants to start dessert."

Jenna peered at him, disappointment in her face. "Daniel, you have been doing so well. Tell Jeff why you won't even try it."

"Yeah, Makoons. Back in the day, the Indians gathered mushrooms for all their feasts. Trust me, you'll like it."

Jeff held the fork up to his lips again. Daniel sighed and opened his mouth. Jeff shoved the mushroom in, then set the fork down.

"Now, swallow."

Daniel sat motionless for an eternity. His nose wrinkled and his lip curled in an expression of disgust. He picked up the fork and spat out a soggy piece of mushroom. His eyes pierced straight through Jeff. Cocking the fork back with his trigger finger, he let the mushroom fly. It hit the kitchen window and slid slowly down, a brown snail leaving a slime track.

Jeff grabbed him roughly by the scruff of the neck. "That was totally outrageous."

Daniel started hacking, wheezing.

"Jeff, stop, you're choking him!"

"I am not," he snapped. "But I'd like to—after *that* stunt."

Daniel slumped to the floor, gasping. Lucky stared at him, his face wrenched with anxiety.

"For *Chris' sakes*. Daniel, *damn it,* sit up." He was obviously faking it.

Daniel began shaking. Jeff pulled him onto the chair and slapped him on the back. Something wasn't right.

"Do something!" Jenna shouted. "He can't breathe!"

Daniel's face flushed red. Jeff smacked him again, hard. He was still hacking. Jeff forced open his mouth, reached in to clear it.

"Oh my god, you've *poisoned* him," Jenna screamed. "They

must be toxic!"

"Don't be ridiculous! we all ate them." Jeff reached around from behind, grabbed his fist with his other hand, jerked upward into Daniel's belly. Daniel gagged, then wretched, but nothing popped out. Jeff pulled again. And again. Daniel's eyes rolled back. His lips were tingeing blue. "Call an ambulance," Jeff yelled. *"Now!"*

He laid Daniel on the floor and tried to force his breathing. He rasped, coughing, choking. Lucky started to cry. Daniel's face puffed out, purple and yellow, blotchy . . . pulse racing, then suddenly weak. Jenna was on the phone with 9-1-1. She gasped, pointing at his neck. Covered with blistered mounds of hives, Jeff watched it swell to twice its size.

Daniel's pulse was fading fast. Jeff pumped on his chest. Daniel's eyes cracked open, unfocused, gazing blankly up at him. Desperate fingers reached out, clutched at his arm . . . then fell away. A camera flashed in Jeff's brain . . .

❊   ❊   ❊

The EMTs were taking forever. Jeff pushed frantically to force air into Daniel's lungs and make his heart thump. Finally, they sprinted up the covered stairway and surged through the kitchen door. They knocked Jeff aside. One of them fed a tube down Daniel's throat, another opened the valve on some oxygen. They hit him with an Epi Pen, then strapped him to a gurney and hauled him away.

Jeff, Jenna, and Lucky raced behind the EMTs to the Loyale Hospital. Jenna and Lucky were freaking out, reinforcing each other's fear with the looks they traded. In his head, Jeff was still screaming—"Breathe!" . . . "Breathe!" . . . *"Breathe!"*—as he bent over Daniel, pumping his chest, terrified he would not respond.

Jeff tried to calm everyone down, including himself. "Look, it might not actually be as bad as it seems. Once he makes it to Emergency, they have instruments to open his throat, keep it clear."

Jenna wasn't having it. "Jesus, Jeff, didn't you see his neck? He's suffering from a serious reaction. He could be in a coma . . . or *worse.*"

No one said anything more until they arrived at the hospital, but Jeff knew they were all thinking the same thing.

In the emergency room, the staff couldn't seem to stabilize him. They rushed him by ambulance to the Northwest Regional Medical Center, battling to save his life.

❊ ❊ ❊

Jeff, Jenna, and Lucky ran out to Jeff's car. The Med Center was a forty-five-minute drive across the Bridge. They made it in thirty-seven.

A volunteer ushered them into the waiting room. An emergency room doctor burst through the door and grilled them: What had the little boy been doing? What he had eaten or drunk? Had he touched or smelled anything unusual? Did he have any history of allergies, asthma, or other illnesses?

Jenna told him about Daniel's inhaler and what she recalled from his medical records. Jeff described the ingredients in everything they had eaten and drunk. He related the mushroom incident that made them think it might be food poisoning.

"No, it's not mushrooms," the doctor said. "He's experiencing anaphylaxis. It's a severe allergic response. The body launches a full-scale attack on something that might seem harmless—eating peanuts or shrimp, taking an antibiotic like penicillin, handling latex, being stung by a bee. Might be almost anything."

For the next few hours, the three of them sat there—fearful, silent, morose. At last, Lucky fell asleep, his head in Jenna's lap. There was nothing to do but hope for good news and twist with anxiety over the other possibilities.

﹡ ﹡ ﹡

Late that night, the doctor pushed through the doors again. Jeff glanced at the wall clock. It was twenty minutes after midnight. He tried to read the doctor's face. It was drawn, haggard.

Jenna jumped to her feet.

"Is he Okay?" she blurted out.

"He's stabilized. We think he'll make it."

"Can we see him?" Jeff asked.

"No, he's in the ICU. Go home and come back tomorrow. He should be able to receive visitors then. Possibly, even discharged."

"So, what was it?" Jenna asked.

"We're still not sure, specifically," the doctor said. He turned to Jeff. "You cooked the meal, right?"

"Yeah, I—"

"We'd like you to bring in samples tomorrow of everything that was on the table."

﹡ ﹡ ﹡

When they left the med center, it was dark, cold, with a light snow falling. Lucky stretched out in the back seat, sound asleep. Jenna was leaning away from him, elbow on the door rest, chin in hand, staring out the window,

Jeff was exhausted. The stress had pumped him into an adrenaline high. Now that Daniel appeared to be out of danger, his guard crashed down. The snowfall was hypnotic, as flakes swirled at the windshield. He could hardly keep his eyes cracked open.

Jenna's phone snapped him upright. She picked up the call.

"Hello—yeah, what's up? . . . at the med center. Daniel got sick . . . no, he's okay . . . had a reaction to something . . . oh, no—when? . . . Oh, god, that's terrible, couldn't be worse. Okay, thanks for letting me . . . headed there now. I'll tell them . . . Bye."

She hung up. She peered at Jeff, then glanced into the rear seat.

"Rachel just passed," she whispered.

"Oh, Jesus, that's the last thing we need. How do we . . .?" He motioned with his head toward the back.

"I'll tell him . . . and Leah, when we get home."

❆ ❆ ❆

As they pulled up to Leah's house, Jenna roused Lucky, then escorted him to the entrance. Jeff remained in the car. He couldn't imagine what she would say and was relieved when she asked him to stay behind.

She rang the bell, then knocked several times before a light came on and Leah opened the door. They disappeared into the house, Jenna's hand touching Lucky's shoulder. Leah shuffled behind, head bowed.

Jeff sat in the darkness, hands on the wheel, waiting for her. His eyelids hung from his brow like lead weights as his mind replayed the night's events in double-time. The burden of it—Daniel nearly dying—slowly crushed him into the car seat. The boy's swollen, mottled face. Its drawn appearance as he lost consciousness. His fingers as they last grasped for Jeff's arm. He had pledged to himself he would never hurt, let alone kill another person, and now, his impulsive, combative actions had almost *murdered* a little boy. The thought of it and his fatigue made him queasy.

Jeff wished he were back with Jenna on Steeple Rock, far away and not agonizing in the pitch-black confines of his car, mentally writhing while he waited for her to inform Leah and Lucky of Rachel's death. How would they tell Daniel tomorrow when they picked him up at the hospital? It would be one more blow to the boy's fractured life, perhaps more than that. He couldn't bear to think about it.

The door opened, and Jenna slipped into the car.

"Take me home," she said. She crossed her arms and stared blankly ahead at the falling snow. A few flakes melted in her long red hair, leaving small, clinging pearls of precipitation.

"How did it go?"

"I don't want to talk about it," she snapped.

"I'm sure it was—"

She gave him an icy stare. "Jeff, what in god's name was that tirade over the mushroom sauce about? You almost killed him!"

"I know . . . I can't understand what got into—"

"No, you don't realize, this is a huge problem."

"Hey, I get it. I've been sitting here trying to reconstruct what hap—."

"You really *don't* get it." She glared at him with an expression of disdain. "Tomorrow I have to report this to the Department and to Belker. Who knows what he will do, especially when he learns that while you were choking my ward, the boy's grandmother was dying in the hospital. I'll probably be fired."

"But you didn't do anything."

"Exactly, I didn't really *do anything,*" Jenna snarled. "Belker will be all over my director to have me at least suspended, if not removed." She shook her head, blew out a long breath.

"Aaahh . . . he won't do that," Jeff replied.

"New employees are all on probation for six months. One word from him or the Judge, and I'm *gone.*"

"Com'on home with me tonight—or what's left of it," Jeff said. "It will all look better in the morning. I'll make it right."

She punched him in the arm. "No. That's disgusting. I'm not having sex with you tonight. Take me to my house. I'm tired. *You* didn't have to tell Lucky—or Leah—that Rachel was dead. Do you know what that was like? And Daniel tomorrow. You need to spend some quality time with your *own* behavior issues."

"Hey, I'm really sorry," Jeff offered. "I'm not sure what else to say."

Jenna turned away to stare out the side window, arms still crossed. Her breath fogged up the glass. Her silence was intense. He turned on the radio.

❀ ❀ ❀

Late the next day, Jeff tried to call her. The phone flipped to voicemail.

"Hi, it's me. I'm just checking whether we need to pick up Daniel. I have to bring those food samples in and was wondering if you wanted to ride together. Call me. I'm leaving around two."

At two, he tried again with the same result, so he returned to the Med Center alone. He stopped to speak with Daniel, but he was sleeping. They told him to come back later or wait until they released him the following day.

Jeff drove back across the bridge to Loyale. It was late in the day, and he dropped by Jenna's office to see how she was holding up.

"It's a big mess," she said. She wiped the tears from her face. "They just called to confirm Daniel has an undiagnosed allergy to sulfites."

Jeff groaned. "Sulfites? From the homemade wine sauce?"

She scowled at him. "Yeah. The lab results showed it was laced with the stuff—it was suffocating . . . *deadly* . . . he almost died!"

"I know . . . I know," he said. But she wasn't listening.

"Now I have to figure out what to do with the boys . . . and Leah . . . and arrange the funeral for Rachel."

He tried to think of some way to show how much he cared about her. "If it would help, I can call a minister and . . ."

"That wouldn't be a good idea." She turned away. They were both worried about the kids, but a fissure had opened between them.

❊ ❊ ❊

Rachel's funeral was held at the Catholic Church. Aside from the priest and the organist, five people were seated in the front pews—Jenna, Leah, Daniel, Lucky, and Roger—when Jeff arrived and took a seat on the end. Rachel's plain, gray metal coffin lay in front of the altar. It was surrounded by flowers from the undertaker, left over from a funeral the day before. The priest covered it with a white cloth. It seemed tiny, made more so by the dark, cavernous church. They sang the opening hymn.

> *Birds are rejoicing,*
> *O'er hill and dell;*
> *Hushed is thy voicing,*
> *Sweeter that fell.*
> *Friend of our happy days,*
> *Mother of prayer and praise,*
> *Thine own sweet music says,*
> *Loved one, farewell!*

At the end of the first verse, the boys and Leah were all sobbing.

After the service, everyone followed the hearse to the Catholic cemetery on a wooded hillside overlooking the Straits. The attendants had dug a small hole in the back of the cemetery in an area set off for indigents and the unknown dead. The casket was lowered into the grave and covered with gravel. No headstone. That was that.

Jeff tried to console Daniel and Lucky, but before he could speak more than a few words, Jenna started to shepherd them away to her car.

Leah said, "Thank you," virtually the only words other than 'yes' or 'no' that she had ever spoken to him. Daniel stayed quiet, sullen. His face and neck appeared bruised and splotchy. Lucky asked whether he would still be coming over.

"Of course." But then added, "Well, if it's okay with Jenna."

The hard set of her jawline let him know it wasn't. She put them in the car, then stepped back for a word.

"Look, my Director says there will be a department investigation."

"Investigation?"

"Yeah, that emergency hospitalization cost over ten thousand dollars. Plus, Belker is making it an issue. Word made it around town that something happened on the Judge's watch."

Jeff grimaced. "But it was an accident."

"Yeah, well, *maybe*." She blurted out, "Jeff, you were way too aggressive. And . . . I . . . should have stopped you."

There it was. He didn't know how to respond. "I—"

"I've been told not to talk or otherwise associate with you . . . until 'this whole disaster is concluded'."

"But Jenna . . ."

Her jaw set. "No! Jeff, I may get fired. In a month, I could be back waiting tables." She thrust her hands out, keeping him at arm's length. "Just . . . stay away."

She wheeled around and strode back to her car, then drove off with Leah, Daniel, and Lucky. Everyone else had left too. He scanned around the cemetery. He was utterly alone.

❆ ❆ ❆

A few days before Christmas, Jeff sat at his desk, alternately making prospect calls, and staring off into space. What would come of the Social Services investigation? What would happen to Leah and the boys? And his relationship with Jenna?

His office phone rang. "Hey, you have a visitor," the receptionist said. "Your dad's here at the front desk."

Jeff hadn't spoken to him since the blow-up. He didn't know what to think, but hoped it wasn't about . . . "Okay, send him back," he said.

As his dad walked towards Jeff's office door, Ray yelled out, "Hey, Jack. What's up? You here to see me, or . . ."

"Nah, just came in to check on Jeff . . . and his new girlfriend."

"She's something," Ray said, giving him a wink. "Right, Jeff?"

Jeff nodded half-heartedly.

"Oh, hey, Jack, what time should we be at your house for the party on Christmas Eve?" Ray asked.

"Aah, four-thirty, five. I'll set up the bar in the basement."

"Okay, let you go, then. We'll be there. With bells on."

Jack dropped into a seat across from Jeff's desk.

"Hey, I know you're busy, Jeff, but that's actually why I dropped by. Your mom asked me to see if you and Jenna are coming to the party. We've heard so much about her from your aunt and uncle, we're really hoping to meet her."

Jeff slumped in his chair, shook his head.

"Everything all right?"

"No, it could hardly be worse," Jeff said. He raised an outstretched palm. "But I'm handling it."

"I'm sure you are," his dad said. "The rumor mill is churning pretty good around town, so I'm not surprised by your comment. Wanna talk about it?"

Jeff glanced up from his lap. His dad had never asked him a question like that.

"Not really, and it's confidential. But here's the short version." He filled him in. "Plus, he and his brother will probably be placed in foster care, likely out of county, or even some institution. Judge Deichman—"

"Deichman? You want me to talk to him?"

"No. Don't do that. I'm already in enough hot water—with Jenna—without that."

"Okay. Well, if you change your mind . . . I know Art Belker too—from high school."

"Look, dad, I'll ask her again," Jeff said. "But I don't think Jenna's going to be at the party. She's been told to stay away from me until the investigation is over."

"Aw, Jeff. That's too bad. Hey, you don't need a lawyer—?"

"No, it's nothing like that. Just her director doing some CYA. I think. But she's also pretty upset about the entire mess—and me. I'm not sure she'll even talk to me."

"Jeez, Jeff, I hope it works out. From what I've heard, she seems like a hell of a girl."

"She is, Pop. I'm really worried I may lose her."

"Hey, uh, about our fight. I . . . just wanted to say I was wrong to grab you like that. It's the way I was raised, but it was a mistake. I've regretted it ever since."

"I know, Pop. But thanks for saying it. I'm going through the same soul-searching about Daniel. In my own way, I pushed him too far. Way too far."

Jeff agonized the rest of the day. Was he really about to lose her? What would happen to Daniel . . . and Lucky? He had to speak with Jenna, no matter what she said. He could not just let her slip away.

❋ ❋ ❋

The next morning, Saturday, he drove over to her apartment to try to make amends. The weather was wet and windy, sleet mixed with snow.

She came to the door, opened it a crack. Her face was even more striking than the mental image he had stored from their first acquaintance. He threw away his script.

"J-Jenna, let me in," he pleaded. "I want to talk with you about Daniel—and us."

"No, you can say whatever from right there."

"Look, I'm sorry, it was an accident, I feel . . ."

"Jeff, you pushed too hard. Way too hard."

"I was just trying to create some . . . structure. Like my dad. It was an impulse. How could I know about the allergy?"

"But you almost killed him." She burst into tears. "It would have been like burying my own son."

"I understand. It's been killing me too." He stopped to regain his composure. "What's going to happen to Daniel? To Lucky?"

"Look, Belker is pressing the Judge to send them to a new experimental residential school for 'pre-delinquents.'" She made air-quotes with her fingers. "It's a Tribe partnership with CMU. They were setting it up when I was in school there."

"That sounds terrible."

"It is. It's funded with Indian casino money, so the County doesn't have to pay anything."

Jeff shook his head. "Typical." He hesitated. "B-but, what's going to happen to us?"

"Right now, Jeff, there is no *us*." She wiped her eyes with a finger. "You have to leave now." She started to close the door.

He reached out to hold it open. "But I love you, Jenna. Surely, you love me. How can we move beyond this? Can't you find a way to forgive me?"

"No, not today. Not tomorrow." She shook her head, glanced away. "Maybe . . . *some* day . . . somehow. Look, it's freezing, I just need to be alone."

Then she closed the door.

❊   ❊   ❊

That afternoon, Jeff headed into the office, trying to bury himself in his workload. It was no use. He had lost the ability to concentrate. His relationship with Jenna was all but over. He had been set adrift again, just when he thought he would touch solid ground.

Without Jenna, there was nothing for him now, except selling insurance for the rest of his life. That prospect depressed him even more. Coming back to Loyale been a terrible mistake. He knew what had to be done but dreaded the thought of it.

❄ ❄ ❄

On Monday, the day before Christmas Eve, he told his Uncle Ray he would be quitting to move downstate.

"Gosh, Jeff. I really need you," Ray said. The pained expression in his eyes confirmed Jeff's anxieties. "Why are you leaving?"

Jeff filled him in on his last conversation with Jenna and his soul searching over the weekend.

"What are you going to do for a living? Do you have a job lined up?"

"I've been looking online," Jeff said. "It may take a while. I'll try not to leave you hanging."

He had to get out of the office. Combing his hand through his hair, he remembered he needed a haircut before attending the Christmas Eve party. He bundled up in his wool overcoat, pulled the lapels and collar around his neck and chin, then walked swiftly through the wind and sleet to Roger's barber shop.

It was mid-afternoon, no one but Roger in the shop. He sat in the first chair, reading the Informer, Loyale's weekly newspaper. When the bell over the entrance jingled, he glanced over top.

"Hey, Jeff, why the long face? It's almost Christmas. The sugar plum fairies are supposed to be dancin' in your head."

Jeff smiled faintly. "Lately, the sugar plum fairies are dancing *on* my head."

"So I've heard," Roger confessed. "What's the latest on Makoons? And Lucky? I've been thinking hard about those kids since the funeral."

"Honestly, Roger, I don't know. I'm out of the loop, but it doesn't look good. They may get moved out of county."

"Oh, that's not good. What's your girlfriend say? Doesn't she do the juvy placements?"

"Yeah, but she's not speaking to me. Hey, you got time to cut my hair?"

"Oh, yeah, sure." He motioned to Jeff. "Here, hop in the chair."

Jeff flopped down in the second chair. Roger gave the pedal a few pumps to adjust the height. He wrapped a barber's cape across Jeff's chest and fastened it and a sheet of tissue paper around his neck.

"As I was saying," Roger continued. "I've been thinking about Makoons. Seeing him and Lucky at the funeral reminded me how much I liked that kid when he came in here for his haircut."

"Hey, Roger, giving him that Ojibwa name made a huge impression. It was a stroke of genius."

"Nah, it was nothing. I do that with all the kids first time I cut their hair. Say, Marilyn and I have been talking. Hardly nobody knows this, but we can't have any kids. We've been thinking seriously about applying to become foster parents— for the two boys."

Jeff sat up. "Roger, you guys would be perfect," he said, excited. "Daniel really looks up to you. And Marilyn would smother both of them with puppy-love and kindness."

Roger chuckled. "Yeah, that's what I'm thinking. We're going to call on Thursday, right after Christmas. But what about their mom?"

"If I had to guess, she's headed for an adult foster home. That seemed to be the thinking just before the funeral." Jeff peered at him through the mirror. "You have to do it, Roger. They really need you."

Jeff left the barber shop, elated. Was it possible it would all work out? He had no illusions that his affair with Jenna was totally in the dumpster, but at least Daniel and Lucky might be salvaged. That was a prospect to feel good about, unless something else happened.

❊ ❊ ❊

A couple of weeks after Christmas, Ray gave him a heads-up on a job in Grand Rapids, working for an insurance company. Ray had long been one of their agents. It was a decent position in a big firm. Jeff drove down for an interview, and with Ray's recommendation, he landed it.

By the middle for February, he had moved into a new apartment, a converted carriage house in the Heritage Hill section of the city. Despite Grand Rapids's stodgy, conservative reputation, Jeff found that he loved its underlying energy and soon made many friends. It seemed like a good place to restart his life.

He tried to contact Jenna off and on, but mostly they listened to each other's voicemails. He learned that the investigation was over and she had been reprimanded. "It's mainly to satisfy Belker," the message said. "Also, Roger and Marilyn received court permission to foster Daniel and Lucky. It seems to be working out. They're planning to adopt."

At one point he tried to convince her to transfer to West Michigan so they might be together.

"I need to stay here at least a couple of years to build my resume," she said. That was the last he heard from her. Two years after he moved, Jeff learned from Sharon Wisinski that Jenna had married some schoolteacher.

❊ ❊ ❊

Now, a decade later, he rarely made it home anymore, other than a few days during the Christmas holidays. His company loved him and over the past twelve years he was rapidly promoted. He had no time for his old life. But he tried to keep in touch with his parents, aunt and uncle, and one or two others.

Out of the blue one day, Aunt Charlotte called in a panic.

"Did you hear what happened to Daniel?" she asked.

"No, what are you talking about?"

"Jeff, it's terrible," she said. "I thought sure you would have heard. It was in the paper. Anyway, Ray and I were out at Benton's Shed…"

Jeff recalled she and Ray liked the Friday night fish fry there.

". . . Daniel was in the bar, shooting pool against a couple of guys. I hadn't seen him in a while. He's grown a lot, he's a taller than you, Jeff, and he's put on some weight. Roger told Ray last month that Daniel had just turned 21. He's been working as a deckhand on the ferries."

"So, what happened?" Jeff asked.

"One of the pool players started needling him—real personal—because Daniel had taken twenty bucks off him in the previous match. He was working hard to get his money back and started calling Daniel insulting names and making rude comments, trying to rattle him."

She related the incident that had taken place.

"Hey, Hiawatha, why don't you try a bow and arrow?" the kid said, smirking over his clever slur.

At first, Daniel seemed to ignore him. But then he started missing shots. Everyone in the bar could see it was getting to him as they all had a few more beers and the trash-talk grew nastier.

After Daniel sank a tough bank shot, the guy waved his arm in a tomahawk chop. "Nice shootin', Crazy Horse."

Daniel was down to the eight-ball. He pointed with his cue to the corner pocket, took the shot, length of the table, and missed.

"Hi-yo, Silver. Even the Lone Ranger couldn't save that one, Tonto."

His buddy let out a big horselaugh. Daniel had no one but

himself, and there were two of them. Charlotte said it was obvious they thought they could say or do whatever they wanted. A few other guys joined in, guffawing at each insult, thinking the bigmouth was a real wit.

He sneered. "Move over, Rover, let the Master take over." He leaned across the table, eyeing the eight-ball. "Time to go cry to mama . . . or sister . . . or whatever the hell she is." He looked over his shoulder for a laugh from the crowd that continued to gather. Full of himself, He tried to show off and miscued, leaving a short side-pocket shot for Daniel.

Daniel stepped up and leaned over to sink the ball. Just as he pulled back to release the stroke, the guy reached down and snagged Daniel's elbow. The ball skewed to the right and ricocheted off the cushion.

Daniel cracked. He wheeled and jerked him up by the collar. Punched him square in the face. The guy staggered, reeling backward. His buddy started for Daniel. Daniel whipped around and let him have it with the cue-ball. The guy's teeth scattered like buttons across the pool table. Daniel gripped the cue stick by the thick end and continued to flail, first one, then the other. Splinters flew like darts around the room.

"Customers scattered," Aunt Charlotte said. "Especially those jerks at the bar who knew the police were already on their way."

When the cops poured through the door, they found the two guys lying on the floor, bloody and unconscious. Between them stood Daniel with the shredded cue, chest heaving, his face and his green and white company shirt splattered with gore.

"So, who were the assholes harassing him?" Jeff asked.

I don't recognize the one on the sidelines—they called him 'Zombie'—but the mouthy one was that Mettner kid.

"Mickey? Mickey Mettner?"

"That's him."

Jeff swore. "He pulled the same stunt back in elementary school, grabbed Daniel's leg during recess when he was batting. Daniel hit him in the face with the baseball bat. Fortunately, he had on a catcher's mask. Or Daniel would still be doing detention. That entire family thinks they're entitled."

"Yeah, well, they got him this time," she said. "The Informer reported the entire incident. They arrested him for assault and attempted murder—they pretty much threw the encyclopedia at him."

"You're kidding! Oh, god, Roger and Marilyn must be really upset."

"Yeah, Ray said Roger is beside himself. Daniel's court-appointed lawyer tried to plea bargain. It didn't work, and that really upset Roger. Especially since Judge Belker sent Daniel down to Jackson."

"Belker? You mean the old Juvenile Officer is a judge now?"

"No, his son, Chucky. You might recall him from high school."

"That bullying son of a bitch!" Jeff railed. "Excuse me, Aunt Charlotte. Chucky Belker has always been an overbearing, belligerent, hardass. That really ticks me off."

"You should have been there," she said. "Once they arrested him, Daniel never stood a chance."

"Yeah, I've felt that way since the first day I met him and Lucky. Did you testify?"

"No, they didn't ask me."

"Seriously? What a sham." Jeff paused to think about it. "At least Mettner got what was coming to him."

"Yes, but at what price?" She asked pointedly.

"Jesus, you're right, Aunt Charlotte, a terrible price. That's very depressing. It just makes me sick. I hope they appeal."

"Me too, but that takes money—so, hey, let me give you the good news."

"What's that—you and Uncle Ray retiring?"

"No," she chuckled. "I'm talking about Lucky."

"Lucky? What about him?"

"Jeff, you would be so proud. He's working up at the Big Boy as a cook for the summer. We saw him a few weeks ago. Turns out he's a terrific golfer."

"Golfer?"

"Yes, Roger taught him. He landed a golf scholarship to Michigan State. He's been cleaning up the links this spring in Big Ten matches. Roger says he'll soon be the Ojibwa Tiger Woods."

"Wow, that's hard to imagine. He was so small back when he was eight."

"Well, he's not small now. You wouldn't recognize him. He's almost six feet—and he's studying pre-law."

"He wants to be an attorney? Who would have guessed?"

"No, a judge. He told Roger he's going to come back to Loyale and run against Belker. Said, quote, 'I'm going to kick Judge Belker's ass.' I think he'll do it too. Belker's a real blowhard."

"Just like his old man," Jeff added. "As for Lucky, more power to him."

✳ ✳ ✳

After Jeff hung up, he walked to the fridge and pulled a large orange from the produce drawer. The constant stress of his job made him vulnerable to chronic colds and bronchitis, and he couldn't afford to miss any work. Vitamin C was supposed to prevent that.

He peeled the orange, releasing a whiff of oil. It reminded him of his first encounter with Jenna McCauley and the perfume scent that trailed her out of the Lakeview Hotel bar. And the afternoon they first climbed Steeple Rock.

Anything and everything seemed conceivable then . . . even

undeniable.

Now, he was married to a good woman, with kids, house in the suburbs, exec job, large bank account. Now, no longer drifting. Now, possibilities closing off, exchanged for stability.

How different it all might have been, Jenna, Daniel, Lucky, and him. How different for all of them, especially Daniel. He had almost . . . killed him. Over what, food? No, a contest of wills, like he and his father. And now, somehow, it had ended with Daniel locked in prison.

Makoons—Little Bear—standing up for himself. This had always been his struggle, his plight. And he, Jeff, who thought he was helping, had succumbed to his own demons and sent Daniel flying down the wrong trajectory. What if everyone—he—had taken the other road?

Makoons caged in a cell. Jeff shuddered, imagining the situation. Now, years too late to fix, yet too unjust to ignore—system failure, culture failure, personal failure—most of all, his own failure.

He promised himself he would call Roger in the morning. Ten thousand dollars would mount a serious appeal and release Makoons from that hellhole in Jackson. Lucky would not be the only one to kick Chucky Belker's ass.

Jeff popped an orange section into his mouth. It was citrusy sweet. Sweet as the first time he spied Jenna McCauley, legs crossed, peering at her cellphone, waiting for the Island ferry. How sweet it might all have been.

Oh, man, he had it so bad for . . .

RUNTLEY GOES ROGUE

Let me not equivocate. I hate dogs. They're always slobbering on you, shedding mangy fur and dandruff everywhere, peeing on every bush and lawn chair. And this old saw about 'his bark being worse than his bite'—bull-*pucky*. Dogs stare at my ankles and think, *turkey drumsticks*. The first one was Gerald Garvey's Rottweiler down the street. He nailed my bike tire on the second morning of my paper route. It's been downhill ever since.

So, when my wife Margot suggested we purchase a dog for our two boys, Junior and Mackie, for Christmas, I put my foot down with a clunk. "Not 'til hellfire freezes into little pink snowballs!" It had been a bad day.

"Quiet, Ed, the boys will hear you. It's supposed to be a surprise."

"I'd rather own a boa constrictor with diarrhea...," I whispered. "...Or a pair of rabid tarantulas."

"Eeew, Ed, do you have to be so g-r-o-s-s, gross?" Margot said. She always does this when she's making an indisputable point—spells the key words. It's part of being an elementary school teacher.

She went to work on me with her "schoolmarm" one-two punch of logic and persuasion, vocally punctuating the end words of every sentence to make her argument. "Ed, children need a *pet*. It teaches them *responsibility*. A dog can be a real *companion*. Haven't you ever watched *Lassie*?"

"*Seriously*? Everyone knows Lassie was just a midget in a cheap fur suit. Dogs are so disgusting. They have fleas, they drool, they bark. They . . ."

"Ed?! Ed! Get a grip." She laid her fingers on my shoulders, kneading them to soften me up. "Can't you imagine a cute, cuddly puppy sitting under the tree on Christmas morning with a big red bow around his neck? I'm thinking a nice little beagle . . . like Snoopy."

"Oh, my god, oh my god, Margot, that would be the worst," I wailed. "Billy Sims had a beagle when I was a kid, and that mutt never shut up. 'Humphrey.' You'd hear ol' Humphrey about two a.m. every night, baying like a yowling banshee. The dog was possessed. He must have stolen my lunch bag fifty times at elementary school. I don't think Sims's ever had to feed him. Talk about a garbage scow. One time, Humphrey ate a whole pan of spareribs and sauerkraut, plus two pies that were cooling off in Bernie Pfeiffelman's garage."

Margot folded her arms and drilled me with a look of exasperation. "Well, they probably shouldn't have left the garage door open."

"They didn't. The garage had a little shelf with a trap door for home milk delivery. Humphrey crawled up a step ladder they had out to fix the gutter, jumped across to the ledge, and snuck in through the opening."

"How did they know it was Humphrey? Maybe somebody stole it?"

"Are you kidding? That dog crapped sauerkraut and blueberries all over the neighborhood. Right after that, Old Man Pfeiffelman bought a handgun."

"Okay, Ed, TMI. I don't think we require every d-e-t-a-i-l, detail. The kids need a dog and that's that." She stared into my eyes with a look of disappointment and pity over my inability to understand the simplest of self-evident facts. I had witnessed this before. "You think about it. You'll see I'm right."

The discussion was over.

❄ ❄ ❄

Six weeks later, I found myself in the family minivan driving to Cincinnati to pick out a new puppy. More precisely, the owner's Kentucky address was just under halfway between there and the other nearest large city, Huntington, West Virginia.

In the intervening time, Margot had scoured the Midwest for a dog. My final instructions to her were, "Well, at least try to find something unique. At a minimum, anything but a beagle." She researched dogs on the Internet and at the public library and homed in on a French Curly-Haired Newt Spaniel, a relatively new import breed to North America. She bought a dog magazine, *Modern Canine*, and called a number from an ad. A rather proper older lady answered the phone. Let's call her Mother Goosey. According to Margot, the conversation unrolled something like this . . .

"*French Curly-Haired Newt Spaniel Breeder's Society of America (FC HNSBSA)*, where good breeding is a way of life," Mother Goosey said. "May I help you?"

"My husband and I are interested in purchasing a Newt Spaniel," my wife lied.

"Madam, *French Curly-Haired* Newt Spaniel," Mother Goosey corrected.

"Right, right," Margot said. "Do you know where we might find a puppy?"

"Yes, of course. That's what we're here for. Where are you calling from, might I ask?"

"Indiana."

"Oommh, one of our more *agrarian* states. Well then, let me see . . . there are currently two available. You'll want the Denver puppy," Goosey said. "Not champion stock like the Baltimore whelp. But, well pedigreed, nonetheless. Would you like me to call the breeder for you?"

"How much do the puppies run? Say, the Denver puppy?"

"Frankly, madam, this is not the closeout department at

Macy's. That question isn't generally asked by members of the FCHNSBSA, at least until after they have been properly introduced to their new companion," Goosey sniffed.

"This is a pet for our children. So . . ."

"Madam, our puppies have been purchased by some of the finest families for their children." Goosey rose to the full height of her telephonic oratorical powers. "As our late President Carver DuPont used to say, 'good breeding is everything and has no price.'"

"But, certainly, you could give me a ballpark figure."

"Well, speaking hypothetically you understand, for a true champion conforming to the breed standard, the sky's the limit. Last year at Westminster, champion High Boy Peckinpaugh Rumsford Bonbon was sold for . . ."

"What about a more 'garden variety' pup?"

"Well, madam," Goosey said, "there are, frankly speaking, few of these available. However, occasionally, the less *uncommon* variants may be had for, say, $2500. In all candor, I should recommend against such a course of action. Shall I call the Denver party for you?"

"No. No, we'll need to think about that. I'll call you back."

"Don't dally," Goosey honked. "They are very popular, especially with upstanding professional people."

At that point, it became clear to Margot that a French Curly-Haired Newt Spaniel would not become part of the Grimwald household, and Junior and little Mackie would have to suffer through childhood without the benefits and advantages that other professionals' children were likely to experience through exposure to good dog breeding. She politely, but firmly rang off.

But Margot is nothing, if not a determined, liberated woman. Soon she was hunting the aisles of dog shows, sniffing out likely breeds. One day she burst through the front door, breathless over a Jarvey Terrier. "Ed, Ed, they're just the cutest *thing.* They have this little turned-up *nose*, like a Pug, and long silky *hair . . .*"

"Sounds like a walking floor mop."

"No, Ed. No, not like that at *all,*" she sputtered, face clouding over. "I talked with the breeder, and he'll have a litter available in two weeks. We can have our choice. All we need to do is send him the application." She thrust a six-page form at me.

"Margot, I refuse to apply to buy a dog!"

"Well, he says they don't sell them to just anyone, Ed. They're trying to maintain *breed integrity.*" She glared at me sideways with her little pouty-lip thing to let me know I shouldn't take it any further.

Well, at least a beagle wouldn't require an interview, I surmised. Or bank references. Or a home equity loan. "Oh, sweet Jesus!" I yelped, throwing up my hands. "I can see you won't be happy until there's a flea-covered, butt-sniffing, face-licking, shoe-chewing, fur-shedding, leg-humping, slobber-drooling beagle terrorizing the household. Go ahead. Go ahead, don't let me be the party crasher."

Margot rolled her eyes, but then a faint, surreptitious grin passed across her lips. Once more, the fates had lined up against me.

So, there I was, heading east on the freeway, an empty shoe box lined with a dish towel on the seat next to me. Perhaps, it was my destiny, perhaps, a lack of will. I can't say anymore.

First, we had looked on Craigslist. There were beagle/red ticks, beagle/dachshund, beagle/pit bulls, not to mention "begals." But no beagles.

"Seems like the kind of dog that can't say no," I quipped, referencing my favorite character in *Oklahoma.*

"Eew, Ed, do you always have to be so c-r-u-d-e, crude?" Margot replied.

"Well, anyway, I'm not buying a dog from someone who

can't spell his product. I'm not *that* gullible. Plus, you never know what you're getting into when you agree to meet someone in a parking lot to buy a dog out of the back of a pickup truck. He might be infested with rabies . . . or measles."

Thunderheads rolled across Margot's brow. "Ed, dogs don't get *measles*."

"Okay, okay, just kidding. Let's try the classifieds," I said. "At least they use proofreaders at a newspaper."

I checked the local rag. No beagles.

"Not to worry, Margot, there will be some in Sunday's Indianapolis Star," I suggested.

No beagles in the Star, nor in the next week's Star.

We went to two pet shops. Nothing but labs, chesapeakes and shepherds.

"We'll try the Chicago Tribune," I said.

No beagles.

"Call your friend Annalise. There's bound to be a mob of beagles in Michigan. That place is infested with rabbits."

Margot didn't say anything but threw me a dirty look. She's from Northern Michigan, near Loyale.

She texted Annalise. Over the next few weeks, Annalise checked the Grand Rapids, Lansing, Flint and Detroit papers. Probably, even the Escanaba Sea-Stack Oracle—who knows? She was on a mission for her BFF.

No beagles.

One evening after Margot put the kids to bed, we were sitting in the living room. I had a tumbler of Old Grand Dad going. Margot was reading American Kennel magazine.

She looked up.

"Hey, Ed, I just remembered. Annalise says we should check out the animal shelter. They might have something."

I choked, spewing bourbon down the front of my pajamas. "Oh, yeah," I gasped. "That's rich. Annalise never met a cause she didn't fall in love with." I put my head in my hands at the horror of it. My chest started to constrict. I was having trouble breathing. "S-so, lemme picture this. We go to the dog prison, secure a slobbering little mutt-waif from his pitiful incarceration. Six months later we find out why he's going through a 50 lb. bag of dog chow every week—he's half Shih-Tzu, half St. Bernard. Will Annalise be around with a front loader twice a week to scoop up Dog Poop Mountain? No, she'll be off trying to save the rainforest in Zimbabwe."

Margot shook her head. "Ed, there's no rainforest in Zimbabwe."

"No, not anymore, but that wouldn't stop her from trying."

"Sometimes you can be so c-r-u-e-l, cruel. Anyway, it was just an idea." She turned back to her magazine and flipped rapidly through the pages.

Having avoided a calamity of biblical proportions, I slogged over to the bar and poured a second OGD to calm my nerves, hoping this might be the last of it.

But by now Margot had become determined, if not obsessed. Every day she drove to the public library and searched the Internet, then combed through the classifieds of a dozen regional dailies. One fateful Tuesday, three days before Christmas, I got the call.

"I found a beagle in Cincinnati!" Margot shouted. "I phoned and told them you would be over this after*noon*."

"What about you and the kids?"

"They're still at daycare and school." I could feel her staring at me through the phone. "Ed, there's NO TIME!"

To this day I still can't believe that the entire supply of beagle puppies in the Midwest had been consolidated to a small barn on a high bluff in Kentucky overlooking the Ohio River. It was like a bad 50s science fiction movie, *Alien Beagle Abduction*. Yet here I was, taking a half-day of personal leave to track down—and purchase—an atomically radiated, genetically mutated, extra-terrestrial, fur-covered sleeper agent.

I had my marching orders from Margot and the following directions: '*1st the f-way, X over the river, exit Rt to a 4-ln, then off on a 2-ln, take the S fork of a Y to a grav rd, follow along the bluff until it Ts into a 2-trck, from where you can see a gate to the Rt with a brkn hinge.*' Pass through the infernal gate, plunge one-quarter mile down a washout, through a field, and thump on the door with the broken window at the second farmhouse. '*Three puppies left.*'

As I rolled into the yard, a zombie posing as a skinny young man wearing a Cincinnati Reds baseball cap and a ZZ Top t-shirt strolled out on the porch. He was chewing a large cud of tobacco. I've repressed his Christian name. Let's just call him Jethro.

"Y'all the party's called about the dog from Indiana?" Jethro said.

"That's me," I said, disregarding the tangled syntax.

Jethro thrust his hands into his over-all pockets. "You gonna hunt him?" he asked. "They's real good hunters. Just listen, you can hear his daddy back in the woods there, chasing rabbits."

"No, pal, it's a pet. For my kids."

His smile faded like the paint job on a '63 Corvair.

"It's my wife's idea."

He perked up, seeming to understand. "Well, if you decide to hunt him, they's *real* good hunters." He motioned me around the side of the house. "C'mon, I'll show you the dogs." He spat in the driveway.

A moment later, Jethro produced a squiggly armful of puppies. "Got two males and a female left." He set them down in the back yard. "Had eight, but they's real desirable for huntin' round these parts."

"What about that female?" I asked.

"Yup, she's a good'un. She'd make a real good hunter." Jethro picked her up by the fur of her neck. "Real healthy too." He flicked a tick off her right ear. "Got a few bugs on her, but most do, don't they?" He passed her toward me.

I gingerly held my hands out. A pair of needle-studded jaws clamped down into the fleshy part of my palm. "Yeeoowww!" I wailed, yanking it back.

Jethro chuckled. "She's a feisty little devil. Got real spunk, ain't she?"

I winced. "Maybe a little too much." I looked at the other two dogs. One was tearing at the owner's pants cuff, growling through his clenched teeth. The other was over near the barn, cowering behind a tractor tire disguised as a petunia planter.

"What about that one?" I said, pointing at the shivering ball of puppy fur.

"Him? You mean Runtley?" Jethro asked, glancing at the alleged, then back to me. "Well, frankly, sir, he ain't much of a dog. We call him Runtley on account of . . . it just appears like to fit him."

I peered at Jethro, skeptical why he was underselling his product.

He chawed a few times, then spit between his tennis shoes. "'Course, that ain't his official moniker. On the papers he's Maximilian Hightower Bonaventure III." He held up three fingers as proof. "But trust me, he won't amount to much. Don't have the natural enthusiastic attitude . . . or the nose…to be a respectable hunter."

I picked up Runtley. He peeked up at me, quivering, through a pair of big, brown, goopy eyes. He whimpered. His ears were acorn-tan, his saddles black as boot polish, and across his forehead streaked a blaze of white lightning. His nose was big as a handball. It was soft and slimy and crusted with dirt from rooting in the planter.

"How much?" I asked.

"Well, I usually get a hundred dollars, since they got papers and all," Jethro said, looking at his feet.

"You said yourself he isn't much of a dog," I countered.

"How about twenty-five?"

He spat another gob. "No, I got to get seventy-five, minimum."

"Forty dollars." I set down the dog.

He picked up Runtley and handed him to me. "Fifty."

I held my ground. "Forty."

"Forty-three, and I'll throw in the collar."

Through the preceding negotiation, Runtley hadn't made a peep. I reached for my billfold.

"Well at least he's quiet."

Jethro gave me a peculiar stare. He took the bills and tucked them in the large trucker's wallet chained to his belt. "I'll get his papers in the house."

I placed Runtley in the box in the back seat of the car. He immediately crawled into one corner and closed his eyes. I congratulated myself on my choice.

A few minutes later I was bouncing along the two-track, headed toward civilization. I made the "T" onto the gravel road and was thinking about my other Christmas shopping. Absent-mindedly, I flipped on the radio to check the weather report.

"BAAAARRROOOOOOOORR!!!!" A razor chill shot up the back of my neck. A sound filled the car that could only have emanated from beyond the gates of Hell. I glanced into the rearview mirror. Sitting up in the box, his bulbous nose arched skyward, was *Runtley*.

"My worst goddamn nightmare," I cursed between gritted teeth.

"BAAAARRRR*AA*ARRROOOOOOOOOORRRRR!!!!"

"Shaddup!" I bellowed.

He bayed again, louder.

"BAAAAAAAAAAARRRR*AA*ARRROOOOOORRRRR!!!!" Then, "BAAAARRRR*AA*ARRROOOOOOOOORRRRR!!!!" just to show he meant business.

"I'll wheel around and take you back to the mother ship," I threatened. "Don't make me do that."

"BAAAARRRR*AAA*RRROOOOOOOOOORRRRR!!!!"

He called my bluff.

I tried to scrunch down behind the seat to make a sound barrier. For two more hours, Runtley bawled like a wounded moose. By the time I reached home, my head ached worse than a walnut in a shop vise.

As I pulled in the driveway, Margot came running out. "Oh, Ed, did you get him?" She squealed, looking in the car. "Look, he's so *cuuuute*.!!"

Runtley stared back at her, tail wagging, dirty nose pressed against the side window.

"Oh, he's cute all right. Wait 'til he starts barking! Then you'll see how cute he is."

She picked him up. "Oh, do you make a *wittle barkywarky*?" she said, giving him a kiss. She glanced my way. "He's so small, he's like a teacup beagle. Is he a teacup beagle, Ed?"

"I wouldn't kiss him until we can have him checked for Lyme disease."

"Nonsense, he's just a puppy," she replied. "A *cute wittle puppy*."

"BAAAARRRR*AAA*RRROOOOOOOOOORRRRR!!!!"

"Goodness!" Margot looked up at me, wide-eyed.

I shook my head. "I tried to warn you. I *tried* to warn you."

Junior came running around the house from the back yard. "Dad! Dad!" he shouted. "You're home!"

Mackie chugged up behind him like a semi-tractor in low gear. Margot turned to face them, doing her best to hang on to the squirming ball of dog flesh between her outstretched hands. Their eyes grew big as gumballs.

"Pup-py," Mackie said.

The cat—more precisely, the canine—was out of the bag.

❉ ❉ ❉

By the following summer, we had been more or less integrated into Runtley's life. In the intervening period, we discovered several more of his idiosyncrasies, in addition to his penchant for baying. One, unless chained to a stake in the yard, he would run away. Two, he would sometimes run away even if staked in the yard. Three, he would not fetch a ball, a stick, or any other material object without meat on it. Four, he liked to bite his toenails, and, five, he was prone to the canine equivalent of Grand Mal seizures. Yes, our dog was an epileptic, perhaps the only one in North America and undoubtedly a byproduct of the trauma of his original alien abduction.

"What do I do about this, Doc?" I said to the veterinarian, whom I have referred to since as Dr. Doolittle.

Dr. Doolittle pondered the correct answer for a moment, peering at me over a pair of tortoise shell reading glasses.

"Mr. Grimwald, you are faced with three choices," he stated. "You can medicate him with a pill every day. It won't stop all the seizures, but it will decrease their frequency and severity. Unfortunately, it will be an ongoing expense. You probably don't have prescription coverage for your dog, do you?"

Bewildered, I shook my head 'no.'

"Well, it's something to consider," Dr. Doo stated. "More and more people these days are purchasing a small policy for pet medical . . . and dental. No sense being surprised by a large surgery bill."

So, what's the second choice?" I asked.

"You can have him put down . . . I assume you don't want to do that."

I looked over at Runtley. He was drooling out both sides of his mouth onto the examining table. He gave a short, pathetic whimper. I hesitated, considering Margot's reaction. It was a tough decision. And the children. "No, I suppose not." I let out a deep sigh. "What's my third choice?"

Doo shrugged "Well, you can just live with it. But at least twice a week you'll be cleaning up vomit, urine, and/or feces around the house."

I groaned. "Okay, start us on the pill."

Thus, began my perpetual morning ritual. I quickly learned that dogs do not naturally take pills. A certain technique must be mastered which involves the placement of the object in question between index and middle fingertips, grasping the dog's jaws at the hinge, squeezing to force them open, and injecting the pill between beartrap teeth into the esophagus with a quick plunging, lance-like motion. Then one hand is used to hold the snout closed while the other massages the trachea. Too quick and the pill is mashed against the dog's upper lip, dropping to the floor and rolling into the register. Too slow and the pill is dredged onto the back of the tongue, ten seconds later to be expectorated into the food dish or behind the refrigerator. A wet slimy pill is more difficult to insert than a dry one, so a second thrust rarely succeeds. When timed correctly, the proper action is not unlike the instant when a matador drives his sword between the shoulder blades of a Spanish fighting bull; in other words, a moment of art and high drama.

However, as the doctor predicted, this only somewhat moderated Runtley' s seizures. A dog experiencing a seizure is a pitiful sight. First, he begins to drivel spit across the carpet or new hardwood floor. Simultaneously, his eyes dilate and seem to twist independently in their sockets, so he looks like a drunk about to fall off a mile-high bar stool. He will take a few tottering steps, sometimes dragging his hind legs, or teetering from side to side. Usually, about this time, the vomiting commences, as well as the loss of bowel control. Then he does a full "crash and burn," falling to his side or collapsing into a heap on the bathroom rug. There he lies for an hour or so, quivering like dog gelatin.

The effect of this sequence on daily family life can only be described as similar to the scramble in a submarine about to be fired on with depth charges: I am lugging him to an easily cleanable spot; Margot is racing to the utility closet for the sponge, towels, and carpet cleaner; Junior and Mackie are jumping for cover so they won't see him pee, poop, and puke or, god forbid, be required to help clean it up. Boys who a moment ago were picking their noses or watering the floor around the toilet or expectorating wads of "gristle" at the dinner table now exhibit the delicate sensibilities of 19th century debutantes and cannot directly observe the grim details of everyday doggie life. "Daaaaaa-ad!" they say, rolling their eyes when admonished to sop up a yellow puddle on the kitchen floor. "It's not my turn. He's not even my dog." And so it goes.

Then, imagine this post-traumatic scene in the "recovery room." Here is poor Runtley being cradled in Margot's arms, shivering and sad-eyed, his insides more or less liquefied, a great tidal wave of drool and slobber rolling off his chin, his paws limp as month-old celery, watching television on the couch. And about to devour dog biscuits and canned gravy or some other form of canine comfort food.

After several months of fussing like this over the dog, I noticed one day a curious phenomenon. As he lay there on the davenport, head flopped across Margot's lap, paws tucked up under his corpulent torso, eyes closed, breathing long, deep, heaving sighs, I happened to walk into the room. Margot was absorbed in a TV game show. Just as I looked at him, he opened one eye and periscoped around the room as if to check whether anyone was watching. Then he shot me a look that I can only describe as Machiavellian. A calculating, crafty smirk of self-satisfaction that let me know he had in some Pavlovian way figured out that a couple of well-timed retches followed

108

by a wobbly, helter-skelter walk toward a dark corner of the living room carpet would produce a seat upgrade on the davenport, complete with snacks, a thorough rub-down, and eventually a gourmet doggie meal.

"The little bugger, he's faking it," I groused, pointing at the culprit.

Down periscope. Runtley gave out a weak, low moan.

"What??!" Margot said, scowling at me, then glancing sympathetically at the comatose mutt. "Oh, that's a terrible accusation, Ed. Poor baby, don't listen to him." She placed her hands over his ears.

"You'll give him a complex," she said. "Dogs have feelings too, you know."

"If he keeps pulling his little stunt, he won't have feelings for long," I threatened. But I might as well have been talking through the TV to Oprah. And so it went for the better part of a year.

Now, you would think a dog with so many creature comforts might stick close to home, but not old Runtley. Open the door a crack to shoe off a Jehovah's Witness, relax a grip on the dog leash to swat a mosquito, or crank open a second story window for a little fresh air, and Runtley would bolt for the wild blue with the determination of someone attempting to beat the land speed record at the Bonneville Salt Flats. Many a night I have driven around the neighborhood, a bag of dog treats and a length of rope on the front seat, looking for our prodigal mutt in every canine club house and doggie den of iniquity. Where he went on these spontaneous jaunts I have yet to determine; in a day or two he would return, redolent of last week's trash, often with a scratch across his nose, a bleeding paw, or a stomach bloated up like a rugby ball, as happy and nonchalant as he had been green-eyed and driven to bolt at his departure. And so it was that I became not only Runtley's personal physician, but his warden as well.

Which brings me to the Crisis.

❉ ❉ ❉

Margot and I own little place up on Lake Michigan, a sanctuary really, where we often go with the kids on weekends during the summer. It's not much, a step up from a house trailer. But Junior and Mackie can play in the surf and throw sand at each other. Margot can sit under a beach umbrella with a wine glass and a romance novel. And I can guard Runtley on the front porch while sipping a bourbon and sometimes squeeze in a short afternoon nap. It's also about halfway between our house and the town we first met—Loyale—near where her parents live.

This past May we made our annual caravan to open the cottage. Margot had loaded our van with the usual supply of non-perishables, linens, beach toys, National Geographics, and garage sale plunder stockpiled over the winter. Everything else, including Runtley, had been packed into my car. Margot no longer lets Runtley in the van because—and I forgot to mention this before—the little control freak becomes car sick about a block down the road from our house. Actually, I timed this once, and it took two-tenths of a mile, exactly twenty-three seconds.

So, we had developed a ritual each time we traveled to Michigan with Runtley. First, we stopped feeding him twelve hours before leaving. The purpose of this was to minimize what became known in our household as the "chunky" effect. Second, we packed up everything except Runtley and his traveling pet carrier, known alternately as the HMR Palanquin. Third, we brought out a large roll of paper towels and covered the floor of the enclosure. The remainder of the towels was placed conveniently next to the cage. Fourth, we placed the cage in the back seat on top of a large plastic garbage bag. Fifth, we all climbed into our respective vehicles and Runtley was brought out on a leash and forcibly pushed into the crate. (After a few upchucks, he had developed a certain phobia about getting into the car). Sixth, we roared off down the road to see how far we could make it before Runtley began to retch.

On this occasion, we made it 1.7 miles, almost to the freeway ramp. I pulled over at the Amoco, and Margot swung in behind me. She rolled down the window.

"Well, he's getting better," I said, matter-of-factly. "At least, this time it's the clear stuff, not like that yellow cheesy mush after we went to your sister's house.

"Eeewww, Ed," Margot said.

"Hey, if you think I'm gross, you ought to try wiping up this cage," I said, glowering at her, then Runtley. "You fur-covered slime bucket."

Runtley gazed back at me through jaundiced, bloodshot eyes. He burped.

"Margot, I'm gonna murdelize this dog, I swear it."

"Take it easy, Ed," she replied. "He's still just a puppy. Besides, we don't have time right now."

This last comment was vintage Margot. Margot, who is normally mild-mannered, gets wound up like a dime store alarm clock whenever her parents come to visit. They had announced their intention to meet us at the cottage the following weekend so, naturally, Margot was already thinking of all the sweeping, cleaning, dusting, and tidying up she would be doing over the holiday. The last thing we needed was a problem or delay.

Which was exactly what we were in for. Murphy's Law should have warned us that if anything could go bonkers, it would do so. And at the worst possible time. The evidence was all there: one, it was Saturday of Memorial Day weekend, when no one is available to help. Two, we hadn't been to the cottage since last fall. Three, her parents were practically on their way; and, four, every time we had opened our cottage in the past three summers, we had experienced an "incident." Initially, it had just been an aggravation, but with each new travail, we had grown more leery. Were we jinxed? We papered over our increasing dread with a thin veneer of humor.

"What will it be this time?" I said, melodramatically. "Another burst pipe? Thank god, I needed a shower that day. Or a burnt anode in the water heater?"

"No, I think we've learned our lesson on that one—'don't flip da circuit breaker 'til da tank's done fillin','" she said in basso profundo, lampooning the plumber who had given us that advice exactly one year and one day ago.

"Well, my vote goes for the electrical. I don't care if we did install new 100-amp service, that big blue spark I saw still makes me tingly all over."

"My money's on the septic pump." In fact, it was the refrigerator. A few hours later, as I peered into the back of the freezer, a small glacier which had flowed over and around the frozen cooling fan made it clear why the milk jug felt warm to the touch and the lettuce looked like frozen spinach.

"Seems to me like there's something wrong with the thermostat," I said. "The fan keeps running, creating an icy build-up which blocks air circulation between the upper and lower parts of the device. It's actually quite interesting, I never noticed before how the . . ."

Margot erupted. "Oh my god, oh my god, Ed, what are we going to do? All this food, no fridge, and my parents coming next weekend. That's just typical, just typ-i-*cal*."

When Margot says "typ-i-*cal*," my antennae immediately go *sproing*. Usually, she starts bawling, but every once in a while, she goes ballistic and starts hurling things. And I own a typewriter with a bent "h" key and two broken bowling trophies to prove it.

"Aww, Margot, now don't worry," I said. "I'll run up to the Shell Station and get some ice and an extra Styrofoam cooler.

I'll call the Sears guy and get someone out this weekend. They have emergency people on call for just this sort of thing."

"Right. On Memorial Day weekend? I think you better just plan on buying a new one. This junker hasn't been right since the day we moved in. I can't live like this, cooking out of a Styrofoam cooler. We'll all end up with food poisoning—salmonella, botulism, e coli—Ed, do you want your children to *die*?"

"Margot, no one is going to get food poisoning," I said to reassure her. "You find some ice and I'll call Sears." The last thing I needed was Margot looking over my shoulder while I negotiated with the repair center. As she rolled out of the driveway, I dialed the 800 number.

"Hello, Sears Repair Center," announced the nasally voice on the other end of the line. "What state are you calling from?"

"Michigan," I replied.

What are the last four digits in your telephone number?"

"Four-seven-nine-four."

"And your zip code?"

I gave her the zip code.

"And now your mother's maiden name."

"*Diebelwacker*. For Chris' sake, aren't you going to ask me what my problem is?"

"Of course, Mr. Grimwald, we're just trying to maintain security."

"How did you get my name?" I asked.

"Oh, it's all right here in the database. By the way, how is the anode in your water heater . . . still functioning?"

"Yes, it's marvelous. But my fridge isn't. It's *kapoot*."

"Oh, one moment, Mr. Grimwald," she interrupted.

A recording came on telling me that my phone call might be recorded for quality control, litigation, and training purposes.

"Okay, now, Mr. Grimwald, exactly what is the problem?"

"My refrigerator won't work. It's a Kenmore Superfrost II. I think the thermostat is busted, because the fan is all iced up in the freezer, and the fridge is as balmy as Charleston, South Carolina."

"Where is your fridge? In Charleston? I thought you were calling form Michigan."

"I am," I growled. "I was making a… never mind, can you send someone out? My hamburger is turning gray, and the pistachio ice cream looks like clam chowder."

"You should get that on some ice right away, Mr. Grimwald. It wouldn't do to get food poisoning, especially on Memorial Day."

"I know, I *know*," I muttered. "When can you send the repairman out?"

"Well, they're all busy. It is the holiday. Except for our man in Sioux Falls, South Dakota. But I suppose that's a bit far for him, isn't it? Where again did you say you were calling from in Michigan?"

"I didn't, but you've got the database. Look me up. We're about two and a half hours north of Chicago."

"No need to be a smarty pants, Mr. Grimwald, We do the best we can, but technology can't solve *every* problem."

"Great, so check your database and tell me when the next available repairman in the Midwest can make a service call."

"Well, we can't send just any repairman," she noted. "We have to send someone certified to work on the Kenmore Superfrost II. That model hasn't been manufactured since 1967. Let me search for a moment. Yes, you're in luck. One of our five nationally certified technicians works out of Grand Rapids. We should be able to put him right on it. He can be out on Wednesday."

"Wednesday?" I bellowed. "You don't understand. I don't live here. My wife's parents are coming. Your man will come out on Wednesday, and he won't bring a thermostat. He will have to order it from some warehouse in Tuscaloosa, Alabama. If I pay the fed ex charges, it will come on the following Tuesday. I will have gone to Indiana and come back again. My in-laws will have arrived at our dumpy cottage and found our broken refrigerator. My wife will be mortally embarrassed and will have committed hara-kiri with a steak knife from the gift set we received when we opened our new credit union savings account. My children will be MOTHERLESS!"

"Calm down, Mr. Grimwald, Shouting doesn't solve anything. Now I can get him out on Tuesday first thing. That's our best offer."

"That's the best you can do? I'll be forced to take a day off work," I groaned. "Tell you what, lady, put me down. But I'm going to call some independents to see if one of them can be here sooner."

"That's your choice. But remember you won't be getting Sears quality. And be sure to cancel within forty-eight hours, or we will be required to charge your Sears Card. Now, do you have your Sears Card handy?"

"I don't have a Sears Card," I said, dejected.

"Would you like one, today, Mr. Grimwald?" she said warmly. "If you apply immediately, I can offer a 10% discount on your repair work next Wednesday."

"Tuesday!"

"Oh, yes, Tuesday, first thing."

"No, I don't want another credit card. I'll give you my Visa card number."

"Don't leave home without it," she said, breezily.

"That's American Express."

"We don't take American Express. Just Visa or Mastercard, and, of course, the Sears Card."

"I know, I know," I said, giving up.

As I hung up the phone, Margot came through the door. I was about to let her in on the good news when the phone rang again. It was my sister Bucky. Bucky is not her real name—it's Victoria—but we've called her that since she was a kid. She's always been a tomboy. For some reason, when she was around six or seven, she took to wearing cowboy clothes, and one day my dad said, "hey, cowgirl, you look like a real Buckaroo." The name stuck.

Bucky and her husband Don Dobroski live in Okemos, near Lansing, the state capital.

"Whatcha doin', Eddy," she said.

I told her about our refrigerator fiasco. "You know darn well that repair guy isn't going to get the blasted fridge fixed, and Margot will have a saber tooth kitten when her mom shows up next weekend. Then her dad will spend all weekend taking it apart. They'll leave Sunday, and I'll be stranded with refrigerator parts spread from one end of the cottage to the other."

"That's a real conundrum," Bucky said. Apparently, she was still doing work on her vocabulary to keep sharp on crossword puzzles.

Sis always has an angle on everything. So why was I not surprised when she said, "Hey, Eddy, I got a cerebral tornado. You can have my old fridge! It's sitting out in the garage waiting for the Amvets to haul it away. They pick up anything, you know, so Donny called them about our appliances. Wait 'til you see our new kitchen. You can bring your fridge over and swap it out. Then, you can see our remodeling job, too. We'll put some burgers on."

So, the proverbial die was cast. It seemed deceptively simple: One, pull the dead fridge. Two, load it into the van. Three, drive one and a half hours. Four, swap the units in the garage. Five, pig out. Six, retrace my tracks. Seven, plug in the new ice box. Eight, as the sun goes down, drink a properly chilled adult beverage. Nine, congratulate myself on a job well done. Ten, reward myself with another adult beverage.

That was before I discovered that the cottage must have been built around the fridge. To understand how this could have happened, you need to know a few things about our little Taj Mahal. It's a one-room affair with two lean-tos for cooking and sleeping, cobbled together from the detritus of a hundred remodeling jobs along the Lake Michigan coast. We have fixtures from a '20s bungalow, gingerbread from some long ago demolished Carpenter Gothic, Greek Revival farmhouse clapboards, early subdivision windows (stained maple) except for the sleeping porch, whose windows are repurposed French doors nailed into a frame of salvaged two-by-fours, and—there is no way to adequately describe this—doorways, some of which appear to have been part of a turn-of-the century hotel and saloon, and others which apparently once graced the residence of Bilbo Baggins.

Of course, the shortest path from the kitchen to the van required that the refrigerator pass through both the door openings. In truth, it was the only path.

"Margot," I bellowed. "Bring me a tape measure." Sure enough, a quick measurement produced the following conclusion: first entry with door fully open, twenty-eight inches wide; second entry with door fully open, twenty-seven and three-quarters; refrigerator, twenty-eight and three-sixteenths. Refrigerator wins at the threshold.

"Aha!" I shouted. Not quite hopeless. If I took both doors off their hinges, I would gain the requisite one-half inch, and the fridge would pass through by a frog's whisker. I would need a furniture dolly, and with both doors off, someone to keep an eye on Runtley, but theoretically, it could be done and back in time for sunset on the porch with cocktails.

So, there I was, after a run to town for a dolly, loading the fridge up and maneuvering it into position in front of the doorway. Then, using a cold chisel and my trusty Estwing hammer, I drove the hinge pins, and the doors dropped away

117

from their casings like losing cards from a blackjack shoe.

"Open house—guard the dog!" I yelled into the kitchen. Margot said he was out with her on the porch.

I rolled the fridge into place and began to wiggle it through the door casings. It wedged on the second one. I dropped down on my hand and knees to see where it was jammed. The drip pan louver was buried about 1/4 inch into the pine door stop. With a little luck and a thin pry bar, I could pop the louver off the fridge, once free of the casing. Unfortunately, the prybar was located in the drawer just on the other side of the fridge. "Margot," I yelled, "Hand me the pry bar through the doorway, so I can . . ."

Margot opened the porch door. "What's that, Ed?" Something black and white flashed by her. Then, I knew how Custer felt at Little Big Horn. Runtley came bounding across the living room floor. Using the first threshold as a springboard, he hurled himself against the open doorway. I threw up a hand to stop him, a Cubs outfielder at the wall trying to prevent the game-winning home run. Runtley sailed over the refrigerator and landed in centerfield.

In a flash he sprang onto the driveway and in another, he was across the street and bouncing toward the beach. Runtley, one-to-nil.

"Jesus H Christ," I yelled, watching his tail disappear over the bluff. "You better be back by Sunday, or you can *hitchhike* your mangy little butt to Indiana!"

So, there I was, a hearse driver at the head of a funeral parade, the dead refrigerator lodged like a snow-white casket in the rear of our minivan, motoring along the Gerald Ford toward Bucky's house. As I pulled into the driveway, up rose the garage door. There stood Bucky in full wrangler gear and behind her, like the monolith in *2001: A Space Odyssey*, a vintage Frigidaire, complete with its Art Deco chrome logo.

"C'mon around to the patio," she said. "Donny's burning

some meat on the grill."

"Okay, but give me a sec," I said. "I want to offload my boat anchor and slide your Frigidaire in its place."

She took off her Stetson and let it flop behind her, hanging by the cord around her neck. "I'll give you a hand, Eddy."

We wrestled the fridge out of the back and rolled it into the garage. I measured hers. It was a little taller but would just fit through the cottage door. "You won't believe the problems I had pulling this fridge out of the house. Oh, and Runtley managed to jump through the doorway and was last seen headed for Southern California."

"That little scamp," she said. "Probably going to Hollywood. That dog is the biggest drama queen I've…"

"Sorry, not in the mood, Buck," I said. "I got the kitchen door laying against the side of the house, the kids are combing the township for our renegade mutt, my in-laws are probably pulling out of their driveway as we speak, the ice cooling our fridge food is rapidly turning into bath water, and Margot is on the verge of her own total meltdown…on second thought, I should probably skip the burger and just get back home before the stove goes out too."

"I see your point, Eddy, that's calamitous, if not catastrophic," she said, scoring twice on the crossword page. "Let's load the Frigidaire, and I'll wrap you up a couple of McDonny burgers for the road."

An hour and a half later, I was back at the ranch. I slid the replacement fridge out of the van, stood it up and rolled it on the dolly toward the kitchen doorway. The mosquitos were thick as L. A. smog and just as lethal.

Margot appeared from the screen porch where she had taken refuge. She glared at me with one of her 'how could you?' looks.

"It's Avocado!"

"Hey, it's FREE…I can spray paint it any decorator color

you'd like—including *arctic white*!"

"By next weekend?" she said, folding her arms.

"Let's just get it in the house and plug it in—before the ice in the coolers succumb to global warming."

With the door off, it was relatively simple to slide the green monster through the opening. I slipped it into place in the kitchen, leaving some space so I could reach around and plug it in. I squeezed between the fridge and the side wall. I grabbed for the plug.

Margot opened the freezer door. "Arrrrrrrggh," she screamed.

I stepped around and looked in the open box. An odor of decomposing mushrooms wafted toward me. The inside was coated with what appeared to be blue-green rabbit fur.

"It's moldy," she cried. "The whole fridge is full of mold."

Junior burst through the open doorway to the house.

"Dad. Dad. You're home," he said.

I got down on one knee, looking him in the eye. "Did you find Runtley?"

Mackie flew around the corner. He reached up and grabbed my face, twisting it around toward him. "Runtley is in a house."

"Where?"

"Over at the trailer park," Junior replied.

"In a house," Mackie repeated. "He was in the window."

"Show me."

"Ed, what about the fridge?" Margot asked, pointing to the freezer. "I can't believe your sister didn't clean it."

"We'll deal with that later, we've got to go find Runtley, don't we boys?"

They nodded.

"Come on, Dad," Mackie said, pulling on my arm.

I stood up and looked at Margot, shrugging my shoulders.

Margot put her hands on her hips. "Ed, you should be ashamed of yourself, using your little sons for an excuse like that. At least, put the door back on the house."

I rehinged the door and we set off across the street. As we reached the entrance to the Gloria's Lakeview Sunset Trailer Park, a Sheriff's vehicle turned out of the driveway, heading away from us. Staring out the rear window like a prisoner on his way to the county hoosegow, taking a last regretful gaze at the past mistakes and misadventures of his life, was Runtley.

Mackie ran after the patrol car.

"Dad. Dad. Where are they taking him?" Junior asked.

"Doggie jail," I replied.

The vehicle disappeared over the hill, and the source of all my consternation and turmoil for the past seventeen months, our beagle Lassie-wannabe, was gone.

The boys and I trudged up the driveway.

Margot saw our long faces. Her eyes darted from me to the boys.

"Where's Runtley?"

"He got arrested," Junior cried.

"By the police." Mackie said. "They're locking him up."

They burst into tears.

She knelt down and gave them a big hug. Over their shoulders, she stared a hole through me.

"Ed, what is going on?"

"I don't know. Maybe, they found out about his Kentucky juvenile record."

"Ed, that's not funny. Now, you get on the phone and call that Sheriff. We want our Runtley back—don't we boys?"

They both nodded, tears streaming down their dusty cheeks.

"Shouldn't we leave well enough alone? I'm just saying."

"Ed, that is so c-a-l-l-o-u-s, callous. Call 9-1-1." She pulled Junior and Mackie closer to her. "Our precious little Runtley has been *abducted*." She glared at me.

I looked down at Junior and Mackie. They both stared up

at me, frowning. No one said a word.

I groaned. "Oh, all right, give me the damn phone."

Margot stepped into the house and handed me the phone off the kitchen wall. I extended the antenna and dialed 9-1-1. It rang twice.

"Allowahegon County. Office of the Sheriff, Elmer T. Jenkins, Deputy Elmira T. Jenkins speaking," the dispatcher said in an authoritative voice. "Who am I talking to.?"

"Edward Grimwald, and I…"

"Where are you now, Edward?" she asked.

"I—I'm home."

I meant, what is your address?"

It's 2125 Lake—look, my dog has been stolen by one of your deputies."

"Stolen?" she shot back. "Sir, the Sheriff does not steal people's dogs."

"Well, I have two witnesses who can confirm that one of your officers was seen driving out of Gloria's Lakeview Sunset Trailer Park with the dog in his back seat. This is a champion beagle Maximilian Hightower Bonaventure III," I said, encouraging her to treat the circumstances with the proper level of gravitas. "If anything should happen…."

"Sir, the Sheriff does not steal people's dogs. He has all he wants or needs at the animal shelter."

I thought about warning her that at any moment Runtley was likely to puke, so there would soon be plenty of evidence of his whereabouts, but given her denial of the reality of the situation, I decided to let them ascertain that on their own.

"Sir, this is an emergency line—for people. If your dog is lost, you need to call the Sheriff's Office main number and speak with the duty officer." She read me the number and abruptly hung up.

"Okay, you too," I said to the dial tone.

Ed, what's happening?" Margot asked.

I put my hand over the phone receiver. "Never mind. I'm handling it."

I dialed the Sheriff's Office. A man came on the line.

"Allowahegon County. Office of the Sheriff, Elmer T. Jenkins. Deputy Ernest T. Jenkins on duty."

"One of your officers took my dog."

"Sir, who am I speaking to?"

"Edward P. Grimwald."

"And you. Edward, are alleging that your canine was taken into custody by one of the Sheriff's deputies?"

"Yes, Ernie, less than an hour ago at Gloria's Lakeview Sunset Trailer Park. I have witnesses."

"And would this be the same small beagle that vomited in the back seat of the deputy's car, destroying public property?"

He had me there. "Maybe," I said.

"Well, Edward, he's been incarcerated at Sheriff Elmer T. Jenkins' Animal Control Facility. I'll transfer you."

"I'll just come and pick him up…." But the line had been put on hold. I glanced over at Margot and the kids. They were huddled together on the patio. Her jaw was clenched.

I gave her a 'be patient, everything's under control' finger wave.

Someone took the line off hold.

"Allowahegon County. Sheriff Elmer T. Jenkins' Animal Control Facility. Officer Edwin T. Jenkins speaking."

"Look, Edwin, I was transferred here by Ernest. He says you are in possession of my dog. The one your deputy, whose name is probably Jenkins, abducted from Gloria's Sunset Lakeview Trailer Park an hour ago. My kids are crying. My wife is sizzling in her own juices. I've been playing hopscotch all over your department, and I want my dog back. Where is he?"

"Who is speaking, sir?"

"Edward Parker Grimwald. I am a property owner here."

"Well, Mr. Parker, your dog is unlicensed. We're required

to hold him 24 hours for rabies observation."

"What! My dog is not rabid. He's been vaccinated and licensed in Indiana. Check his tag."

"He doesn't have a tag, sir."

I glanced over at the kitchen table. There was Runtley's collar and tag. I groaned, remembering that Margot had taken it off to give him a doggie bath in a futile attempt to reduce the malodorous aftereffects of his journey north.

"...From our viewpoint, Mr. Parker, he's a rogue animal. We have to treat him as a public health hazard. Plus, he vomited in one of Sheriff Elmer T. Jenkins' vehicles. We will undoubtedly need to replace the seat. You, as the alleged owner of the reprobate, will be responsible for the Sheriff's expenses. Plus, the rabies shot, and the County Dog License—assuming that you are right that he doesn't have rabies. If he does, well that's a whole different kettle of fish."

"Look, Edwin. Let's not go down a rabbit hole here. If I produce the tag, can I simply drive to your facility and remove him from your responsibilities? I'm certain you have lots to do."

Yes sir, Mr. Parker. That's a factual statement."

"Okay, I'll be right over. Where is he?"

"Not so fast, sir...he's here at the animal control facility in the Sheriff Elmer T. Jenkins Correctional Complex in the City of Allowahegon. However, it's closed to the public until Tuesday."

"You mean I can't pick my dog up until Tuesday?" I shouted.

"First thing Tuesday morning, 7:00 a.m."

I wanted to say, "Well, you keep him then," but I looked over at Margot and the boys and decided in the present circumstances that would be an unwise course of action.

I rang off and filled in Margot on the details.

"Well, you'll have to take a day off, Ed. I need to be in

school on Tuesday. It's our final week. The boys and I will leave on Monday." Turning to Junior and Mackie, she said, "Daddy will bring our sweet little Runtley safe and sound back in Indiana on Tuesday, won't you, Daddy?"

"Unless he tunnels out of doggie prison and steals a car," I responded.

"That's nothing to joke about, Ed." Turning to the boys, she said, "Daddy didn't mean that. He's just making another of his insensitive wisecracks. Ed, the boys are traumatized. Look at them."

They both were wearing hangdog looks.

"Yes, I'll pick him up on Tuesday. The sheriff told me they were having salisbury steak tomorrow for the holiday—and pie and ice cream—and he would make sure Runtley got a double helping."

They both perked up at that news.

Margot turned to face me. As her shoulders drooped, she shook her head, giving me a glassy stare. She silently mouthed the words, "Typical. Typ-i-*cal.*"

Sunday morning, I woke up to the smell of Pine-Sol. I looked into the kitchen where Margot was washing out the refrigerator.

"I can't believe Bucky didn't clean out the fridge before she called Amvets. Your family, sometimes…." She continued scrubbing vigorously.

"With all the commotion during their remodeling, she probably didn't think about it."

"What a mess…"

"If you're done, I'll plug it in," I said, attempting to steer the conversation. I squeezed between the fridge and the side wall, reaching for the plug. I pushed it into the outlet.

GZZZT. I jerked my hand back.

"The fridge light blinked off!" Margot said.

"Yeah, I know. I got a heck of a shock."

"Oh my god, don't tell me this one's dead, too," she wailed. "Ed, you need to go buy a fridge. Pront-o!"

"Relax, it's probably just the plug, easy to fix…"

Margot screamed. "Fire! Fire!" Black, acrid smoke poured out of the fridge. "Grab the kids. We have to evacuate."

Junior and Mackie ran into the room.

"Dad, Dad!" Junior said. "The fridge's on fire!"

"I'm hungry," Mackie added.

"Stand back!" Margot placed her outstretched palms against the boys' chests. Then she ran to the sink and grabbed the sprayer near the faucet.

"Don't spray water on it." I pushed the fridge door shut. "It's an electrical fire."

"Ed, you get that Shrek thing out of here."

"No problem, let me turn the power off, so I can unplug it."

"And bring it back to Bucky. Or…*whatever*." She threw up her hands and rolled her eyes. "Typical. Typ-i-*cal*."

I flipped off the kitchen circuit breaker and jerked the plug from the wall socket. Margot turned on a large fan in the living room and pointed it toward the back door. As the smoke cleared, the upper half of the fridge door was now covered with a thick layer of soot, black and green and smokey as Jabba the Hutt. I contemplated another funeral procession toward my sister's garage and appliance mausoleum in Okemos.

Margot's stare had an air of lethality. Unless I got control of the situation, any minute now, household objects could start flying in my direction.

"You guys head to the beach," I said in a cheery tone. "I'll run into town and shop for a new fridge—and figure out how to dispose of the old one." That seemed to calm everyone down.

As I headed toward town in the minivan, I watched Margot, followed by Junior and Mackie, fade into the distance through the rearview mirror. They marched single file across the street to the park, a goose and two goslings, sporting identical neon green plastic sunglasses and purple paisley bathing suits.

She lugged the yellow landscape cart I had purchased for her birthday the previous summer. I knew from experience it was laden with towels, blanket, suntan lotion, soda-pop-filled ice chest, aluminum folding chairs, boom box, romance novel, coloring books and crayons, plastic sand pails and shovels, swim masks, inflatable floaty toys, potato chips, a baggie full of celery and carrot sticks, a tub of cantaloupe chunks and fresh strawberries, napkins, and individually wrapped peanut butter and jelly sandwiches, cut in quarters. In other words, pure Margot, my schoolteacher/ mother/ wife/ paragon of organizational virtue.

If I hustled to the appliance store, I could return in time for a plastic tumbler of Old Grand Dad followed by a soothing afternoon siesta on the porch davenport—*sans* Runtley. Lord knows, I had earned it.

After a trip to the big box stores in Grand Rapids, I lay on the screen porch couch, empty bourbon glass on the concrete floor below my pillowed head. Ethereal visions of a placid, dogless heaven swirled about my addled brain.

The screen door slammed.

"Waaaah!" I jolted awake, bewildered. Margot towered over me. With her wet auburn hair, oversized bright green sunglasses, and purple bathing suit, she appeared to be a giant insect.

She shook me. "Ed! Wake up! Where's the new refrigerator?"

I flinched, involuntarily wrapping my arms across my face. I peeked between them. Behind her stood Junior and Mackie, similarly attired. My conscious mind finally broke the surface of my brain.

"Oh, no problem, Margot. Gosh, you scared me. They're

delivering it tomorrow. And hauling away the old…"

"Ed, what is *that*?" She pointed at the back of the minivan.

"You mean the big-screen TV?"

"Exactly, Ed, exactly, the big-screen TV."

I sat up, rubbing my eyes, as I gathered my thoughts.

"Oh, ah…that. Well, when I arrived at Ahab Appliances, they were having a terrific Memorial Day Sale, up to 40% off storewide, and I got to looking at all the TVs and everything, which are right by the door as you enter. And I remembered how you're always encouraging the boys to watch PBS with its wonderful educational programming, and I thought…"

"So, you bought yourself a TV."

"No, no, not just for me, Margot. For the whole family."

"Ed, where are we going to put *that thing?*" She pointed again. "It must be six feet long."

"No, now that's not true, Margot, not true, it's only 70 inches, diagonal. You'll see, it's really great. I was thinking it could go on the family room wall near the…"

"Ed, we can't afford that. We're buying a new refrigerator, or did you already forget?"

"No, no, it's all being taken care of. See, that's the beauty of it. Kind of a BOGO. See, the Ahab salesman, Jerry, he saw me looking at it and he asks me, am I in the market for a new TV? Of course, I said no, I'm here to buy a fridge. But Jerry says, okay, I just thought you looked mighty captivated. Which, to be honest, I was kind of interested. I just never saw a TV with a picture that clear and bright and, the colors Margot, just like reality. In fact, better. They had a video going on the Grand Canyon, and that's when I got thinking how great it would be if Junior and Mackie could see that video. It was like you were standing on the rim looking down into a million years of natural history…"

"Ed, get a grip."

"Right. Sorry, Margot, I'm still a little groggy."

"So how many bourbons *did* you drink?"

"Just the one, Margot, just the one. Well, maybe two. Anyway, so the salesman Jerry points out that since the fridges are all on sale at up to 40% off, a $1595 refrigerator only costs 957 bucks, a savings of 638. And a $795 TV only costs 477. So, you take the $638 savings on the refrigerator and put it on the TV. For that, you get both appliances, and you put the change—$161—in your pocket. Or you can take $99 back out and buy the extended warranty, so you don't ever need to worry about your fridge catching fire—for five years." I held up my outstretched palm. "I knew you would want that, and we still come out 62 bucks ahead . . . which I thought it would be nice to take everyone out for dinner tonight since you guys are all heading back tomorrow, and I have to stay behind to get poor little Runtley out of hock and wait for the fridge delivery."

"And the old fridge? What about that?"

I could see she was softening. "That's the best part, Margot. Well, almost. See, I was still reluctant, like you. It's a lot of money even though we were getting the TV for free. Actually, kind of getting a rebate back, too. So, I told Jerry, 'Well, I don't think I can swing it. Our old fridge is dead, and I have to pay someone to haul it to the dump. But he says, 'Oh, I'm sorry, Ed, I forgot to tell you. We haul it away for you when we deliver the new fridge. But wait, there's more, Ed. We give it to a local charity like Goodwill or the Salvation Army, then we send you a receipt from them with your extended warranty, which gives you a charitable tax deduction that pays for the cost of the warranty. So, see, it's free.' Well, I couldn't really argue with that, Margot."

I smiled at the boys. "Who's ready for some dinner?"

"Dad. Dad. I am," said Junior.

"I want chicken fingers," Mackie added.

"Oh, Ed," Margot sighed, shaking her head. "There really is no hope for you."

A few miles from our cottage, on the outskirts of Jenkinsville, is the Wye-Knot Inn. It's a railroad-themed bar and grill that has been our neighborhood haunt since we bought the place.

"Everybody get changed," I said. "We can pick up some more ice at the Shell Station on our way back home."

❆ ❆ ❆

Monday morning, I helped Margot get the kids around and pack up her car. The traffic down the freeway toward Indy can be brutal at the end of a weekend, so she always tries to make an early start. It was sad to see them go. On the other hand, I looked forward to having the day to myself. Well, mostly to myself. I still had to cancel the Sears repair guy and wait for the refrigerator delivery.

At quarter to eleven, I had cancelled Sears and was finishing the Sunday paper, enjoying a second cup of coffee on the screen porch. Up the driveway rolled a delivery truck from Ahab Appliances. Two gorillas hopped down from the cab and headed toward me. The driver held a clipboard.

"Roll it around to the back," I said through the screen. I walked into the cottage and greeted them at the kitchen door.

"Mr. Ed Grimwald? I'm Bob from Ahab, but everyone calls me 'Plumb.'"

"I get it—'Plumb-Bob'—clever."

He checked his paperwork. "We have a Whirlpool fridge for you."

"And I'm Fetch," his partner said. Apparently, someone had fetched a few of his teeth, hence, the name.

"You sure the fridge will fit through the door?" he said.

"Absolutely positive. I've been loading fridges in and out of here all weekend."

They gave me a confused look.

"Hey, it's a long story."

130

Plumb-Bob checked his paperwork again. "It says here, you also have one to pick up."

"Yeah, it's right there in the kitchen."

"You mean that burnt one?" Fetch asked.

"Yeah, the burnt one."

"Does he have a nickname? I like it when people name their appliances. Makes it more personal."

"We call it Avo."

They looked puzzled.

"Avo Cado."

Plumb-Bob glanced at Fetch and laughed. "He's putting you on, Bro'."

Fetch grinned. "Okay, Mr. Cado, let's go for a ride." He tipped the fridge and Plumb-Bob caught the top corners. The two of them waddled out to the truck, the fridge straddled horizontally between them. They set it down and, raising the liftgate, tipped it up, rolled it back and strapped it against a side wall.

"I own a dolly," I said. "If you want to borrow it."

"Thanks, but we have one too," Plumb-Bob replied. "We broke it yesterday."

Fetch pulled some cardboard and strapping off a fridge on the truck. He rolled it to the liftgate and lowered it to the ground. Tipping it toward Plumb-Bob, they reversed the process of loading the previous fridge. I pulled the door back so they could ease it through the entryway.

They set it upright in the kitchen. It was too easy.

"Where's your water line?" Plumb-Bob asked.

"What water line?"

"For the ice maker, in-door water dispenser, and coffee machine."

"Oh, Christ," I muttered. "I forgot about that. We don't have one. Margot will kill me."

"Hey, no problem, Boss, happens all the time, we got your

back," Plumb-Bob said. He opened the sink cabinet and bent down, using his cell phone as a flashlight. "We can tap the cold-water inlet and run a quarter-inch line behind the fridge."

"That would be great, but I need to leave tomorrow morning."

"No, Boss, we'll do it right now. Fetch, get the water line kit."

"Whoa, wait a minute, what's this going to cost me?"

"Only a hundred ninety-nine dollars."

I grimaced. "How much?"

"If you pay cash, we can do it for one-fifty."

"Okay," I said. "Put it in."

"You're going to need a water filter, too."

"It doesn't come with a filter?"

"No, not for the sale price."

"You mean I have to go back to Grand Rapids and buy a filter? Bull-*pucky*!"

"Naw, relax, Boss, we're taking care of you. We carry a spare on the truck."

"What's that cost?"

"They're cheap, Boss. Forty-nine ninety-five."

"No cash discount?"

"No, sorry, that's the sale price. But they last six months."

"You mean every six months I'll be replacing the filter—at fifty bucks a pop?"

"Hey, don't blame me, Boss. Talk to Jerry. He's supposed to explain all this. We're just delivery guys."

"What else do I need? If you tell me the compressor is extra, and you have one on the truck, I'm…"

"That's funny," Fetch said.

"No, once we put the line in and install the filter, you're good to go," Plumb-Bob added. "But I did notice the TV in your van. You're going to want a wall mount for that."

"Don't tell me, you have one on the truck."

"Funny you should bring it up…"

"How much…?

"Seventy-nine ninety-nine, but we can do seventy bucks, cash."

"I scowled at him. "All right—add it to the bill. You know, you're cutting into my drinking money."

Fetch retrieved the wall mount. I told him to stick it in the back of the minivan, with the TV and the dog carrier.

Plumb-Bob hooked up the water line and ran a glassful from the fridge door.

"Okay, that does it," he said. "You'll need to run about three gallons more to clear air out of the line and remove any filter sediment. But right now, I have to unplug it to give the refrigerant an opportunity to settle. You can turn it on in twelve hours."

"Twelve hours? You must be kidding," I said. I looked at my watch. It was 12:05 p.m. You mean to tell me I have to wait until midnight to plug in the fridge?"

"Yeah, sorry, Boss. It's right here in the manual." He pointed to a paragraph ambiguously titled *Breaking In Your New Whirlpool Refrigerator.*

"So, all day, I'll be forced to run to the Shell Station to feed the goddamn ice chests while my fridge gets over its belly ache? Seems like you would stock some Pepto Bismol on the truck."

"That's funny," Fetch said. "I don't care what you say."

"Hey, look," Plumb-Bob said. "I'll knock off ten bucks. Go up to the Wye-Knot and drink a couple of cold ones on us. The tourists are all headed back to Chicago. It'll be nice and quiet. Midnight will be here before you know it."

It wasn't a half-bad idea. The fridge was installed, that was the most important thing. There would have been bullets flying next weekend with no fridge and Margot's parents knocking on the front door. I had a new TV, and the delivery guys had fixed my water line. True, my appliance deal was now $270 negative, but all things considered, maybe, it was the most I could expect.

"Naw, you guys keep the $10. Consider it a tip," I said. "Tell Mr. Ahab I insisted."

"That's funny right there," Fetch said.

"Yeah, there is no Mr. Ahab," added Plumb-Bob.

"But it's called Ahab Appliances."

"There's a story behind that," he said.

Fetch smirked. "A funny story."

"But kind of tragic, too,"

I bit. "So, what is it?"

Plumb-Bob lit up a cigarette. "Well, the company founder, Calvin Clybourne—Jerry's great grandpa—was a New Englander and a graduate of Boston College. In his youth, he had a thing about the novel Moby Dick." He looked at me through a cloud of smoke. "You know the book?"

"Yeah, I think every college kid in America had to read that damn "doorstop" in their freshman lit class. Not to mention the movie."

"Well, Mr. Clybourne was apparently as obsessed with the book as Captain Ahab was with the whale. For years he tried to write a sequel. The family had a little money, but he realized he needed a way to support his literary aspirations. So, he took a job in a hardware store that sold appliances. Eventually, he bought out the owner and renamed it Ahab Appliances."

Plumb-Bob took a drag on the cigarette. "One evening after a marathon bout of drinking and writing, he suffered through a terrible nightmare. In his dream, *He* was Captain Ahab, and he was chasing Moby Dick, but instead of a whale, it was a giant white refrigerator. There he was, standing on the bow of the little longboat, pitching and rocking in the middle of the Atlantic Ocean, being circled by this giant white enamel lev-i-athan. But every time he hurled the harpoon, it bounced off the fridge. All night long he tried to annihilate it with no success. Finally, it turned on him and crushed the whaling boat, pulling him down into the depths of the roiling sea. He burst awake early in the morning, screaming over and over, 'To the last I grapple, from hell's heart I stab, for hate's sake I spit my last breath.' After that, he was never the same, and doctors later determined he had suffered a minor stroke.

"Jerry's grandfather took over, building Ahab Appliances into the retail chain we recognize today. Everyone in the company knows this story. It's the first thing they tell you during training."

"But what's the point to all that?"

Plumb-Bob stubbed out the cigarette on the liftgate. "Don't get carried away by the appliances."

There was a Zenlike moment of silence as we each contemplated this company parable.

"And don't drink a lot right before bedtime," Fetch added.

"Wait, you guys are messing with me, right?" I glanced from one to the other, grinning, looking for a "gotcha" moment of recognition. Neither cracked a smile.

"No, it's the gospel truth. All documented in a book Jerry's dad, Clarence, wrote, '*Chasing the Impossible Dream: Calvin Clybourne's Transcendental Journey.*' You can buy it at the store."

"Right, I saw it—up by the register. But if Jerry is the owner's son, what's he doing in Grand Rapids? Why isn't he in Boston at company HQ, training to fling the Ahab harpoons at the next giant, threatening appliance?"

They chuckled.

"Jerry? Oh, he fell in love with a Dutch girl from Hudsonville," Plumb-Bob said. "They met in Ann Arbor. Her dad's a minister. She wouldn't leave West Michigan, so Jerry's dad built a store in Grand Rapids for them as a wedding present. It's become our flagship. Turns out Evangelical Christians really love appliance sales. Who knew?"

After they packed up and headed out the driveway, I walked

back inside to admire our new fridge. It was beautiful. But the Ahab story placed it in a new context.

I reflected on my own circumstances. Perhaps, *I, too,* was a bit like Ahab—and Runtley, my Great White Mini-Whale. Despite his numerous shortcomings, perhaps, he didn't deserve some of the abuse I had heaped on him over the past seventeen months. True, he was a conniver, but I was forced to admit, he was also just a dog, and a diminutive one at that.

I spent the rest of the afternoon and evening at the Wye-Knot, one eye on the clock, the other on the establishment's dwindling supply of Old Grand Dad, pondering what I had come to know as the "Runtley Predicament" and related life-altering questions.

It was midnight bar-time when I stumbled off my stool, fell into the minivan, and made my way down Lakefront Drive toward the cottage. Fortunately, there were no Jenkins family members lurking in unmarked squad cars. Or I might have found myself in the same grim situation, and possibly even the same holding cell, as Runtley.

❄ ❄ ❄

Tuesday morning, I woke to the phone ringing in the kitchen. It was undoubtedly Margot, checking in on her way to school. I sat up in bed. My head was pounding like it had been dribbled on the driveway by Shaquille O'Neal. As I fought through the brain-pain, I could already hear the questions: 'Did you get the fridge? Is the food okay? Did you get Runtley? Is he all right? Are you on your way back?'

"Ed, how's everything?" she said.

"Smooth as silk, Margot. The new fridge is in, the old one's gone, and I'm packing up to go rescue Runtley. Then homeward bound."

"Great, there's terrible construction around South Bend. So, plan on a half-hour of sitting in a parking lot. Is the food okay?"

"Well, not so good. I had to pitch it."

"Pitch it?"

"It's a long story, but the fridge couldn't be turned on until midnight because of the break-in period. Meanwhile, they ran out of ice at the Shell Station. But, hey, we own a new icemaker. The appliance guys installed it. Your dad's going to love it— not to mention Junior and Mackie."

"Actually, Ed, that's what I'm calling about, Mom and Dad canceled out for next weekend."

"What? Why's that?"

"Oh, I don't know. Some problem with the boat. Dad wants to fix it Saturday. Mom says they'll be down around the Fourth."

Margot's dad was always working on his boat, but I sensed she was a bit distraught. I tried to strike the appropriate tone. "Wow, that's too bad."

"Yes, Junior is terribly upset. And Mackie too, but he's…."

"Well, I'll be home soon with Runtley, and everything will be okay."

She perked up. "Yes, Runtley. Everything will be back to normal."

After she rang off, I finished packing and headed for the City of Allowahegon and the Elmer T. Jenkins Correctional Complex and Animal Control Facility. On the seat next to me lay a double-thick two-inch-wide nylon leash with a locking titanium clasp made from military-grade parts. I had bought it six months ago. Once the clasp was fastened to his collar, Runtley's care-free cruising days as a canine delinquent would be *over*. In anticipation, I pressed the accelerator.

Arriving at the Sheriff's Complex, I parked the minivan and was quickly checked through security.

"Where's the Animal Control Facility?" I asked the officer at the information desk.

"Through that hallway, then keep hanging a right until you get around to the third leg of the pentagon. Just follow the signs."

I noted the officer's name tag, Sgt. Everett T. Jenkins. I was beginning to fear that I had wandered into the realm of some arcane religious or military cult called "The Family," undoubtedly an offshoot of the Branch Davidians or the Church of Scientology. Each member wore the same neatly pressed black shirt, the same gray camouflage cargo pants, and the same polished black combat boots. Over the right breast pocket above their Jenkins Family membership pin and name plate, each one sported a patch with an eagle slinging lightning bolts. Above the left breast pocket atop their gold badges, was sewn the motto, "WE FIGHT AS ONE." I wondered what there was to fight about in a rural county with less than 75,000 residents. Perhaps their feral pet problem was more serious than I had first surmised.

I strolled up to the bullet-proof service window at Sector 3. According to her nameplate, it was staffed by Animal Control Officer Esther T. Jenkins, Deputy First Class.

"I'm here to pick up my dog," I said. "I called Sunday. They told me you have him and I could retrieve him today."

"What kind of dog? We have over a hundred."

"A hundred? Seriously?"

"Yeah, people come up from Chicago all the time and drop them off in the woods. Cats too. Even parakeets. Sheriff Elmer T. Jenkins is mighty tired of dealing with their urban irresponsibility. He's working on a bill for the Legislature that would make it a felony."

"My dog is a beagle. A ridiculously small one."

"With a big mouth?"

"Yeah, that's the one. We call him Runtley."

"Well, you should have named him 'Robocall.' That mutt hasn't shut up since he arrived."

"I feel your pain," I said.

"And he puked in the patrol car."

"Yeah, I heard about it. So, where is he?"

"Back in the Tombs. We'll process him out shortly. Here's the itemized list of charges."

She slid the paper through the steel tray under the glass.

"Charges? You mean like criminal charges?"

"No, fees and costs. Sheriff Elmer T. Jenkins believes the Allowahegon taxpayers shouldn't be required to subsidize the costs of dealing with scoundrels and reprobates."

"My children's dog is not a scoundrel. He comes from champion stock. And I have the paper to prove it!"

"Terrific, now you have one more," she said.

I looked at the invoice.

—Transport 32 mi @ $.57/mi	$18.24
—Intake Fee (Weekend/Holiday)	$39.00
—Veterinary Exam	$55.00
—Rabies vaccination (per State contract)	$35.00
—Allowahegon Co. Canine License	
(1 year, renewable)	$25.00
—Room/Board, 3 nights @ $47.00/night	
(Holiday Rate)	$141.00
—Gym/Activity Fee, 3 days @ $11.00/day	$33.00
—In-Room TV, 3 days @ $8.95/day	$26.85
Local Channels	$5.00
Regional Sports Package	$7.00
HD	$10.00
On Demand Videos @ $4.95 each:	
—Old Yeller	$4.95
—Lassie Come Home	$4.95
—Isle of Dogs	$4.95
—Marley and Me	$4.95
—Turner and Hootch	$4.95
—Air Bud	$4.95
—Benjii	$4.95

Premium Channels: Animal Planet	
—Westminster Kennel Club Dog Show	$14.95
—Energy Surcharge	5.00
—Allowahegon County Franchise Fee	$1.61
—Beverage Fridge:	
Doghead Beach Jamaican Ginger Ales,	
11@$7.00	$77.00
—Release Fee (Standard)	$45.50
SUBTOTAL	$605.40
—Sales Tax @ 6%	$36.32
—Tourism Development Commission @12%	$72.65
TOTAL	$714.37

"That is totally outrageous!" I yelled. "I'm forced to pay more than $700 because your deputy stole our dog?"

"Hey, if you can't do the time, don't do the crime."

"I guess these places really *are* Holiday Inns!" I shot back.

"Mr. Grimwald, do I have to call in the SWAT team?"

That sobered me up. I flashed my AAA card. "Don't I at least get a discount?"

"No."

Okay, do you take Mastercard? I don't carry that much cash."

"Yes, but we will have to add a convenience fee of $3.95." She pointed to a legal notice taped on the window beside me.

I shook my head and pushed my credit card through the glass window.

She processed the card, then passed it back. "Sign at the bottom. Your copy is the yellow one, and I have attached a coupon for $10 off admission to the Sheriff Elmer T. Jenkins Annual Round-Up Rodeo and BBQ on July 4th. It's a family event."

I pictured taking my Mother- and Father-In-Law, Margot, Junior, Mackie—and Runtley—to the rodeo. My chest tightened. My head continued to pound. "Gee, thanks," I said, faking a smile.

"Have a blessed day."

The double doors next to the window burst open, and a young man in Jenkins family attire strode toward me. Swaddled in his arms, shivering like a drunk after a three-day bender, was Runtley. He handed me the prodigal pooch and held out a clipboard and pen attached on a string. It was a release form and arbitration agreement. I wanted to argue for my litigation rights, but Runtley burped, and I knew what was coming. I caved and signed, then scampered toward the minivan.

I looked down at him. His eyes were raw and red. "One too many Jamaican Ginger Ales?"

He burped again.

"Well, I hope you didn't get too addicted to prison chow, 'cause when we hightail it to Indiana, you're going back on Walmart dog food and, I don't care what Margot says, no warm milk to make gravy. No bottled water either, strictly tap—oh, and, did I mention, you're grounded—until further notice."

He let out a long pitiful sigh.

I opened the rear of the minivan.

"*Buenos Dias, Sen-ior!*"

I turned toward the voice. An older Hispanic couple four cars down stood next to a beat-up, blue Ford station wagon with the tailgate up.

"Sen-ior, you wanna buy a dog—for free?" the man said.

I glanced at the back of the wagon. There, sitting smartly upright in a cardboard box, was another beagle. A momentary *déjà vu* flashed through my inflamed brain. During the night I had passed and been eternally banished to reside in Hell.

"She's a very good dog. Very quiet. We can't take her back to Mexico," he said. "She has all documents."

"Sorry, sorry," I said, waking from my nightmare. "I already own a dog. One's enough."

I turned to go. Runtley lifted his head up from where it rested against my forearm and peeked around me. Their dog barked.

"Barrror-rraaar," Runtley whined. It was a pitiful, high-pitched howl—pleading, pain, and protestation wrapped together in one feeble cry.

I looked down at him. His nose was all slimy, his eyes wet and goopy.

I took another step toward the minivan, then hesitated.

"I must be insane. Actually, totally insane," I muttered. "Oh, alright."

I wheeled around and walked over to the couple.

"What's her name?"

"Gracias, Senior, gracias" the woman said. In her outstretched hands, she had wrapped a large, black rosary.

"We call her 'Frida,'" the man added. "You know, the great artist Frida Kah-lo."

I looked down at Runtley. "Did you hear that? Frida. I hope you're up for this. Seriously, Dude."

He looked at me with a big dog-eyed expression, then licked the back of my hand.

"Okay, let's do this thing."

The couple walked Frida over to the minivan and said their goodbyes. They were both crying when they left her with Runtley in the dog carrier.

I closed the tailgate and headed for Indiana.

"BARRRRORRRAARRRR!" Runtley crowed. Then he belched again.

I looked through the rearview mirror. "I'm glad *somebody's* happy."

When I arrived home and pulled in the driveway, Margot and the kids rushed out of the house to greet me.

"I have a surprise for everybody," I said. I opened the tailgate and pet carrier and out jumped the newly released miscreant, followed by his refugee Mexican bride.

Margot squealed. "Runtley, you brought home a girlfriend!"

She boxed his ears, then gave him a big kiss on the forehead.

"Look, boys. Runtley has a new companion."

Junior gave Runtley a big hug.

Mackie picked up Frida by her hind legs and started wheelbarrowing her around the front yard.

"Careful, careful, you'll hurt her," Margot said, releasing Frida from his grip. She looked up at me. "Ed, she is so precious. Where did you find her?"

I told her the sad tale, ending with her name.

"Fri-to," Mackie repeated.

"No, Frida—like the Mexican artist," I corrected. But by then, it was too late. Junior and Mackie marched around the yard, chanting, "Fri-to, Fri-to, she's really nea-to!" And soon Margot joined in. Then both dogs started barking at all the noise and commotion. I stood there, silent, helpless, reeling from the consequences of my momentary lapse of iron will.

❊   ❊   ❊

A few weeks later, as we were dressing for bed, Margot said, "I think we should make an appointment for Frito, I mean, Frida. We should probably have her spayed, don't you think?"

"Because of Runtley?" I scoffed. "I doubt there's much danger. He can't even fall off the couch to finish his dog chow." I thought about it for a minute. "On second thought, I suppose you're right. The potential consequences would be too dire to contemplate."

The following Tuesday, when I arrived home from work, Margot was waiting at the door.

"Ed, I took Frito to the vet today."

"Everything go alright?"

"Well…," she said. "Not exactly."

"What, she can't be spayed?

"No. Actually, yes. The vet says it's too late for that."

"You mean…?"

"She's pregnant!" Margot shouted. "Isn't it fantastic?

143

Runtley's going to be a daddy!"

"What!? That's impossible!" I yelled. I raised my hands to my face, trying to block out the surge of traumatic images triggered by her revelation.

She put a finger to her lips. "Shhh, he'll hear you." Her voice dropped to a whisper. "You're right, the Vet says she's been pregnant for three weeks. So, they can't actually be his."

"They?" Then it dawned on me. Canines don't give birth to only one or two puppies at a time. Through my head poured the image of a swollen river of dogs swirling about my pantlegs as they flowed between kitchen and dining room. Worse yet, they could be half Greyhound, or Sheepdog or, god forbid, Great Dane. The food bill alone…what had I done on that fateful day in the Sheriff's parking lot? How many circles of hell would I have to pass through down my personal road to perdition?

Forty-two days later, we had our answer, or answers—all thirteen. And they weren't part Airedale or Malamute or even Jarvey Terrier. No—they were half Chihuahua.

"Aren't they cute, Ed?" Margot said, picking up one of the females. It was the size of a coffee mug. "Here, hold her."

Gingerly, I took the puppy from her hands. I could feel its little heart ticking like a watch on steroids. I stroked her tiny nose. Her eyes were barely open.

"Don't get too attached, Dad," she said. "You know we can't keep them. Or at least most of them."

"That might be harder than you think, they don't have any papers."

"I've been thinking about that, Ed. I picked up an idea when I was researching dogs."

She went on to explain the current rage in pet ownership: mixed breed canines, such as labradoodles and cockapoos. "We could initiate a new novelty breed," she said. "I think we might be able to get five hundred dollars apiece. I even have a breed name picked out."

I did the math. "Wow, Margot, that's sixty-five hundred bucks—for one litter. So, don't keep me in suspense—what's the name?"

"At first I was thinking Cheagles," she said. "But now I've settled on Beagihuahuas."

That's my Margot. Wife, mother of my children—and soon, new business partner. "Brilliant," I responded. "Absolutely brilliant."

First Kill

"Never hunted before, eh?" Halvor lifted the shotgun from the rack over his living room couch. Rolling the old single-shot in his calloused hands, he inspected, then presented it to his nephew's young boy, James.

"No, not deer. Not a real gun—only a BB gun." James received the firearm from his tall, steel-haired great-uncle. He clutched it, fearing it might drop and break. It weighed heavy, pitted and rust-splotched, the forearm attached by several windings of black tape. It smelled of wood smoke and machine oil. On the receiver, he read the words *Iver Johnson—12 Gauge*. He rested the gun stock on the cabin floor, keeping his hand tight on the barrel.

"It doesn't look like much, but a good piece to learn on. We'll shoot a few rounds before dark. Practice for tomorrow and Sunday." Almost to himself, he said, "Can't figure your pop, should have hunted two years now."

"Pop told me if I wanted to, I should go ahead and try. Said if I liked it, he would buy me a deer rifle for Christmas. Otherwise, I could have a bike . . . or something else."

Halvor smiled. "I suppose you're facing a tough choice." "Seems your pop may lean toward the bike."

"Yeah, told me Gramps had spoiled it for him, but he said I could decide—."

"How's that?"

"Pop said they were sitting in a blind one time when a big doe came over the ridge. Gramps drew a bead and dropped her. Right after, two fawns circled around the doe. So, Gramps pulled up again and killed them too. That soured him."

"Guess I'm not surprised," Halvor said. "Your Gramps was

a hard-old SOB. It was how they raised us. We were fishermen back in the day, making our living out of the lake. The way your Gramps looked at it, those fawns wouldn't last through the winter on their own, so might as well make use of them. He gave me one of those hides—on the recliner there." James turned to where he pointed, a small, red-brown, spotted deer hide draped across the rear cushion. "Didn't realize your pop was there when he shot 'em."

James reached out with his free hand and gingerly stroked the fur. It was smooth, soft. A shadow crossed his face. He returned the weapon to Halvor.

"Does it kick hard?"

Halvor chuckled. "No worse than a government mule . . . you'll get used to it. Shoulder the stock tight—so it doesn't slam. Don't worry, I'll help you." He broke open the breech and gazed through the barrel at the ceiling. "I know you have the jitters. Everyone does. But when the action starts, you forget that. The hunt takes hold—no sensation like it." He peered at James. "Not like . . . video games." After scrutinizing the inside of the barrel a moment longer, Halvor lowered the gun and snapped the receiver shut. A dry, metallic clunk sounded through the room.

❊ ❊ ❊

After supper, they hopped in the car for a ride. Halvor's pale-green Ford sedan drifted through the woods along an overgrown logging trail.

"Suppose you don't drive yet, either?" Halvor asked.

James gave him a worried look. "N-no, I'm only twelve—well, almost."

"When I was your age, I'd been driving two years already, and that was a stick shift. Heck, when your pop was ten, your Gramps and I taught him to drive." Halvor stopped the car. "Since he started work in Loyale at the bank, he sure has fallen off on your schooling." With a twinkle in his eye, he added, "When you go back Sunday night, you tell him I said that— here, switch places."

James hesitated, then slid over and Halvor sauntered around the rear and dropped into the passenger seat.

"Okay, James, here's what you do," Halvor said. "You start the engine by twisting the key away from you and let go when it catches. The car won't move until you shift out of *Park*. Pull the long lever towards you and slide it into D for *Drive* or R for *Reverse*." He pointed at the floor pedals. "On your left is the brake. On your right, the gas. Some people use both feet, but I suggest you take your right foot off the gas to press the brake. Turn signals are on the short lever. You push down to signal 'left' and up for 'right.' Unless you are shifting or signaling, keep both hands on the wheel. Everything you need to know. Fire up the engine."

James stared up at him, eyes the size of quarters. "What if I crash into something?"

"You can't—nothing to hit out here."

James peered around. On both sides of the road was a deep meadow that stretched away two football fields. "Okay, I'll try." He turned the key, and the motor came to life, then a loud chattering gzzzzzzt noise.

"Let go the key," Halvor said. "You're chewing up the starter." The engine dropped into a purr. "Now drop the shifter into Drive. And hit the gas with your foot."

James tromped on the pedal and the car jumped forward. He stomped the brake pedal with both feet. They slammed headlong toward the windshield. He flipped the key off.

"One more thing, let's put the seat belts on," Halvor said, rubbing his hand where he had caught himself against the dash. "And go easy. You just need to touch the gas pedal to set the car in motion. Fire up."

After fastening their belts and adjusting the seat distance,

James tried again. He made a few more false starts, but the car traveled farther with each try. Soon he was piloting the big Ford along the two-track with relative ease. Every few minutes, Halvor reached over and tugged the steering wheel to realign the vehicle. "You got it, don't oversteer." He flashed a thin smile. "Can't go shining without a competent wheel man."

James beamed. He felt the throb of the engine through his hands. It was scary but exciting. He gave the engine a bit more gas, and the car surged ahead with a growl. He glanced at the speedometer. They were doing twenty-five. It seemed like a hundred.

"I would've taken the pickup," Halvor said. "But learning to drive is easier if you don't need to shift gears and press a clutch while you're trying to steer. Plus, she makes too much noise—muffler's shot." He leaned back, relaxed.

James looked over at the twelve-gauge resting beside him, the wood stock dented and cracked, the finish long gone.

Halvor noticed his stare. "First gun I ever used. 'Course, it was newer."

James broke his concentration and stared ahead at the rutted trail.

"Shot my first deer when I was ten. Lot more since then. Some legal. Others not so . . ." He winked. "The best was that first one. Wish I was in your shoes, James. I surely do."

"M-maybe we will both get one." James offered.

Up to the right was a turnoff to Dolomite Road. Halvor gestured to turn and directed him to stop the car at a small, abandoned rock quarry. They stepped out on a trail that led to a low sea stack overlooking the deep pit. The pungent odor of ripe, moldering trash caught James by surprise. They were at the township garbage dump.

Halvor glanced around and spotted a patch of low plants with bright red berries. He picked a handful and gave a few to James.

"Here, try chewing this. Wintergreen berries. Should help block the stink."

James popped the berries into his mouth. The skins were waxy, the insides soft with a pleasant, almost minty flavor.

After a minute, Halvor spat out the chewed remains of the berries. James followed suit as Halvor loaded the vintage single-shot and handed it to him.

"Pick something in that pile and squeeze."

James lugged the twelve-gauge to his shoulder. It wasn't easy to hold steady. He closed one eye and sighted over the barrel.

"Relax more, but hug her up tight on your armpit. Don't aim, you point . . . like your finger, and tighten your whole trigger hand."

The barrel quavered.

"Easy now, ea-sy."

James aimed, then shut his eyes. He clutched the gun stock, trying not to jerk the trigger. He squashed it, like a toothpaste tube. Harder.

"It won't fire."

Halvor smiled. "Pull back the hammer."

James cocked the hammer and raised the shotgun again. This time with a snug grip, he pointed into the heap. His hands clenched tight, jerking the trigger. The firearm exploded, slamming the butt against his body. Through the cloud of smoke, a shovelful of trash splattered off the top of the pile. He lowered the barrel and shook the ringing from his head. His arm hurt as if someone had whacked it with a bat.

Halvor laughed. "Couple more rounds, you'll get the hang of it. Squeeze the trigger this time. Remember, snug up against your shoulder."

James fired three more shots. A cloud of acrid gun smoke enclosed him. He coughed. Halvor smiled as he took the weapon.

"James, you're a regular Deadeye Dick."

By the time they returned to Halvor's car, the gray specter of dusk had descended on the woods. James sat in the driver's seat. The Ford's headlights turned the trailway into an incandescent tunnel.

"This is when you see 'em," Halvor said. He waved his long arm out the window. "Off the roadway or back in the fields."

James sat forward, eager to spot something. Halvor withdrew a shell from the pocket of his Mackinaw coat and slipped it into the chamber of the gun on the seat between them. James threw him a cautious glance.

"You know, a game warden told me once, without local poachers, the deer would starve during winter. The extra kill keeps the herd from overgrazing, same way you thin carrots in your garden. If you don't pull half that come up, they crowd each other 'til they all die." Halvor scowled. "But lots of people—most of them politicians—think they know better."

A crescent-shaped field surrounded by dense, twisted bushes and trees extended into view on the left. Halvor motioned James to pull off. The car rolled to a halt. James gripped the armrest.

"I put a salt lick out this summer by an apple tree back of that meadow."

He groped beneath the seat and extracted an enormous chrome flashlight. Aiming through the open window, he switched it on.

"We should see something."

James's gaze followed the beam. His mouth went dry as sand. The circle of light swept several times across the field.

"Damn," Halvor whispered. Out blinked the light. "Guess we're going tomorrow after all."

James slumped back. "Guess so."

❈   ❈   ❈

When James awoke the next morning, he heard a commotion like someone opening drawers and shuffling through papers. He peeked out and saw Halvor slouched over his desk.

"Hmmh," Halvor muttered. "Where the heck is that tag?" He motioned to James. "Did your pop buy you a hunting license?"

James nodded.

"Let me look at it." James started back toward the bedroom. "Oh, never mind, I found mine—stuck under the bills." He peeked at James with a sly grin. "Thought for a minute I might have to make my own."

A knock thumped at the kitchen entrance.

"That'll be Squint—Com'on in!"

The door opened to reveal a short, plump, schoolteacher of a man covered head-to-toe in red wool, except an orange camo vest he held in one hand and a scuffed-up gun case in the other. From beneath a butch haircut, he blinked through an oversized pair of brown plastic glasses.

"Hey, Squint, in here. Meet my nephew's boy James . . . from over in Loyale."

Squint offered a chubby hand. "Glad to meet you, James. Glad to meet you—first time, eh?"

"Yeah," James said.

"Well, you're lucky to have such an eminent instructor." Halvor shot him a skeptical look. "He can knock the left eye out of a baby gnat at two hundred yards."

"We probably ought to head out, Squint, before you pile it any higher," Halvor replied. He turned to James. "Sorry, I meant to warn you." He threw on his coat and an orange ball cap and took a last slurp of coffee. "Well, they won't come looking for us." He reached up and pulled the shotgun and a long, octagonal-barreled, lever-action rifle from the gun rack.

James stared, fascinated.

"Gift from your great-grandfather," Halvor said. "Took a long time to earn."

"A rifle like that would be worth it." James continued to admire the long-gun.

"Gets the job done. But it's the man that counts. The one who pulls the trigger—or misses the shot." He stared at Squint.

"There you go . . . there you go again," Squint cried. "Couple years of bad luck and a man's friends vanish like jackrabbits."

"Well, today is the end of that jinx," Halvor said. "Right?"

"Yeah, right. Let's roll." Squint shooed them through the door.

Twenty minutes later, the Ford pulled off the gravel to the grassy shoulder of Silver Lake Road. They creaked open the doors, and Halvor removed the guns from the back seat. He passed Squint an old thick-stocked Springfield rifle.

"Why the heck don't you invest in a new piece? You couldn't hit a bull in the backside with that blunderbuss . . ."

"Hey, if it worked for my great-grandfather killing Krauts in World War I, it will put meat in the freezer today." Squint slung the ancient bolt-action rifle over his shoulder. "We'll be back with a buck," he called out as he ambled away. "Big one."

Halvor glanced at James. "Hate to say it—he's a good man and a great friend—but he won't hit nothin'," he confided. "We've been hunting together for seventeen years, and in seventeen years he's never shot one thing. A lesson for you. You need to have . . . the instinct. Have to want it."

"He doesn't seem worried."

"Nah, he likes to go tromp around the woods, all right. He's like your pop, except one thing—."

"What's that?"

"Squint can't see he doesn't have it. Blames it on luck."

James inspected the gun in his hands. "How do you tell that?"

"You just know. You can feel it. When you're deep in the woods, you can almost sense a deer. You don't see him, but you know he's near. You freeze right there, scan around, sit tight. Then, an explosion. On your side, a big buck arches off. Behind you, a doe and fawn disappear down a trail into the swamp. Something you're likely born with . . . or not."

Squint vanished into the undergrowth. They loaded their arms and slipped through a barb-wire fence that bordered the woods.

A deep brown mulch pressed beneath their feet. The fallen leaves were fringed with frost needles, dissolving in the advancing morning light. Naked hardwoods thrust tangled fingers into the gray-blue sky. Everywhere hung the odor of mushrooms.

Halvor picked through the downed limbs and thorny brambles, a hound on scent. James kept up on his right, the shotgun clenched in both hands. For an hour they traveled like a dog and his shadow deeper into the forest. Ahead lay a fallen beech tree. Halvor searched the woods expectantly. James followed his gaze but saw nothing.

Off to their left, a shot boomed and reverberated. Halvor whirled around. Another blast, two more.

"You think he got one?" James clasped his gun with both hands.

Halvor drew a finger to his lips, his body poised, catlike. The clatter of crashing brushwood faded away. He spat in the wet leaves. "Damn, missed again—let's head out and hear what he has to say this time."

He stepped up a quick pace and in half an hour they plunged through, a few hundred yards from the car. Ten minutes later Squint trudged puffing from the woods.

"Almost had him. You should've seen, rack like an elk."

"He should be big. I've been feeding him all summer." Halvor lashed Squint with a withering glare.

155

"He's a big one . . . a big one."

James looked. Squint's hands trembled.

"Sure you didn't wound him? It'd be a shame to leave him."

Squint's face flushed. "No, clean miss, I checked, but no blood trail."

"Aw, heck, just as well," Halvor relented. "Give me a chance to get my salt money back."

James polished and polished the worn gun stock with his sleeve.

They hunted until after dark. They spotted tracks in the soft mud of a footpath along Otter Creek, tracks that had weathered overnight. Twice, they came upon "deer coffee" cold as the wet turf. Yet no odor of deer lingered, no presence of deer across the ridges or in the marshes or on the edges of fields.

At last, they unloaded and drove St. Martin Portage, a narrow road, back toward Perkins settlement. Squint sat munching a chocolate bar, while James sprawled in the back. Halvor stared at a distant point over the wheel. He and Squint shared a bottle of wine.

"Here, James, try a swig." Halvor passed the bottle over the front seat.

James hesitated.

"Just a little plum wine Squint makes every fall. Won't hurt you."

James yielded, took a short draw. It tasted sweet, fruity, warm in his mouth. He handed the bottle up to Squint, who downed a long pull.

"You know, makes you mad," Halvor grumbled. "Used to be lots of deer. You could always kill one opening day, at least one more by end of season."

"Everything's all changed, Halvor. More hunters, less woods. Not to mention the DNR, they got a season for every reason." Squint licked his fingers, guzzled another swig from the wine bottle.

"Yeah, plus Great White Hunters from Detroit. With their scoped rifles and fancy camps."

"And ATVs, GPS, assault rifles," Squint chimed in. "The deer don't stand a friggin' chance."

"Spot on, Squint, spot on." Halvor's hand tightened on the wheel. "Sometimes I wish they never built that bridge across the Straits." He glared into the windshield. "Well, venison 's still to be had for the ones who can ferret it out."

"Sure, Halvor . . . that's right," Squint echoed.

James drifted off to sleep curled against the guns, in his stomach a warming glow.

❄   ❄   ❄

The next day, Sunday, they dressed before dawn. As they rode east on the state highway, the sun rose like a red-orange balloon released from the outstretched grip of the slate brown trees.

Squint was only half awake; Halvor had taken up the driving.

James sat blinking in the gloom of the rear seat. He stared again at the guns. The octagonal-barreled long rifle captured the sunlight in a blue-white glint. Squint's army weapon was a dull gray; its stock, rough coffee-colored wood. James's scatter gun lay rusted, taped and scarred. It had killed many deer. It would kill one more in the right hands. James touched it as he had several times in the last two days. The machined steel receiver felt cold, and he drew his hand back.

The Ford wheeled on to Silver Lake Road. As they approached the area where Squint had missed the big buck, they spotted a blue Dodge truck angled off the shoulder. In the bed were stacks of wood boxes full of gill nets. Beside them hunched a wolf-like man and three taller youths bundled up in orange and red clothing.

"Gundersen and his boys," Halvor said. They pulled

alongside, and Squint rolled down the window.

"Seen anything, Carly?" Halvor called out.

Gundersen's grizzled face filled the window frame. He poked a thumb toward the oldest boy. "Auggie seen tracks, big fresh ones. The rascal's in the bush here. We're gonna drive him out t' other side."

"Squint got a shot yesterday," Halvor said casually.

Gundersen struck a flinty laugh. "No need t'ask if he hit the rascal."

"I got a good glimpse," Squint said, trying to make up the shot. "He's a big boy, all right."

"Why don't Squint and the boy there and Auggie wait on the blacktop. Us four will beat him out. See if we can't put venison on the table tonight." He slapped the car door for emphasis. His right hand was missing two fingers.

Halvor agreed. Squint and James climbed in Auggie's pickup.

Gundersen pulled out a pocket watch. "We'll give you ten minutes."

Auggie sped away in the Dodge. After a couple of turns, he stopped on the Millecoquins Cutaway, a tar road parallel to the one they had left earlier.

Auggie's face appeared to James in the rear-view mirror.

"We'll leave you on the corner here; Squint and me will stand further down."

Squint pushed open the door to let him out.

"Now keep an eye on both them streets," Auggie warned. "The rascal's liable to come off the side."

"Okay," James said and stepped into the chilly, dank air. The pickup sped away a hundred yards and shimmied to a stop for Squint. A few minutes later, Auggie pulled the truck over for himself.

James remembered the shotgun. He drew a shell from his jacket pocket and turned it in his hand. The brass shone dark yellow. Through the translucent red casing, the buckshot floated like round gray phantoms. He loaded the receiver. The breech snapped shut. The gun hung between his coat and sleeve, heavy across his forearm. He looked down the blacktop. Auggie was resting against the truck door, Squint kneeling on the shoulder's edge. James gazed up the unpaved road. It faded back, flat, brown, dusty.

A half hour passed. He drew the shape of a deer in the loose gravel with his boot, then scraped it away. Squint was standing now. Auggie lounged against the tailgate, upraised double-barrel supporting his right side. James could hear the beaters making a racket, coming closer. He watched for any movement.

He could view no silhouette in the dense undergrowth, only the stark lines of leafless trees. The sun warmed his wool jacket, but his hands stayed cold and clammy. His chest pulled tight—from the morning air, thick clothing, anticipation.

The buck stepped out on the gravel road. James's hands froze to the gun. He was big, soft brown and massive. Eight points at least. He glanced left, then right, surveying the landscape—his domain. James stopped breathing. He softly cocked the trigger, inched the shotgun into position. It hung there like an anvil. The deer stood broadside to him. James sighted along the rusty barrel. It trembled. He forced the gun steady, hands still icy white. He closed his eyes. When he opened them, the buck turned and stared straight at him. A full minute passed, deadly quiet.

The deer turned away, flicking his tail, and crossed over, then sauntered into a dry, grassy field. James followed him with the gun, eyeing him at the end of the sight-bead. He stood there, head raised, sniffing the wind.

Up the road from behind the buck flew a shiny black Lincoln Navigator. It roiled long snakes of dust as it skimmed along, growing ever larger. When it reached the field, it dragged to a halt, fishtailing on the loose surface. James let the shotgun fall.

A skinny young man with a shaved head and tattoos on his neck leaped from the SUV, camo-coated assault rifle in hand. He shouldered the high-powered, military-style weapon and peered intently through the laser-sight. A hot-red bead appeared on the deer's neck, right as he bolted. The rifle recoiled. A triple whip crack ricocheted through the forest. The buck sprang in one sailing motion, then rolled and crashed to its shoulder in the long, dry grass. It lay there kicking feebly as its blood pumped into a steaming puddle on the half-frozen sand.

The other men vaulted from the vehicle, screaming rowdy whoops. James watched them pound their buddy on the back, dancing and hollering toward the slain buck. Squint and Auggie sprinted out of the woods and stood gasping at his side.

"They shot him," James rasped.

"Them sonuvabitches," Auggie snarled, his eyes bright-hot with anger. "Them road-huntin', downstate sonuvabitches."

They stood there several minutes longer, watching as the shooter posed with his trophy for cellphone photos, then field-dressed the buck with a gleaming, heavy-bladed, sheath knife. Toward the SUV stomped Auggie and his two companions. When they approached it, the men were dragging the deer by the horns across the shoulder ditch.

"I guess there ain't a whole lot to say," Auggie groused. "Thank god, Pa ain't here."

"Yo!" shouted the man who had fired the shots. He raised both arms in a victory wave.

"Hey," returned Squint. "Just happened to drive along here, eh?"

"Yeah, bro', can't believe it—incredible. First one I ever shot, took him right down with this new AR15—got a bump stock. Right down—doornail dead—that's what I'm talkin' about. Woo-ha!"

He gestured with a bloodstained finger toward the futuristic, hi-tech rifle, now in the hands of one of his buddies.

"'Course, should have expected it with Jerry here." He pointed to his pal, who was nearly wide as he was tall and sported a full neckbeard and designer sunglasses. "When it comes to hunting, he's got serious mojo, right, Jer?"

Jerry grinned like a slice of musk melon. "Gotta be a state record, Scotty—for sure. Gonna set real nice over that stone fireplace in your new camp."

Auggie stood stiff as a fence post.

The third guy opened the back of the SUV, and together they heaved the steaming carcass across a sheet of black plastic and secured the hatch with a bungee cord. Its hooves stuck out over the chrome tailpipes.

"Yo, hope you have the same luck today, bro'," Scotty said, struggling to cut away Auggie's hostile gaze.

"Yeah," Squint responded, a chill in his voice. "See ya." He wheeled around to leave.

Auggie hesitated a moment, glowering until Squint grabbed his lanky arm. "Com'on, we got more hunting to do."

James tagged along at a distance. When they reached the corner, the SUV flashed by. Through its tinted windows, Scotty imparted a vigorous farewell wave.

"Bastards!" Auggie yelled as the vehicle grew smaller. He shook his fist. "Lousy De-troit bastards!"

After the SUV disappeared, the three of them lingered, waiting for the others to emerge from the woods.

Squint pulled James aside. "You know, Halvor would never slaughter a deer like that," he said. "'If it's that easy,' He'd say, 'what's the point?'"

James agreed.

"You're lucky he's your teacher. He may bend the law from time to time, but he wouldn't ever pull anything as disgraceful as those guys. You couldn't have a better friend, whether you keep hunting—or not."

"I know. That's what pop says."

Auggie was still steaming when Halvor broke through the wall of brush. One-by-one, the others appeared behind him, wheezing for breath.

Auggie related to Gundersen what had happened. He smoldered, silent. Then, he detonated a blistering curse. Up went his rifle by the barrel. With a powerful swing over his shoulder, he hurled it gyrating toward a birch thicket. The weapon hung there, trapped in the branches. Gundersen stood, scowling, huffing like a pair of bellows, eyes burning out of his face.

Halvor spat on the road. "God damn it," he said.

James and Squint stood motionless to one side. James leaned easier on the old shotgun.

❊ ❊ ❊

That evening James's dad arrived at Halvor's house to take him home. "How did he do?" He asked Halvor.

Halvor laid a hand on James's shoulder. "Oh, he's a deer slayer. Had a shot at a huge, ten-point buck. But he got robbed by a couple of jerks from Down Below."

"How's that?"

James and Halvor recounted the afternoon's events.

"What a shame," James's dad said. "At least you had an opportunity to know what it's all about. You'll get another crack at it."

"Lots of 'em," Halvor stated. He smiled at James. "We had a good time, didn't we?"

James nodded. "Thanks for teaching me, Uncle Halvor."

"Anytime, James. Reminded me of when me and your Gramps first took your dad out." He glanced at James's dad. "Jesus, I'm getting old."

They both laughed.

❄ ❄ ❄

Monday was a school day, workday for mom and dad. James was eager to see his two buddies, Evan and Stan.

"You went deer hunting?" they asked, incredulous. "Did you kill one?"

"No, but I almost did, a ten-pointer, and I got to shoot a gun, a twelve-gauge."

"Whoa, that must have kicked," His buddy Stan said. "I shot a 20-gauge once. That was bad enough."

"Yeah, and I drove a car too—for a little while," James bragged.

They both looked at him in awe. "No bull?" Evan said. "Wow, cool."

James held off on the part about drinking the wine. They might not believe him, anyway.

Over the next few days, he would have a lot more to tell his friends. In a couple of weeks, things would change back to regular. In a month, school would be out for the holidays, and maybe a new red bike would be leaning by the Christmas tree.

THE BARFLY

They huddled inside the back entry of the Sea Stack Tavern for some time before Doc arrived. His keys jangled in the frigid air as he turned the lock.

"There's a good nip this morning, Doctor." Bakker's deep, gravelly voice spilled into the darkened barroom. "Radio claimed she dipped below forty last night."

"Won't be long now," Doc replied. "Won't be long."

They took their usual seats around the L-shaped bar: Bakker, half-standing, with his back to the door; Flynn the stonemason catty-corner to him; Buddy off their right; Old Ned on the end by himself; and Doc behind the counter.

The summer visitors had long since departed. With the approaching pall of winter, the Island was reverting to its customary life. Doc flipped on the lights over the bar, finished hanging his mackinaw, and poured them each a drink.

"S'pose you'll be hauling in your tomatoes soon, 'eh, Bakker—or losin' 'em."

"Picked 'em last week, Doc," the big Dutchman replied. "Just the little ones, though. Had to pack 'em high as ten to the peck." He paused, glanced around the room, took a slurp of brandy. ". . . Still, they was all slicers."

Everyone chuckled.

Bakker smacked his lips. "Aaah, that draws the chill."

Doc stifled a rasping cough.

"They say you got a regular jungle out there," said Buddy. Whether he was attempting to reopen the subject or didn't realize it had just been closed was uncertain: Buddy wasn't known as a bright light. He extended the hook that protruded from his right sleeve and scooted his glass across the bar to his

165

other hand. "A man who can't do no spadin' gets missing them fresh tomatoes," he stated, glancing at Doc for the nod.

"Aah, bullshit." Flynn took a slug off his jigger. "Them sort of tomatoes won't be found in the gardens you're used to frequentin'. And if they was, you couldn't handle yer little spade there neither." He wriggled a crook'd pinky in Buddy's unshaven face.

A snicker echoed around the bar. Buddy managed a half-hearted smile. Since his divorce, common knowledge had it he was looking to put his hooks—or hook—on Doc's new night barmaid.

"Well, you can write me down as meat and potatoes," Doc said, redirecting the conversation. "Always have been, boys." He looked each one in the eye. "Say what you want about your vegetables, but mark my granite, a man don't live on bread alone—remember that." Doc had been a semester to seminary and a year to pharmacy school, so he had not gained his present role entirely by accident.

"Ay, you're right on," Bakker said. "I'll drink to that."

"Me too," Buddy echoed.

". . . Or cut my stone, 'He never made a stew he couldn't eat.'" Doc's hand blocked the phrase word-by-word in the air. He broke his momentary pose, scanned the bar. "That venison do eat so good . . ." He tipped a big swallow of beer and squinted into the morning dimness. The half-light, half-shadow falling across his bald pate and face gave his smile a melancholic twist.

"But no frigging tallow," Buddy added, remembering a prank at Doc's last game dinner.

Bakker burst out with a hearty laugh, Flynn following with a hoarse chuckle. Old Ned's lips found a faint curl, though he continued to gaze off at the back wall. Doc cut short his preoccupation and flashed a polite smile.

They topped it with a long drink. A little green fly droned

off the back bar and circled Doc's head. He twisted back and brushed it away from his face.

"Speaking of that, Doc, I suppose you'll be heading to Wyoming soon," Bakker asked. He pushed forward his empty glass, and Doc reached into the gloom of the bar well. The bottles clanked together. "Get yourself one too, Doc," he added. Buddy hurried to drain his. "And the others, what they're drinking."

"None for me," Flynn said. "Got urgent business with the Church." He slid off the stool and disappeared toward the gentlemen's room.

Two matters in the bar were of general understanding. Doc never tested more than one in the morning, unless community "circumstances"—a birth, death, marriage, or divorce—demanded it. Second, standing a round without including Ned signified a major breach of decorum. Ned was on a fixed income, so Doc and his wife Alice looked after him. In return, they let him sweep out and pick up the mail. That left Buddy.

"I'll have whatever Bakker's drinking." He edged his glass forward. Flynn passed him a dry look.

"Thanks, Bakker," Buddy said, unruffled. He winced at Flynn from behind his drink.

As Doc moved to the register, Flynn scowled.

"Well, I suppose you'll be off to Wyoming, eh, Doc?" Bakker repeated.

Doc's hunting trips were legendary. Every fall he drove out to the Rockies. He never returned without a mule deer, elk, or antelope (on one trip, he had bagged both a mountain goat and wild ram) or to invite all his friends to a game dinner. It had grown into a social event on the Island, as only a church supper might have elsewhere, and had assumed the trappings and revelry of a Christmas holiday party.

There were rich stews or a lean red roast and green salads, potatoes, pasties, and hot bread, followed by buttered vegetables, sweet and sour relishes, and crusty fruit pies, plus all the draft they could pump from the barrel—an enormous potluck affair catered by Doc and Alice (who cooked for the bar) and embellished with various specialties of the women of the Island.

"Eat like it's your last meal," Doc would shout, and everyone pushed away from the table with swollen paunches and glazed eyes. It was a spectacular feast, and each year Doc swore 'round and 'round it was the final one, that it couldn't be surpassed, that it was too hard on Alice, and that for one or another reason, he could not do it one more time. This line continued with unwavering conviction into mid-fall, when the penultimate moment would find him discovering to his surprise (if to no one else's) that perhaps it might be topped, that perhaps Alice did not mind being rid of him for a couple of weeks, and that for one or another reason, he had to go— at which point, he dropped into organizing the details of the trip. In this fashion, everyone on the Island looked forward to the next dinner from the end of the last one. And the stories that returned with the expedition somehow carried them into the new year.

So, Doc's reply did not surprise them. His voice sounded flat as he faced the dark wall panel, counting Bakker's change. "Nah, I don't think I'll be going. Too much bother and expense." He hesitated, turned away. "It's a god-awful long trip, and Alice gets stuck running the bar. It takes a month to straighten out the mess, a burden on me and the old lady both." He snatched a beer for himself from the cooler. "I don't think I'll go."

Flynn slipped back onto his customary perch.

"Hell, Doc, you say this every year. We all been looking forward to it," Bakker pleaded. "Surely, you're not serious."

"My mind's made up." He pulled out a cigarette, changed his mind, then lit it. "Damned fly," he said, waving away the little pest in a cloud of smoke.

"Aah, he'll come around," said Flynn. "He always—"

"And no dinner neither?" Buddy asked.

"Last year was the last."

"Hell, Doc, I didn't think a death in the family would keep you from going on that trip," Bakker said.

Doc's face set like a plaster mask. "Why don't you mind your goddamn business, Bakker." He crushed out the cigarette, wiped the counter vigorously.

"Hey Doc, I weren't trying . . . to press you," the Dutchman said. "It was only a joke."

Doc stopped wiping and stood there, the focus of their silence. "Well, it weren't no joke to me."

He peered around the bar, then into the gloom that lingered in the building corners. His lips bunched up stiff, puckering his chin, as he stepped into, and out of the sunlight glaring through a small window behind them.

"Hell, you might as well have the truth of it—from the horse's mouth." There was a husk in his voice. He nodded toward the ashtray. "It's those dad-blamed coffin nails—the doctor's give me notice."

"Wha . . .?" The four of them started together.

"It's true," Doc said. "My number's coming up fast."

"I don't believe it," Flynn stated.

"Doc, if I'd only known," Bakker said, his big palm outstretched. "But Christ, you don't look like a sick man—surely, he's mistaken."

"No mistake. The way they looked me up and down, you'd have thought they were judging a prize hog."

The five of them sat—each with a hand on his drink—letting it soak in.

"When do they operate?" Bakker asked.

Doc shook his head.

"You can't mean—?"

169

"—Six months . . . on the outside," he said, teeth gritted. "A year would qualify for sainthood—*his* words."

"Aah, them doctors—they don't know *crap*," Flynn said. "Go out to Mayo's, Doc, they'll patch you up."

"Nah, it's true, boys. Sure as you're sitting here—I'm a goner." The idea caught in his throat. "Seen the x-rays—myself," he blurted. "Tumors big as rocks—both lungs." He swatted again at the pesky green fly.

"I knew it," said Buddy, breaking the unnatural chill. "I told you, Doc, you were treadin' the same path as Johnnie Robertson. First time I heard that cough."

"For the love o' Mary, shut yer pie hole," Flynn snapped. He threw back the rest of his drink. "Goddamn hyena…"

Buddy hunched into silence.

"Gimme another—Jesus, Doc," Flynn growled, tight-jawed. "Jesus H Christ."

"I know, Flynn," Doc said in a vacant tone. He poured out a double.

Flynn reached into his pocket.

"On me, Flynn."

Doc set up a round for the house. They drank with solemnity, extra-long and deep, as if the old burning numbness might have hidden all along a richer, more vital flavor. Each recalled a time when Doc had offered money or a lift or a bed to sleep it off. Their debt totaled far more than any could alone recall. Each man ached with a returning sorrow and a resurgent need to talk that whiskey could no longer suppress. Doc seemed less anxious too, so Bakker chanced a probe.

"Have you said anything to Alice and E. J.?"

Doc grimaced. "Aah, there's the worm. I don't care so much about myself. I've had it good, living on the Island and running this place, not to mention . . . you boys and my other friends." He stopped, gazed down at the bar. "But telling those women . . . might take me on the spot. It's made me sicker than these." He crushed the cigarette pack. "How do you tell a woman you've lived with over twenty years—or your daughter? Since I found out, I've felt like . . . a g-goddamned criminal," he stammered. "Lord—what are you supposed to do?"

He struggled for a few minutes to compose himself.

"Doc, I'd take them on one hell of a tour," Bakker said. "Lock this bar up tight and go. All them places you been dreaming of, that you been wanting to see and telling us about your entire life—here's your chance to do it right. Get off this stinking island and share time with your family."

"Christ, Bakker, I don't have that kind of money."

"You must have *some* savings, Doc. Not meaning to pry, but now's the time to spend 'em."

"A trip would make it easier," Flynn added.

"Nah, it's no use, boys. The chemo and radiation don't come cheap. Insurance will pay most, but there'll be some hellacious bills. And I still owe on the bar."

They knew that was true. Doc was too good a friend to be a sharp business manager, but his confession of it held them in a rigid, uneasy stillness.

"Don't worry, I been tucking some by for E. J.'s college," he stated. "Planned someday she'd escape this island—not just across the Straits to Loyale. It may be alright for the likes of you and me, but I won't leave that girl with no passage to a better life—that's what the money's for. I wouldn't, couldn't touch a penny—*now.*"

His face appeared withered, sallow, and he turned away to stare into his lap. "There's no way out. I start the treatments next damn Tuesday, and the cancer doc says they make you horrible sick."

Doc's last few sentences sapped any further response, each man braced against the counter, with pale, paralytic fingers gripped around his glass. Here they were, wanting to reciprocate all Doc had given but held mute by the disclosure of a blank fact, a cruel impassable dead end that confined each one as assuredly as if he too were soon to depart. They sat in the pallid morning light, in the foreboding silence of brooding, compulsive drinking—silence broken only by the heavy, green housefly that buzzed in aimless circles around them.

It dived again into Doc's eyes. "Goddamn fly!" he cried, face livid. With a brutal swipe, he knocked it to the bar. Reaching toward the floor, he yanked off his shoe. Heel down, he slammed it on the bar top. They all lurched back, pulled their glasses closer. Over and over, Doc battered the counter, crushing the repellent insect. He looked up at the men, the rising glare through the window spotlighting his rage.

"That'll teach the bastard," he snarled, replacing his shoe. "That'll teach him." He stepped away from the fiery light pouring through the dusty glass, slumped back into the shadows, and leaned against the rear bar, breathing heavily. He hacked another deep cough, then shot a fearful look at his friends, punctuating it with an angry nod. "That'll teach him."

WHAT I LEARNED FROM WILKOWSKI

When I heard a peculiar, high-pitched laugh from across the Sea Stack Arena at the Loyale all-class reunion, I knew it could be one only person, Chuck Wilkowski.

I shuffled toward him through the crowded space.

"Gosh, Chuck, must be forty years." I pumped his hand as I surveyed the skinny, wire-haired elf of a man standing before me. He looked older, but in my mind, still the original nerd who transferred in ninth grade when Ojibwa County hired his dad to manage the airport. His thick glasses, clipped red hair and freckles, buttoned-up short-sleeve shirt, high-water pants, white socks, and black tennis shoes had created an unforgettable first impression—not to mention, his strange, penetrating chortle, like Alvin the Chipmunk mimicking Woody Woodpecker.

"I hardly recognize you," I said. "Where you been keeping yourself?"

"Hey, Steve, forty-five years in the salt mines. I arrived in town a few days ago."

"Terrific, how long you here?"

"Here for good." He gave me a 'thumbs up.'

"No kidding? Never thought I'd see you again. Last time I knew, you were headed to Detroit."

"Spot on, I was. I never expected to come back. But three months ago, a 'near-religious event' made me rethink my life." He burst into the same falsetto giggle I hadn't heard since high school.

"I remember you coming over to my house one Saturday morning," I said. "The little bungalow I rented on High Street right after we graduated."

"Oh, yeah? Boy, was that street aptly named, eh?" We both

chuckled.

"It was December, and I thought you came to say goodbye. You were lounging on my couch, red-eyed and hung-over. I said, 'Hey, Chuck, at our graduation party, you swore an oath to everyone to take a full twelve months off and do nothing but party day and night. By my count, it's been nine months—how's it going?' I'll never forget your answer."

"What's that?"

"You said, 'Steve, it's *hard* to party for a whole year—if you do it long enough, it's *work*!' I cracked up, almost fell off my chair."

"Yeah, and right after that I enrolled in meat cutter's school," he said.

We both had another laugh.

So, I asked him, now that he was back in Loyale, what was he planning to do? And this is pure Chuck.

"Nothing." He burst into a short, piercing cackle. "You won't believe it, Steve, but I joined a weekly lottery pool with the crew I used to work with at Farmer Jack's in Detroit. A few months ago, we hit the Michigan Lotto and split a $15 million pot nine ways. My working days are *over*."

"Wow, that's got to be exciting," I said. "But you aren't serious about doing *'nothing?'* I thought you learned that lesson."

"No, no problems. I have it worked out."

"Jesus, I hope you're not going into politics." I leaned backward in mock horror. "Like Heikkinen."

"No *way*!" he said. "I am so over that bromance. A little travel, fishing on my new boat, a couple of hobbies. It's all good."

"Well, I'm envious," I said.

"Say, speaking of Heikkinen, have you seen him—did you catch his latest caper?"

I grimaced. "Oh, Christ, I'm afraid to ask. Why isn't that

guy in jail yet?"

Chuck shook his head. "He ought to be… after his latest stunt."

I felt the hair on the back of my neck rise. "What's that?"

"You should hear it from Dana Defoe. You won't believe it."

"Defoe? You mean Kellerman."

"Defoe's her new married name. She flew in from Arizona, and he was bragging to her, undoubtedly figuring she was leaving in a day or two and would take his dirty little secret back to Scottsdale. Meanwhile, he could score a few points."

"Yeah, he always had the hots for her—anybody in a cheerleader's uniform."

Chuck threw me a feigned look of disgust.

I cracked up, realizing my mistake. Chuck had made his original bones in a notorious cheerleading incident.

Chuck's size and appearance made him an easy target. For months after he first walked through the school doors, he became the butt of every joke. The jocks and anyone taller than five-foot-three pounced on him. Week after week, they pranked and roughed him up. But he simply 'took' it and responded to any humiliation or abuse with his high-pitched staccato giggle. After a while, it became known throughout Loyale High School as a Chuck-Laugh. You could hear it ring through the halls between classes as different students tried to emulate him.

Varsity football reigned as king in Loyale. The Friday afternoon before every game, the Athletic Department staged a rally in the school gym. The Coach and team led five hundred kids in the bleachers through a ritual of speeches, cheers, and pep band music, a script everyone knew and understood. Except Chuck.

One Friday after the event started, he sneaked into the girls' locker room. A few minutes later, in the middle of the head football coach's 'give 'em hell' speech, he burst through the door.

The student body turned to look and erupted into laughter. The Coach stopped in mid-sentence. He whipped around as Chuck skipped across the floor in an oversized purple-and-gold junior varsity cheerleader vest and skirt belonging to Dana and a pair of tall, olive-green rubber "swamp boots." Chuck vamped back and forth, a drum majorette's baton in one hand and a pompom in the other. His antics drove the students into hysterics.

Chuck grabbed the mic out of the Coach's hand and started a cheer.

"Two bits, four bits, six bits a dollar,
All for the War-ri-ors, stand up and HOLLER!
UG-FAY-OO-YAY! WARRIORS GO!"

The students sprang to their feet and joined in two more refrains, each louder than the last. They stomped on the bleachers and yelled until hoarse.

Chuck turned his back to the student body, bent over, tossed up his skirt with a couple of wags, and mooned them all. The pep rally exploded into thunder.

Someone threw a handful of pennies toward center court. Others dug out their pocket change and flung hundreds of coins onto the floor. They rained down on Chuck in a copper shower. Then he laughed into the mic and five hundred Chuck-laughs echoed through the gym.

From that moment, the Two-Bit Chuck-Cheer followed by the Chuck-Laugh became the Warriors' rallying cry that inspired their undefeated season. Chuck's cheerleader stunt endeared him to the students and faculty, including the Coach. At the football awards dinner, the Coach presented him with his own cheerleading skirt and vest. The boosters gave him a standing ovation. No chance he could play football, given his physical stature, so the Coach appointed him team manager.

I was still laughing about Wilkowski as I made my way around the reunion, looking for Dana.

Out of the men's room stepped Randy Heikkinen. We had been "friends" since kindergarten. We both loved football. I was stocky but quick, built to be a linebacker, crashing through the scrimmage line to sack quarterbacks. Randy was tall, lean, and forever on the make. He played offense, a wide receiver known for his "showboat" catches. He displayed a singular knack for twisting every situation to his advantage, and I often thought he executed his leaps and dives into the end zone to appear far more difficult than they needed to be.

My senior year, I expected to become team captain. I mentioned this to Randy and asked for his support. Behind my back, he hounded the Coach for the job and pushed Chuck to lobby for him. It worked, and the Coach picked him instead of me.

I had never warmed up to his "win at any cost" philosophy.

Late in the season, Randy dislocated a shoulder and sat out the remaining few matches. During our final away-game at arch-rival Ste. Marie Sacred Heart. it didn't stop him from executing a "covert operation." His dad was a big electrical contractor in town, so Randy borrowed a few tools and hid them under a black trench coat he often wore. He liked the idea that the coat made him look like Napoleon Solo in *The Man from U.N.C.L.E.,* his favorite tv show.

In the game's second half, he sneaked over to the Sacred Heart side of the field and slipped beneath the home-team bleachers. At that point, the Warriors were down thirteen points. He located the cable that ran between the coaching staff on the sideline and the spotters' booth above the Sacred Heart home crowd. With a pair of massive wire cutters, he clipped the link. In the confusion that followed, the Warriors squeaked by, 21-20, and clinched the conference title.

His last touch was to chalk a large "Z" on the light pole

behind the booth. That idea was classic Chuck, who Randy had recruited. Chuck loved the old Zorro tv series. He told me a couple of days later he expected it might throw off the authorities.

When the game ended, the Sacred Heart coach tramped across the field to the Warriors' locker room. He pounded on the door, demanding to interrogate the team. The Coach told Chuck to let him in.

"What's the matter, Coach.?" he said.

"You know what's the matter. Someone from your team cut our vital communications and cost us the game."

"Whoa, that's a serious accusation, Coach. Maybe you just got outplayed. You have any proof?

"I know it was you, Heikkinen," he said, pointing at Randy standing in the back of the room. "I have witnesses who saw someone in a black trench coat sneaking around our bleachers."

"That's impossible," Randy said. He slipped into the persona of Zorro's alter-ego Don Diego "My arm's in a sling. I've been helping our manager keep stats."

The Sacred Heart Coach glared at him. "I don't believe a word. I'm taking it to the Conference."

Chuck piped up. "Randy was with me the whole time." He played Diego's faithful servant Bernardo to perfection. "Look, here's the clipboard with a sheet for each quarter."

The clipboard Wilkowski produced was the clincher. It held detailed game stats in Randy's handwriting, including the fourth quarter when the wires were cut. But he didn't fool his teammates. In an instant, they figured out the locker room sleight-of-hand that occurred after the Warriors' victory. Randy had honed his skills copying test answers from almost every team member.

For the next month, rumors circulated about Randy's culpability, but he got away scot-free. He should have been taken to the slaughterhouse, but Chuck saved his bacon.

Now, he was Loyale's three-term State Senator, regarded for his ability to work magic on the floor of the legislature. Behind his back, many people called him "Sin-ator So-low" or "Randiego."

"So, *Sinator*," I said with a touch of sarcasm. "Have you talked to Wilkowski yet? He hit the lottery."

"No shit? You mean 'Candy-Ass?'" He snickered. "No, I haven't seen him. But don't you know, Candy-Ass Wilkowski is the one guy who'd wind up a lottery winner. I should hit him up for my reelection campaign."

He gave me a jovial slap on the back.

The "Candy-Ass" nickname referred to another source of Chuck's enduring fame. To celebrate the football team's conference title, local boosters put up the money to send them to a Detroit Lions game.

With the game set to begin, the players roughhoused as they took their seats, letting go the pent-up energy from the six-hour bus ride downstate. As they jostled each other for the best viewing locations, Chuck kept being pushed farther and farther toward the end zone until only two empty spots remained in the row. Randy shoved him, knocking him off-balance, and grabbed the better of the open seats. Chuck sat down hard on the last one.

"Yaaoowww!" he screamed and jumped to his feet. Everyone near him looked to see the commotion. Chuck spun around to reveal a glossy red candy apple that protruded from the rear of his pants.

"Jesus, Chuck, you sat on a candy apple," Randy said. "It's even got a bite out of it!"

"What?" The Coach stood up from the row below.

"Chuck sat on a candy apple! It's sticking out of his butt."

Chuck reached behind and pulled on the apple. It came free, and he held it up, stick and all, to have a look.

"Oh, that didn't feel so good," he said. Several team members near him guffawed, pointing at him and the apple.

"Hey, Chuck, we always knew you were a Candy-Ass!" Randy shouted, breaking up the entire group.

The Coach pushed his way past the other players. He barked out, "Wilkowski, what the heck is going on?"

Chuck explained the situation.

The Coach put a finger to his lips while he mulled over the problem. "Com'on, I guess I better take you to the emergency room." He scowled. "The rest of you guys behave yourselves."

Chuck spent the next three hours being examined by a proctologist. They gave him a shot and released him from the hospital. As he stepped on the bus carrying an inflatable donut-shaped cushion, the team burst into a Chuck-Cheer. All the way home, the Coach made him sit on it. That sealed his fate.

The following Monday, the entire incident, from candy apple to donut, sent a huge Chuck-Buzz through the halls. His new nickname, "Candy-Ass," promoted by Randy, stuck for the rest of his school career. It was a typical Randiego move.

❃   ❃   ❃

A few weeks after the reunion, I was returning beer bottles at the Shop 'n' Go. I fed the empty containers, one-by-one, into a machine at the store entrance, which counted and swallowed them, then spit out a credit slip for the bottle deposits.

It's a chore no one enjoys. The worst part is when the machine doesn't recognize the product because of a torn bar code label or data error. Then you stand in line forever at the customer service counter.

So, there I was, with several bottles, waiting for a refund. The Store Associate, whose name tag identified her as SHIRLEY, asked, "do you have any slips from the machine? I can cash 'em out together."

"Here you go." She took them and handed me two dollars and thirty cents.

Turning to leave, I noticed a bank of lottery ticket dispensers next to the counter. A red light on the Powerball machine was flashing… *$700 MILLION, WEDNESDAY $700 MILLION, WEDNESDAY $700 MILLION*. The drawing was tonight.

I never buy lottery tickets, but that was serious dough. I wasn't sure what a ticket cost, so I asked Shirley.

"Powerball is two dollars."

Out of nowhere, Chuck's face appeared in my head. The bottle deposit funds were the same as found money, and although the odds were astronomical, I mumbled, "If Wilkowski can hit the damn lottery, why not me?"

"What's that?" Shirley asked.

"Oh, nothing, just thinking out loud."

She gave me an odd stare, so I felt compelled to feed my two bucks into the payment slot. Five seconds later, a slip plopped out with my numbers, selected at random. I stuck the ticket in my wallet and moved on to other chores.

Later that evening, I had trouble sleeping. I tossed and turned half the night. After talking with Randy Heikkinen, I couldn't help seething over him and his antics. He gave me an earful on how much good he had done for Loyale.

But I knew better. Toward the end of the reunion, standing in the drink line, I caught up with Dana Defoe. She looked exactly as she did at seventeen when we got to know each other in the back seat of my dad's 1964 Ford Galaxy. I knew she had made a fortune in Arizona real estate, and it was obvious she was spending time and treasure at Scottsdale spas and plastic surgeons.

"Chuck Wilkowski told me you had a story to share about Heikkinen's latest caper."

She rolled her eyes. "Oh, god, Steve, he's been hitting on

me the whole night, even though my new husband Cliff is sitting over there in the corner."

I looked where she pointed at a tall, athletic guy with a deep tan. He appeared to be ten years younger than her.

"Wow, Dana, did pretty well for yourself."

She gave up a hearty laugh. "Yeah, he's my tennis coach. Third time's the charm." She waggled a huge sparkler at me on her ring finger.

"So, what's this Chuck was telling me about Randiego?

She frowned. "It makes me wretch to say it. He claims he elected the President."

"Wha—? No way."

"I think we better sit down," she said. We each grabbed a drink.

"Steve, you won't believe this. After the 2010 Census, Randy got himself appointed chair of the committee that draws the State electoral maps."

"You mean for congressional districts?"

"Yeah, but other offices, too."

"Christ, how did he accomplish that?"

"Some Detroit legislators owed him. He secured the State money they needed for Ford Field."

"Ford Field? That was a $500 million project," I recalled. "The Lions already had a stadium in Pontiac. But Detroit wanted them back for its 'Renaissance.'"

"Yeah, Randy told me he was Chair of Appropriations in the House. Just slipped it in during a late-night session."

I groaned.

"That's not the worst of it. Once he got control of the redistricting process, he spearheaded a Republican gerrymandering effort followed by a massive purge of the voter rolls in key Democrat districts."

"That sounds like him."

"But he was really thumping his chest over the 2016

election. He claimed his political hat trick—appropriations, gerrymandering, and voter purges—threw Michigan's electoral college to the Republicans by less than 11,000 votes. This was their lowest margin of victory in any state. According to him, he single-handedly put the President over the top."

I gagged on my drink and started coughing.

She stared at me. "You all right?"

"Yeah, no, I'm okay—but what did *he* get out of it?"

"Oh, *that*. They awarded his biggest supporter some huge timber leases in Upper Peninsula federal forests. He made a fortune selling the lumber to offset Canadian imports the new administration tariffed out of the U. S. market."

"Which explains why earlier when I spoke to him, he was banging the gong over the hundreds of jobs he created for local woodcutters."

"Well, here's the truth—from the horse's mouth. The largest beneficiaries were Sunbelt homebuilders and his campaign account. His eye's already focused on the governor's seat for 2022. He hit Cliff up for a campaign contribution. Do you believe it?"

"Classic Sin-ator So-low," I said.

❊   ❊   ❊

The rest of the night, I couldn't let go of Dana's comments. At three a.m., I broke out of my drowsy nightmare, fidgeting but still dead-tired. I lay there fretting and fuming over a dozen things.

Then I remembered they had drawn the Powerball numbers earlier that evening. Seven hundred million. I reflected on that colossal sum. What would I do with so much? I started a chain of calculations, hoping it might help me fall asleep.

I reminded myself you don't receive the $700 at once. If you opted for the single payout, after taxes you would net $400. In bonds or something "safe," it would yield $16 million a year. That was still a pile of dough.

What *would* I do with sixteen mil? Pay off the mortgage? Buy a luxury car or two? Build a second house in Florida? Take an extensive cruise? Okay, there's a million—fifteen left.

Give a million to each of our kids. A million to my brothers and my sister. A million to the nieces and nephews. That's ten-mill, total.

A million to my alma mater. Purchase a sailboat. Add a couple of rooms to the house. Acquire an airplane and take flying lessons. A million to charity. Two left.

Once the word was out, a hoard of long-lost "friends" and relatives would overrun me. A half-mill ought to cover it. I'm an art lover, so a little "walking around money" to buy paintings, maybe redecorate.

At last, down to a final million. Plenty to support my enhanced lifestyle, including extra income taxes, at least half of which would end up in Lansing—in *Randy Heikkinen's pocket.*

I cringed.

All that planning was hard labor. Plus, it would take me nearly twelve months to complete. I would have to hire an attorney. And an accountant. The new real estate and the boat would entail a crew for maintenance. Not to mention security. Would I need a bodyguard? Yeah, and one for other family members too. I would have to build walls surrounding my houses. Gates at every entrance. Tracking devices on everything.

On the bright side, we would have one heck of a Christmas. In fact, we could party all year long. Chuck Wilkowski's image flashed into mind. *If you do something long enough, it's work.*

Oh my God. I covered my face with my hands. The day after New Year's Eve, it would start over with another $16 million. What would I do with *that?* I would need a full-time financial advisor and someone to oversee a family trust.

In a few years, I planned to retire to a comfortable, stress-free lifestyle. Now, I had worked myself into a sixty-hour-a-week second job; a demanding, lifelong responsibility to manage employees, relatives, friends, and charities; and the daily threat of kidnapping and robbery. Worse yet, no matter what I did, *Randy Heikkinen would grab a big chunk of it. It might even force me to cheat on my taxes—like Donald Trump!*

NO THANKS.

But what if I had *won*? An avalanche of anxiety crushed me. Wide awake, I lay in bed, rigid, adrenaline flowing. I threw off the covers and tiptoed over to the dresser, trying not to wake my wife. From my wallet, I pulled out the ticket and stepped into my home office, hands shaking. I turned on the computer and searched for the Wednesday Powerball. Up it came. Number by number, I compared my slip with the box on the screen. Then once more to be sure I wasn't hallucinating.

Not a single digit matched.

I slumped in my chair. *Thank God.* I sat there a minute contemplating how close I had come to wrecking my life. I vowed on the spot I would never buy another lottery ticket— as long as I lived. But if I ever did—and won—I pledged to write a big fat check to Heikkinen's election opponent.

The stress and apprehension left me drained. I slipped into bed, curled up, and drew a blanket around me in a cocoon. The rest of the night, I slept like a newborn.

TEATIME AT THE TWILIGHT HOTEL

As he walked through the entry, he saw his mother dozing in a high-backed, upholstered chair. One of her hands was flopped over onto the lamp table next to her and rested on a large red book. He sauntered across the carpet past a Christmas tree in the lobby area and lightly touched her arm.

"Mom, it's me. Harry."

She jumped awake with a snort, glanced around her surroundings.

"Oh—hi, Harry."

He bent down, gave her a brief hug. "Awww, did I startle you? I'm sorry, Mom. We were supposed to meet this afternoon."

She reached up and took his fingers in her hand. "How's my darling boy?"

"Good, Mom. Really good. And what have you been doing since last Friday?"

Her face went deadpan. "Counting from one to two."

He laughed, "That's funny, Mom. You're a card."

She didn't crack a smile. He paused, peered down at her.

"No—No, it's sad! You poor thing."

She stared off, a shadow crossing her face. Harry sat in the empty chair across the lamp table.

"Hey, Mom. I've got a joke for you," he said. "What do you call a fairy who hasn't taken a bath?

She perked up. "Oh, oh, I know this one." She paused for effect. "A PIG-xie!" She slapped her knee. She pushed her nose up into a pig snout, snorted, and made a piglike motion with her hands. "Get it, PIX-ie? PIG-xie?" She slapped her knee again and cackled.

Harry smiled and shook his head, then joined her laughter.

187

"That's good, Mom. You haven't lost your sense of humor. You always crack me up. But the real answer is, . . . 'What do you call a fairy who hasn't taken a bath?' . . . wait for it . . . '*Stink*-er Bell!'"

They both hooted. Her face went deadpan again.

"I like mine better. PIG-xie!" She reprised her pig grunting noise and pig motions. Harry laughed politely.

She peered off toward the door.

"So, what are you thinking about, Mom?"

"Packing."

Harry gaped at her, brow furrowed. "Packing? Why? Are you going somewhere?"

Her mouth dropped open, eyes widened. "Well, I can't stay on vacation forever!"

"But Mom, you're retired—you're on a permanent vacation." He snickered.

"I know that, silly. But if you do it long enough, it's work!" She leaned over, spoke in a whisper." Plus, there's too many old people in this hotel." She waved with a flourish at several bystanders around the lobby.

"Well, yeah, Mom. These days, there's a lot of old people everywhere."

"I don't like old people," she said. "I'm thinking of moving to Australia."

Harry did a double-take, then looked away and smiled.

"Next Tuesday. I just need to find my passport." She poked around, searching the space next to her seat cushion.

"Mom, you can't do that. How would we have our crazy socks contest?" He stood up, lifted his pant legs. "Check these out." He showed off a pair of brightly colored, patterned socks. They were red, with orange and purple zigzags and yellow stars.

She leaned over to examine his feet, then pulled up her pant legs to reveal her own pair. They were gaudy pink with what appeared to be green U.F.O.s that flashed on and off using multi-colored LEDs.

Harry cracked up. "Oh, Mom, you win! You win! Those are the wildest yet."

He lifted her pant legs higher, admiring them. "Marcia has outdone herself this time. I still don't understand why she keeps sending you all those *crazy socks.*"

"She owes me."

"For what? This has been going on for years . . . every month, another pair."

Harry's mom pulled him closer, looked one way, then the other.

"I'm blackmailing her," she said in a stage whisper.

Harry guffawed, slapping his gut. "Blackmail? For what— stealing a buck out of the church collection plate?"

"How did you know?" she rasped. "So, she finally confessed?"

"No, Mom . . . you might have mentioned it. You probably just forgot. But your secret is safe." He patted her arm.

She looked around again. "She's after me. I think the socks have tracking devices. That's why I'm moving to Australia."

"But, Mom, Marcia is one of your best friends. Would she really do that?"

"She sure would. She's trying to steal Earl from me."

"Earl? Who's Earl?" He stared at the irate frown that settled on her face.

"My boyfriend Earl. Earl Grey. We're going to Australia. Soon as Earl finishes packing, we're gonna blow this pop stand." She glanced over her shoulder. "There's something not right . . .," she muttered.

Harry glanced around to see what she was referring to. "What's that, Mom?"

"Oh . . . something. Something needs to be done." She stood up unsteadily, leaning on the walker next to her chair.

Harry put a hand on her arm. He reached for the large book

on the table. "Mom, is this the scrapbook Ellen mentioned to me? She told me she found it a while ago in the attic. When did you make this?"

She turned stiffly. "Oh, I don't know. I just worked on it in my spare time." She sat back down.

Harry thumbed through the pages. "Ellen said it was wonderful. Newspaper clippings. Photos of you and dad. Report cards." He looked over the top of his reading glasses. "Wow, Mom, this article says you sold more War Bonds than anyone else in the US."

She sat up attentively.

"Students, that is," he added.

Harry continued to read from the scrapbook. "Christina Nordstrom, Junior at Sea Stack High School, in Nicolet, Michigan, was recognized by President Roosevelt last week as the top seller of War Bonds among students in the United States. Her sales to date have totaled $212,437." He turned to look at her. She sat up, puffed with pride.

"That's incredible, Mom. Here's your picture with the other top students. How did you do that?"

"I don't know. I just worked on it in my spare time."

"But, Mom, when did you have any spare time?" Harry asked. "According to this other article, you were captain of the Debate Team. And here's one of you giving a graduation valedictory speech. You were Valedictorian—I didn't know."

"I just worked on it in my spare time."

Harry chuckled, patted her arm. "Here's a later one when you were on the school board in Loyale, the year they built the new high school, 1964. You chaired the building committee. I was in the first class. Mom, you built the High School!"

"Well, I just worked on it in my spare time."

Harry flipped through a few more pages. "And here's your certificate from when you were named Ojibwa County Woman of the Year, 1970. The same year you chaired the Chamber of

Commerce board. Plus, you raised me, Ellen, George, and Eric. Four kids!"

She stared up at him, shook her head. "Now, that was a full-time job."

Harry broke up, laughing. "You were such a great mom. I didn't know this stuff about you. All these years, you've been hiding your light under a basket."

She looked around, a worried expression on her face.

"There's something I have to . . ." She started up out of the chair.

Harry pointed at the scrapbook pages, eased her back.

"Mom, look at this one. It's dad in his army uniform. My gosh, this news clip is scary." He read from the scrapbook.

"Lt. Cal Nichols was home on leave this week from his duties in the Army Air Corps 449th Bomb Group. He had quite a tale to tell. 'Sometimes we take some heat out there,' Nichols said. 'A few weeks ago, when we landed, we counted over 300 holes in the ship. A few days later, a jagged piece of spent flak flew through the windshield, hit me smack on the chest and landed in my lap. No injury, but when something like that happens, it makes you think a little.'"

Harry's mom gazed off into space.

"Gosh, he sure was handsome in that uniform. You must have been quite the couple."

Harry stood up, blocked out a headline in the air.

"Dashing War Hero Returns Home, Meets Aspiring Actress at USO Club."

He turned to her. "What was Dad like—when you first met him?"

She thought for a moment. "He was a nervous wreck!"

Harry smiled. "Yeah, I suppose so." He shook his head, put the scrapbook away, then checked his watch. "Well, I have to leave soon."

"I thought you were staying for tea."

"Oh, we're having tea?"

"Of course, every afternoon, three p. m. sharp. The Twilight Hotel Tea Party is world-famous." She gestured around the lobby. "People come from everywhere."

"I didn't know that." Harry paused, put his finger to his chin. "Maybe I did read something . . . I suppose I can stay a bit longer. But only if my best girl will be here." He patted her arm again.

"Why, of course, I am, darling," she said in a voice channeling Kathryn Hepburn. "Whenever I'm a guest here, I never fail to attend. I shall miss it dearly when we travel to Australia. Have you finished packing?"

"Packing? No, not yet."

"Well, you must get on with it. We cannot leave without your bags."

"Okay, I'll keep packing," Harry replied.

She stood up, stepped forward behind the walker, and scanned the lobby. "Something is amiss, quite unsatisfactory. I believe we must call a meeting."

Harry stepped toward her. "It's all right. Tea will be here shortly."

She took another step forward. "Attention everyone, I wish to call the meeting to order. Everyone pay attention now.

She tapped her bony knuckles against the walker frame, as if gaveling atop a table. "Order . . . order. That's much better." She paused, waiting for the room to go quiet. "I know you're all wondering why I have called you here. Before we address that, is there any concern a member wishes to place on the agenda?"

She paused, scanned the room. "Okay, seeing no hands, let's begin on item one. I'm sad to report that the Twilight Hotel will close soon. Tuesday, to be exact. Now, this may shock many of you, especially the regular guests. However, I am happy to report that we have made arrangements, if you so choose. I have booked passage for everyone on a luxury cruise ship to Australia." She paused, seeming to let the membership grasp the news.

"For those who wish to stay behind, you must vacate the hotel by midnight Tuesday so we can fumigate for fairies. Are there questions?"

A door opened, and a young woman in a nurse's uniform strode toward the chair where Harry sat listening. She placed a tray with glasses of iced tea and a paper cup on the lamp table. She leaned over to him. "I see we're having another meeting. Her tea is ready."

". . . Hearing none, a motion is in order," Harry's mom said. "Everyone leaving, step over to this corner. Quickly now." She gestured toward the entry. "Those staying behind, step to that corner." She gestured in the opposite direction.

She made a sweeping gesture behind her. "All the dead babies named Martin, to the rear."

Harry leapt to his feet, alarm on his face. He stepped behind his mom. The nurse stepped to her other side. Together, they guided her back to the chair.

"It's *teatime*," the nurse said buoyantly.

Harry's mom surveyed the room. "Thank you for your avid attention. Meeting adjourned." She sat down in the chair.

"Okay, Christina."

Harry's mom leaned forward, opening her mouth. The nurse took two pills from the paper cup, an oval pink one and a square white one, and placed them on her outstretched tongue. She held a glass of water to her lips.

"Swallow these and . . ." Harry's mom gulped the pills and drank some water.

"Now, here's your tea, Christina, with lemon, just the way you like it."

She set the water glass on the tray and handed Harry's mom an iced tea. She reached for it and grasped it with both hands.

Harry pulled the nurse aside.

"Dead babies? What was that about?" He looked back at his mom.

"Who knows? Could be random . . . could be a miscarriage. Or . . . whatever. . ."

Harry reached for a glass of iced tea and sat down. He studied his mom with a worried expression.

The nurse picked up the tray and turned to leave. "Enjoy your tea, Christina."

Harry's mom leaned forward, hunched over, and took another sip, continuing to hold the glass in both hands. Harry drank some of his tea. She looked squarely at him, pointing with a scrawny finger.

"Don't forget your luggage, Earl. Remember—Tuesday. Australia."

She started to place the glass on the table. Harry helped her, then sat back in his chair, staring off into space, a sad expression on his face. Finally, he took another sip of tea.

His mom slowly lowered her head and fell asleep.

Harry covered her with a blanket draped over the back of her chair. He gestured to one of the staff.

"Can you buzz me out?"

"Sure thing, Mr. Nichols." The attendant punched in the code on the wall keypad, and the steel entry door clacked open. "See you next week."

Harry stepped through. "Next week," he echoed. He turned for a last glance at his mom, then hurried past the sign in front of the building, 'Twilight Memory Care.'

Next week.

THREE DANCES

Prologue

The day before New Year's, an electrical storm "fried" my laptop. For a freelance writer, this was existential. I had spent my money on Christmas and was forced to throw myself on the mercy of Craigslist. After a week combing the Internet, I located an obsolete model. While not ideal, the seller had priced it right at forty-five dollars. An elderly woman answered my phone call. She declined to give her address but agreed to meet at McDonald's.

"We're downsizing," she said. "A whole garage full, you can't imagine. Some of it dates to my parents, some my brother's."

"I bet you'll be happy to get your parking spot back."

She grinned. "My husband will. He hasn't parked inside in a decade."

She took the laptop out of its case. "My grandson posted the ad—I don't use Craigslist. He told me it worked last time he knew, but you can check for yourself."

As I turned on the machine, she mentioned she had removed the data and programs.

"I think I erased everything but promise you will delete any personal or financial info you find."

I assured her.

Later, circumstances compelled me to hedge. I couldn't bring myself to destroy a folder I found. Her ad had listed an email address, which turned out to be her brother's, but my attempts came back undeliverable. I tried to locate her and other family members, sending emails and leaving phone messages, which led to more dead ends. I almost gave up, wondering if I changed everybody's identities, could anyone complain. Finally, a relative called and gave me permission to use the information, but not their names. So, I was, in spirit, able to keep my promise.

❀ ❀ ❀

March 1, 2018 Email to Larry Thorsen
<u>Subject: Christmas follow-up</u>

Dear Larry: It was wonderful to see you and your parents at Christmas. I was thankful everyone made it back to the old family homestead here in Loyale and especially pleased to spend time with you. You have grown over the past seventeen years from a little "bottle-swigger" into a fine young man.

I am starting to work on my staffing plan for the upcoming season. Before you know it, summer will be here. So, I wanted to follow up on our conversation over the holidays about Tower Rock.

I assume you have spoken with your parents, but I haven't heard anything from you or them. Are you still on board?

Let me know,

Your Great Uncle Charley

March 1, 2018 Email to Charles Lochting
<u>Subject: RE: Christmas follow-up</u>

Hi, Uncle Charley. Sorry, I didn't respond before.

I misunderstood. Thought you knew I was planning to work for you this summer. When do I start, right after school gets out? What do I need to do before then?

Thank you for the opportunity,

Your Nephew Larry

March 2, 2018, Email to Larry Thorsen
<u>Subject: A serious proposal</u>

Dear Larry, I didn't mean to press you. I assumed you would work for me this summer. However, after the holidays, my diabetes caught up with me and is destroying my circulation. I have developed a terrible ulcer on my right foot, and most days I struggle to walk. On the last visit to my doctor, he warned me if it doesn't heal soon, they will have to consider amputation. Larry, I don't know how I can work if they cut my legs off. Even more distressing, they tell me that half of diabetic amputees die within two years.

That's why I asked for a confirmation. I may need someone to play a significant part in my business, someone trustworthy. Your visit over Christmas gave me a kick in the pants. I set my sixty-eighth birthday—next week—as a deadline. You will work harder but get paid more.

Please confirm now that you know the situation.

Your Great Uncle Charley

March 2, 2018, Email to Charles Lochting
Subject: RE: A serious proposal

Uncle Charley, I think I am ready for it, but your health problems sound really serious. I'm worried for you. Mom and Dad too. What would you expect me to do?

Larry

March 3, 2018, Email to Larry Thorsen
Subject: A serious proposal

Ok, Larry, in a nutshell, here's the deal—I have no heirs or succession plan. If it pans out this year, I want you to continue working in the business each summer while attending college. After graduation, if mutually agreeable, you will become a salaried manager. Over time, I'll help you acquire the company. If the worst happens, the plan implementation will fast-track.

Aside from my health issues, why am I extending this offer? It has always bothered me that your mom followed your dad to Oakland University and abandoned our enterprise. Your great grandfather regretted to the day he died that she didn't stay in Loyale; we all did.

So, my proposal to you is my way of swinging the wheel full circle to chart a new course, one that will reunite the disparate elements of the Lochting family. I honor my parents and grandparents, who gave me so much, and pass the company banner to the newest generation. This is more than a business proposition—a challenge to you to plant our founder's flag on a loftier height.

Think about it, Larry. You're still in high school, your whole future ahead of you. It's a big commitment. Ready to ascend the summit?

Your Uncle Charley

—Oh, also, forgot I have a small favor to ask. Next time.

March 3, 2018 Email to Charles Lochting
Subject: Re: a serious proposal

Hi, Uncle Charley. Showed your email to mom and dad. They're still in shock. Me too, but I have thought it over. Count me in. We're all sweating the health thing.

You mentioned a favor—what's up?

Larry

March 4, 2018 Email to Larry Thorsen
Subject: an odd request

Larry, thank you for reminding me. It will seem trivial, even though it's crucial to me. So, bear with me while I try to put it in perspective. I don't want you to think I am off my rocker, but it won't make sense unless I tell you a bit of my personal story. . .

For twenty years, I have been fascinated by the Lochtings' genealogy. Our family emigrated to the U.S. in the late 19th

Century, settling in Wisconsin. Over time, many Lochtings fished and farmed on Rock Island. How my grandfather ended up in Loyale is a story in itself. But once there, he noted the large numbers of tourists and the unusual limestone formations called sea stacks. He seized the opportunity to create an observation platform on the tallest one—Tower Rock—to survey the magnificent local vistas. When he gained the property, the rest was history.

I suppose my fascination with our genealogy started with a family reunion, but an incident occurred there that marked my life and haunted me for over half a century. I must run to an appointment right now but will tell you about this in my next email.

Regards,
Uncle Charley

March 5, 2018 Email to Charles Lochting
Subject: Reunion

Uncle Charley, you won't believe this, but I have a new assignment for my World History class. We all have to write a family history. Mom gave me a copy of the family tree you compiled, but any stories about family members you can share will help make it come alive.

Thanks, Larry

March 6, 2018 Email to Larry Thorsen
Subject: Family History

Larry, I would be happy to share some stories for your project. My family reunion story will provide a good start.

Our family in Wisconsin and Michigan had never organized a formal reunion. By the early '60s, a hundred descendants claimed the Lochting name. I had never visited the Island, and

SEA Stacks

I tell you, Larry, it was a trip to another planet. Here I was, an eleven-year-old boy transported in time at least 50 years.

They held the event in one of the two bars there. Since there was no town per se, community life revolved around these "watering holes," more like meeting halls than taverns or pubs. In fact, Karly's Tap, where we gathered, contained a small bar in the front; behind it, a large hall with a stage.

Soon the place filled to overflowing with Lochtings by blood or marriage, abuzz in conversations. Long tables stretched across the hall, covered with food brought by the Islanders, pot-luck style.

I never ate from such a feast, especially so many mysterious dishes. Norwegian meatballs, venison pasties, and smoked fish chowder, plus more conventional dishes—seven-layer salad, scalloped corn pudding, and fresh cherry pie. Outside the tavern, they fed a wood fire for a fish boil—whitefish and lake trout steaks, yellow potatoes, and onions poached in a huge pot and served with thick rye bread and melted butter.

Before long, a band of old-time musicians assembled onstage. Someone pulled the curtain back to reveal the players: guitar, violin, accordion, and a stand-up bass. They struck up a lively tune, which filled the dance hall.

I often listened to my mom and dad's records from the '30s and '40s and my babysitter's 45s. But this recalled no melody I had ever heard. It was music from another time, another land, another culture. The musicians reeled off one song after the next, and dancers soon packed the hall—smiling, laughing couples, embracing, whirling around the floor, marking out intricate steps. It pulsed in rhythm with their feet. The violinist introduced each number, and I learned certain songs accompanied certain dances—polkas, schottisches, etc.

I was desperate to join the others on that dance floor but terrified to learn the steps and dreadfully afraid of embarrassment or ridicule. So, there I sat, paralyzed;

surrounded by relatives, most of whom I didn't know, exhilarated by the music and dancing, but petrified to try in front of a crowd.

At that moment, one of my dad's cousins and my aunt came over to the table. The violinist called out a "Flying Dutchman." The dance consisted of threesomes—gentleman in the middle, a lady on each side, with arms locked behind each other—who proceeded around the perimeter of the floor like skaters on an ice rink.

They stared down at me, smiling.

"Dance with us, Charley?" Aunt Sigrid asked.

My heart dropped into my stomach. "N-no, not really."

"It's easy, we'll show you. Com'on," said Cousin Karen. She held out a hand and wiggled her fingers.

"I just like to listen."

"Are you sure?" they said in unison.

I nodded, my face a mask of fear.

"Ok, we'll check later, in case you change your mind." Off they went to find a different partner.

I slipped away and stayed outside the hall. I wished to learn how, but ashamed that I had lied and turned them down. It haunted me, and I have never told anyone about it. For years, I wanted somehow to make amends. Now, strangely, I may have found a way. It could be my last chance.

That's why I need your help.

Uncle Charley

March 7, 2018 Email to Charles Lochting
<u>Subject: Happy Birthday</u>

Hi, Uncle Charley, sorry about your shyness. Maybe it's growing up in a small town. Mom says, back in the day, times were weird. I asked my friends—they never heard of the dances you mentioned. And a band with no drums? Seriously, you might have been born in the wrong century! Which reminds me…

Happy Birthday—number 68, right?

Larry

March 7, 2018 Email to Larry Thorsen
Subject: More history

Larry, thank you for remembering my birthday.

To your other points, it's true that people have largely forgotten these dances, but a few keep the old traditions alive (more to follow on that, later).

As for not having a drummer, you have to remember that the music was not amplified, and the shouting, shuffling, and stomping of the couples on the dance floor provided the percussion. The dancers and the musicians engaged each other in the performance of the tune, in its own way, an intense experience.

Okay, back to your project and another scrap of my personal history, this one relevant as well to the silly favor I need.

A few years after the Lochting reunion, the Beatles became a phenomenon. You can't imagine the impact on me and millions of other teenagers. I remember an afternoon in 1964, sprawled crossways on my parents' bed, tuning their clock radio to our local AM station. As I listened, the DJ announced "…the new hit record by the BEATLES." Across the airwaves floated the words and melody to "I Want to Hold Your Hand." It was more than energizing, like nothing I had heard. I lay on my back and contemplated this singular moment.

Later, on a Sunday night, I watched the Beatles perform on the Ed Sullivan Show on my grandparents' black and white television. Seeing them live before a screaming audience was one of the most transformative events of my life, as implausible as Neil Armstrong walking on the moon or airplanes hitting the World Trade Tower.

From that instant, I yearned to play in a rock group. When I turned fifteen, four classmates and I started a band called the Beatrayors. Our popularity surged, and we performed around six counties at high school dances, teen clubs, and weddings. The number of groups in those days playing rock 'n' roll music, specifically in rural communities such as Loyale, was virtually nil, so it was easy to grow a fan base.

I had overcome my earlier shyness, in part through daily rehearsal, in part through the thrill of performing before hundreds of teenagers every weekend. Imagine being sixteen, the center of attention, playing songs by the Beatles, Rolling Stones, and Animals; and American groups like the Beach Boys, Temptations, and Mitch Ryder; plus being paid for it. Much better than pumping gas or bagging groceries. From our elevated view on the bandstand, we couldn't help but notice the dancers—especially the girls—and the interaction between various kids in the audience. We received a free, in-depth education in human behavior.

Girls from northern Michigan and across the Midwest arrived on summer vacation by the hundreds with their parents and showed up at the venues where we played. The Beatrayors developed a large following, and they loved us. Often, our fans invited the band afterward to a house party or beer bash at a park or local beach. What happened to me at one of these parties changed my life.

My phone is ringing. It's your grandmother, so I will email you the rest later.

Uncle Charley

March 8, 2018 Email to Charles Lochting
<u>Subject: Rock History</u>

Uncle Charley, thanks for the info on the Beatles. Super stuff for my school assignment. AM radio? black and white tv? I assume you didn't have cellphones either. Hard to imagine. Can't wait to hear the rest.

Larry

March 8, 2018 Email to Larry Thorsen
Subject: Rock History—continued

Larry, sorry to cut my email off abruptly yesterday. The word on my health problems has gotten around Loyale, so I am getting phone calls from concerned people—like your grandma. I appreciate it, but sometimes they talk like I'm already dead. I keep telling them, don't rush things!

As for cellphones, imagine this. We didn't even have dial phones. When you picked up the telephone, an operator came on saying, "Number, please."

You would say, something like, "137, please." And she would say, "Thank you," and connect your call at her switchboard. And then your party would answer.

So back to my so-called teenage "Celebrity Rock Career."

As I mentioned, we would often get invited to a private party after playing at a teen dance. At one of these get-togethers, I first met Angelika Biedermann. In late April 1966, I turned sixteen. We were playing a spring dance in Millecoquins—an hour northwest of Loyale—our favorite venue. The girls there were lively and highly approachable.

Across the hall, I noticed a slender blonde, dancing with another girl. Back then, a lot of guys thought dancing wasn't cool or lacked experience, so it took a while for the girls to entice them onto the floor. Nobody wanted to be the first or only one. The girls danced with each other, while the boys stood on the sideline, waiting to make their moves.

This girl was different. She displayed a unique style,

uninhibited, but precise, someone who had taken ballet or modern dance lessons. I loved the way she moved and was eager for a chance to meet her. All evening, she flirted with several guys vying for her attention.

Afterward, one of the employees invited the band to a county park on a small lake. Across a bonfire, I spied her, the fire's glow illuminating her face and figure against the dark canvas of the night. Flickering light from the blazing wood shimmered and danced along the strands of her long, honey-blonde hair. Her deep blue eyes sparkled, animated by her captivating laugh. I discovered she was a foreign exchange student from Germany staying with Jill McNaughton, who had hired the Beatrayors for a school event. I strolled toward them and Jill introduced us. Although her name was Angelika, everyone called her by her nickname, Schnuki.

"I love your rock-and-roll music," she said. "It sets me free."

"I noticed. I thought maybe you had taken dancing or gymnastics lessons."

"Ah, yes, gymnastics—and a little ballet. You like how I dance?" She tossed me a coy look and smiled.

"Yeah, nice. Best dancer."

"You should see me polka!" She laughed and twirled, performing a few mock steps. "If you learn a polka song, I will show you."

I couldn't tell if Schnuki was putting me on. She flashed another mischievous grin, and I was smitten. The whole way home I sat in the rear seat of the station wagon we used for travel, watching a bright, silent moon float high above, thinking of her.

Over that spring and the rest of the summer, I saw her at every one of our Millecoquins dances. The band played forty-five to fifty-minute sets, with two short breaks. On the breaks, other band members and I hung out with people from the audience, made plans for after the dance, or walked outside to cool off. But the week after I met her, Schnuki and I sneaked through the stage door behind the bandstand.

I was so young—in age and temperament—we grew up in a different time. I naively tried to make conversation, telling her again how much I liked the way she danced. "And how have you been since the bonfire? I enjoyed meeting you and hoped to see you again."

She moved in close. I continued to blather, not knowing what else to do. Without warning, she reached up and wrapped her arms around my neck, drawing me to her. The press of her nimble body sent an emotional shock wave rolling through me. She kissed me, not like the handful of girls I kissed in junior high or high school, but long and deeply, as a young woman. I was breathless, flooded in its intimacy. I wanted to stretch the break into forever.

Over the next four months, we spent more and more time together, less and less with band members and school friends. Even though she lived an hour away, I found other ways to meet her outside our gigs. I didn't tell my parents, but my friends knew.

The more time I spent with her, the more intensely I fell in love. She was stunning, so warm and easy to be with, so delightful and fun, yet for me—a small-town kid—so graceful, so cosmopolitan. Her brilliance overwhelmed me; she stood at the top of her class, spoke five languages. I worshiped everything about her and couldn't believe she was real.

I had only one worry. Toward the middle of summer, it exploded into panic. She was older by more than a year—the heart of a dreadful problem. In a matter of weeks, she planned to return to Germany to finish Gymnasium, the German prep school for university-bound students.

Circumstances had trapped us in a web of desperation. We exchanged address and phone numbers, but international calls were very expensive (as you might imagine) and, of course, no Internet. It seemed impossible I would see her again. I was prepared to do anything. Right before our last night together, a terrible problem arose.

Gosh, sorry, Larry, I need to quit again. My shipper just pulled in, and I have to sign for a delivery. You will get to do this too when you come up here this summer.

Uncle Charley

March 9, 2018 Email to Charles Lochting
Subject: Schnuki—do you have pictures?

Uncle Charley, that is freakin' awesome. I never would have guessed. Do you have a picture of Schnuki? If so, scan and send to me, plus any pics of the Beatrayors. I would be fantastic for my class assignment. No one will believe this. And I haven't forgotten about the favor you want. Just let me know.

Larry

March 9, 2018 Email to Larry Thorsen
Subject: RE: Schnuki—do you have pictures?

Larry, I will look around and see if I can find any pics for you. I had some a long time ago, but where they are, I don't know.

Anyway, to pick up on my story from yesterday, The Beatrayors had a terrible problem arise. One of our band members caught strep throat and could not play our final summer gig at Millecoquins. I asked a neighbor friend, Chaz Burkhart, a college student and exceptional guitar player and singer, to sit in.

Dr. Burkhart, his father, had bought a new Mustang convertible, and Chaz asked to borrow it. He and I rode together so we could talk over the set list and other details he needed to know. I confessed to him my passion for Schnuki and my anguish over this being our last night. In fact, the situation was worse. She couldn't stay for the whole dance. Her host family planned to drive her first thing in the morning to catch a flight out of Detroit Metro, a six-hour drive from their home.

At the break, Chaz handed me the keys to the Mustang. "Take her for a ride?"

I was speechless. Our venue manager expected the Beatrayors to play again in fifteen minutes. The band might fake a few numbers, but they could not perform more than half an hour without me. The people paying us would be extremely unhappy. I didn't care. I grasped her hand, and out the door, we ran.

I had only been driving for five months. When I received my license, my father told me, "Charley, don't ever borrow anyone's car. If you wreck it, they'll cancel our insurance." I promised, but I wasn't going to let Schnuki return to Germany without a night she would never forget.

"Do you drive?" I asked. She nodded, and I handed her the keys. "This will be the best drive of your life."

We headed out of town on a two-lane road. I had in mind a secluded lake nearby where we could be alone for our brief farewell tryst. We were flying fast, talking faster. As we crested a hill, an oncoming car banked around a blind curve to the left. His brights flooded the windshield of the Mustang. We couldn't see the blacktop and slid on a patch of loose gravel. As he flashed by, Schnuki lost control. We skidded over the embankment, taking out some short posts marking the pavement edge. The Mustang plowed through brush and weeds, stalling in front of a small billboard.

I sat there in the moonlight—shaking, scared—in disbelief. I looked over at her. Her right cheek oozed blood from a gash where she had bumped the steering wheel.

"You're hurt," I sobbed. I tried to wipe the blood away.

"*Nein*, I-I'm okay." She looked dazed. I reached to touch her, kissing her over and over—my heart, a scramble of emotions.

"If anything happened, I don't know what…," I cried. "Schnuki, I love you so much, and now I may never see you again."

"I love you too, Charley. Forever."

I held her face in my hands. "I planned everything—our last night—it's all gone wrong."

We spoke rapidly, with passion—time had run out.

"Come to Germany next year and visit me. You must," she begged.

I promised to find a way, next year—at the latest, the year after. In the meantime, we would write. I kissed her once more, long and deeply, as she first kissed me, a seal on our mutual commitment.

We switched seats, and I tried to start the car. We backed out of the field and up onto the highway. When we returned to the dance, I looked it over. A rocker panel was crushed, the aluminum trim dangling from the driver-side door.

I told Chaz that I messed up his new Mustang. I asked him to tell Dr. Burkhart that I was sorry and promised to pay for the repair. He acted pretty cool about it. But I was quite worried what my dad would do.

I have to quit here, Larry. Sorry. Way past my bedtime. I have always been a night owl, but the doctor says I must change my ways. I am making the effort, before it's too late. It's hard.

More to follow.

Uncle Charley

March 10, 2018 Email to Charles Lochting
<u>Subject: Losing your girlfriend—and a wrecked car?</u>

Uncle Charley, That's a really crazy story. What happened to Schnucki? Did you get to Germany? Or did your dad kill you for wrecking the car.

Just kidding,

Larry

March 10, 2018 Email to Larry Thorsen
Subject: RE: Losing your girlfriend—and a wrecked car?

Larry, I will cut to the chase. The next morning, when I informed my dad, I caught a bucket of hellfire. He was even more unhappy to find out about my German girlfriend. After I explained the circumstances in more detail, he said, "Well, Charley, I hope to God you learned something," and let it go. But as our conversation ended, Schnuki was on the road to Detroit, then airborne to Frankfurt.

For more than a year, she and I kept up an ardent correspondence. In one of my initial letters, I recalled the first time we met and how she pressed me to learn some polka songs. I wrote, 'We never actually danced together.' Schnuki replied that if I came to Germany, she would take me to Octoberfest, and we would 'drink beer and dance all night long.'

I continued to promise I would travel to see her. But she lived so far away and had started university. I was in high school, more and more engaged with the Beatrayors. A steady stream of new girls threatened to divert my attention every weekend, and my college and career preparations loomed ominously larger each successive month.

Our relationship inevitably faded. It ended when I informed my parents I planned to travel to Europe for the summer after my college freshman year. Although the band dissolved as we left high school to pursue our respective plans, I had stashed away a stack of gig money, plus my pay working summers for my dad at Tower Rock. I had the cash, especially if I stayed with Schnuki. But my parents were adamantly opposed. For months I kept after my mom until at last she told the truth to make me realize it was hopeless.

My father had fought in World War II. She said he witnessed firsthand the Nazis' ruthless atrocities, something he never spoke of. Twenty-five years later, it still held an iron grip. "Why would Charley take up with a *German*?" he asked. "He doesn't know what these people will do, given the chance—why can't he find a nice girl here?"

My whole life, I have regretted to the core I didn't go. I loved Schnuki profoundly and might have married her; I promised to visit, but later broke my pledge. Most troubling is that I didn't write and tell her why. I couldn't figure an honest way out that wasn't a personal humiliation, so I stopped answering her letters.

Maybe, that's why I never married. Although I hate to believe it is true, through my failure of courage, she slipped away, and I couldn't rebound. Every time I met an interesting young woman, I would spot something—a word, a laugh, a touch—that reminded me of Schnuki. I would fall into the same old funk, wanting only her, but having blown my chances.

Larry, I have gone on way longer than I intended. But without this history, my request for your help might appear peculiar and trivial. I promise to bring the suspense to an end in my next email, a pledge I will keep this time if it kills me.

Best Regards,
Uncle Charley

March 11, 2018 Email to Charles Lochting
Subject: Schnuki

Wow, Uncle Charley. What a downer to lose your girlfriend—especially, so long ago. Have you tried to Google her? Do you think she's still alive? Did she hook up with someone else? Or like you, believe no one measured up?

Is that the favor you need—you want me to find her? It may not be too late!

Larry

March 12, 2018 Email to Larry Thorsen
Subject: Favor next Sept

Dear Larry, it's time I explain how you can help.

Before that, let me respond specifically to your email. your questions are the same ones I think about every day. Although it haunts me, I have never tried to find Schnuki. I couldn't bear to know what happened to her. It would only deepen my despair to learn she died, suffered through an unhappy marriage, or experienced some other life tragedy. I have preferred to remember her ideally, as the young woman I loved with such passion, when I was so young. However, an incident last fall crashed through the lifetime mental wall I had built.

Last September, the 29th to be exact, I took a day trip to Frankenmuth, Michigan. Doubt if you have ever been there, but it's a quaint little town with a strong Bavarian heritage. Its fame rests on a couple of restaurants that serve family-style chicken dinners. The other attraction is Bronner's, the largest Christmas store in the world. Acres of ornaments and decorations. Unbelievable, really.

Two of your grandmother's Florida friends came for a visit. They knew of Bronner's and wanted to make a day trip. I offered to act as chauffeur and tour guide. On the Internet, I discovered that Frankenmuth's famous Octoberfest was opening with a line-up of musical acts, food and, of course, lots of German beer. I suggested we top off lunch and shopping with a Pilsner and some music before heading home, a three-hour drive.

When we pulled into the Octoberfest park at a quarter to four, we heard the music wafting across the street from a tall metal building. Inside, row upon row of long tables pointed toward the dance floor. A German band made up of five older men from Cleveland played on a large bandstand. It was early in the festivities, scheduled to last all weekend. At least a hundred people sat in the audience, many of them decked out in lederhosen, dirndls, and other traditional dress. The hall easily held 1,000, so plenty of good seats were available.

We found an empty table across the dance floor from the bandstand a third of the way back. I left to buy a pitcher of beer. When I returned, a family of four had seated themselves a few chairs in front of us. On one side sat a tall, thin man in a yellow, long-sleeve shirt, slacks, and a small green alpine hat. A jaunty feather poked up from its band. Across from him sat a girl, ten or eleven years old, long hair streaming with ribbons, a garland of flowers adorning her brow. To the man's right, directly in front of me, sat an older girl, thirteen or fourteen, with long blonde hair also entwined with ribbons and crowned by a garland. Across from her, a woman with thick auburn hair cut in a long shag style hunched over the table, weighed down by a heavy cardigan sweater, her eyes dark and sunken. They had brought food and bottled water with them, and it was obvious they planned to make an evening of it.

As the band hit its stride, the man began to dance with his daughters—first one, then the other. Round and round the floor they pranced in a circular course. Fifteen or twenty other couples also danced, and the band—accordion, piano, guitar, trumpet, and drums—hopped from tune to tune, attempting to prevent them from leaving.

The girls were both tall and thin, resembling their father, and excellent dancers, light on their feet. The youngest wore a long, red print dress, white anklets, and little flat, black shoes fastened with a strap and buckle. Her older sister wore the same costume, except her print dress was dark green. Together, they conveyed a cheery, energetic impression on the rest of the audience.

Soon, when one girl wasn't dancing with her father, she was invited to dance by someone else. All the old guys took a turn with one or the other. Once or twice, their father danced with their mother, but they stayed near the table and moved slowly and gingerly on the floor.

Your grandmother noticed this, and remarked, "She doesn't look good. I think she must be ill—or depressed."

The band retired from the bandstand, and another younger group from Wisconsin stepped onstage. Their instrumentation was similar, except that an attractive young woman, hair braided and coiled atop her head and dressed in a short dirndl, sang their songs. She also played a keyboard and several wind instruments. Her voice was clear and bright and her movements vibrant. She amped up the excitement on the dance floor, which was filling as crowds of people poured into the building. But I scarcely noticed, intoxicated with her lively face, honey-blonde hair, and uninhibited dance moves.

I had collided with a lightning bolt and flashed into another world. The singer so resembled my long-lost Schnuki—but ten years older—she could be no other person. A hundred vivid memories flooded my heart.

As I turned away from staring, my eyes came to rest a few feet away on the older of the two girls. She nibbled some raw vegetables while her father danced with her sister. Now, a whole new wave of emotions spilled into my soul. She too was a clone of Schnuki, only this time, how she must have appeared as a young girl before we met at Millecoquins so long ago. I twisted around toward your grandmother, unable to look at them, afraid at any moment to burst into tears.

214

Someone touched me on the shoulder. I turned back to see, standing before me, the bright young girl in the dark green dress. She reached out a hand.

"Would you like to dance with me?"

Larry, those words crushed me. Touched that this innocent girl had the kindness—and poise—to invite a wretched old man like myself onto the dance floor, I choked.

"I-I don't…I don't know how." My eyes teared up. Before my companions behind me noticed, I tried to brush them away.

"Oh, that's okay," she replied with a soft smile. She returned to her seat, and a few minutes later, a young man sauntered over and asked her to join him.

"What a nice gesture," one of your grandmother's friends said.

"Yes," they all agreed.

Devastated, I sat, my back to them, trying to regain my composure. She had extended a hand, put herself out to include me in the festivities. For the third time in my life, I had utterly, completely failed.

I gazed out at the floor, where she danced with her father. They skipped lightly around the hall, and I imagined myself in his place. As they passed the bandstand, I saw the blonde singer, and my heart ached once more. *Schnuki.* I tumbled into the darkest valley of my long life of disappointments.

The band stopped for a break. The young girl in the green dress headed for the concession stand behind us.

"I am going to the restroom," I announced. "Anyone for a last beer while I'm up."

They were ready to leave, and so was I. But first I needed to meet one obligation.

I hung around near the concessions, waiting for her. As she turned with a bottle of water in her hand, I made way toward her, feigning a chance encounter.

"Oh, there you are again," I said. "I wanted to apologize."

"That's okay."

"No. No, it's not," I insisted. "I have always wanted to learn how to polka—for over fifty years—and now I am embarrassed, especially when you were so kind to ask. I want to make it up to you—and myself."

She glanced at me warily, her brow furrowed.

"You and your family come to the Octoberfest every year—right?"

"Yes. My mother is German. We have been coming as long as I can remember."

"Do you always come on opening day?"

"Yes, my father says the crowds are too rowdy on the weekend."

"So, if I learn to polka, and come back next year, you will be here—and dance with me?" My heart was racing.

"Yes." She laughed. "I'm sure we will be here—my mother says we must preserve our German culture. If you come, I'll dance with you."

"And I promise—sincerely—I will be here too, and I'll learn how beforehand. One more thing, may I ask your name?"

"It's Annika. Annika Schneider."

"And I am Charley. Charley Lochting."

She shook my hand and nodded. "Ok, next year, Mr. Lochting."

In another moment she had slipped back to her family, and I to your grandmother and her friends.

"What was all that about?" she asked. They obviously saw me speaking with the girl.

"Oh, I thought I should encourage her. Told her I was sorry I never learned to polka."

"Ha. Never too old to flirt, eh, Charley? Ten minutes from now, she won't even remember meeting you."

Larry, I didn't believe that, but didn't want to argue the point. This brings me to my favor, my "odd request."

I found a woman across the Bridge in Nicolet who teaches dancing. I started lessons, but my leg problems have forced me to quit. Yet I am determined to keep my promise—somehow—to that girl.

I want you to go in my place. I have arranged for dance lessons this summer, and I'll pay you to learn, as part of your job. Next fall, I'll meet you in Frankenmuth. I'll explain to Annika, but I need you to dance with her—for me. You may have to be excused from school a couple of days, so please speak to your parents.

This must sound crazy. If it does, please humor an old man. For me, in some way, it may compensate for the personal failures that have haunted my entire life.

So, Larry, will you do this small, silly favor for me? I'll be forever in your debt. And if that's not enough motivation, let me say, she's lovely and, as I hope I conveyed, most endearing. But when you meet her, you can make up your own mind.

Check with your mom and dad. Please, let me know soon. I am counting on you.

Uncle Charley

March 15, 2018 Email to Charles Lochting
Subject: Trip to Frankenmuth

Uncle Charley, in a hundred years, I couldn't have guessed what you wanted. Mom and dad are okay with the trip. But I hope you will be there to dance with Annika yourself—and around for many years to come.

So, yes, I'll go!

Larry

❆ ❆ ❆

Ed. Note: Several more emails followed on Larry's summer employment. For reasons of brevity, I deleted them.

❆ ❆ ❆

SEA Stacks

Dear Uncle Charley, so disappointed that you can't meet me. I realize how much that meant to you—and me too. Mom said the surgery went well, but we've all been worried. Grandma assures us you are in good spirits— under the circumstances, as good as expected.

Don't worry, I have Frankenmuth <u>covered</u>. My friend Ben is going with me. He'll record everything and make a video. I know it won't be the same as being there, but I hope you'll enjoy it.

Thanks for the dance lessons. I have it nailed. Most of all, thank you again for the wonderful job experience this summer. I am already looking forward to next year.

Only two weeks until Frankenmuth. I'll give you a full report.

Take Care,

Larry

October 1, 2018 Email to Charles Lochting
Subject: Frankenmuth—sit down, before you read this!

Dear Uncle Charley, you must be anxious to hear about my trip to Frankenmuth. You are going to be so blown away. Let me give you the Twitter version. My buddy Ben is editing the video he shot, and we'll post it on YouTube soon.

Ben and I arrived at 3:30 p.m. from Rochester and shot straight to the Octoberfest Hall. The band had started, but not many people were there yet. We found a seat right where you told me to sit, and Ben set up his camera tripod with a fantastic view of the dance floor.

But Annika wasn't there. It didn't worry me because your description convinced me she wouldn't let you down. After an hour, the place was filling, the second band onstage, yet no sign of her or her family. I had all but given up hope, when three people walked past and sat at the table on our right.

I knew straight away it was Annika—her blonde hair was real long, strewn with ribbons and a garland crown. Her younger sister was also just how you described. A tall, thin man with graying brown hair and a mustache—their father—sat with them. But her mother was nowhere to be seen.

I gave them a chance to settle and stood up to introduce myself. Right then, her dad asked her sister to dance and off they went to the dance floor. They skipped and spun around in time with the music, exactly how you described. I watched for a few minutes, amazed by how they moved, then saw my opening and stepped forward. Annika turned toward me with a look of expectation. but a middle-aged guy from the next table stood up, touched her arm, and asked her to dance. She nodded, turned again, and shrugged, leaving with a melancholy smile.

After that, it was her turn to dance with her father. He swept her across the floor, even more elegantly than her sister. I was determined not to let my next chance pass.

She must have been thinking the same thing because as her father swung her around near our table, she glanced back at me. The music ended, and they returned to their seats.

Or so I thought. But she continued toward me.

"Would you like to dance?" We both said at the same time, followed by an embarrassed laugh. I took her hand, and we headed back to the floor. And that is how I finally danced with Annika Schneider.

After the music stopped, we remained near the bandstand. I thanked her and told her I was certain I knew her.

She shook her head and threw me a wary glance. "How is that possible? We only just . . ."

"I have been waiting to dance with you for six months," I

teased.

She blushed.

"In fact, you're Annika Schneider."

She pulled back, stared at me with a puzzled look. "But—?"

"I'm Larry, Larry Thorsen. My uncle is Charley Lochting."

Her face brightened. She crinkled her nose. "Charley?"

"Yeah, a year ago at Octoberfest, you asked him to dance, and he was so embarrassed he didn't know the steps that he promised to learn and meet you today."

"Yes, he apologized." She sighed. "He was kind of *emotional*." She peered over toward Ben, then around the hall. "Where is he? I thought he would come."

So, I told her about your amputation, Uncle Charley. How you asked me to go in your place and how Ben was recording everything. Her shoulders slumped, but when I told her you made me take dancing lessons, her eyes sparkled, and she laughed.

Here's the amazing part, Uncle Charley. I asked about her mother—was she okay?—because you said she might be ill.

She perked up and chuckled. "Mom? Oh, she's great. But last year, she wrecked her car and hurt her back. She's a terrible driver. This makes my dad crazy—he's an engineer with General Motors. She was in severe pain but wouldn't miss Octoberfest for anything. She insisted on going."

"But she's not here today."

"That's a whole other sad story. Mom grew up in Rüsselsheim, Germany. It's how my dad met her—at Opel. A few weeks ago, my Grandma Biedermann fell and broke her hip, so mom flew home to Frankfurt to help her."

Uncle Charley, I couldn't believe what she said—.

"Biedermann?" I asked. "What a coincidence. Uncle Charley—actually, my great uncle—told me last spring he had a girlfriend by that name in high school. She was a foreign exchange student."

Her eyes widened. "Shut *up*. That is so weird. Mom told me grandma was a foreign exchange student—here in Michigan. Is it possible…?"

"Uncle Charley said her name was Angelika, but everyone called her Schnuki."

"Oh my gosh, they still do, it's been her nickname *forever*. People still call her that."

"He told me they were in a car accident together."

"Yeah, she has a little scar under her right eye. She calls it her 'love mark.' My mother won't believe your uncle knows her. How crazy!"

Uncle Charley, I was totally brain-blasted. I didn't know what to think, let alone how to tell you, especially since Schnuki is bedridden. But you needed to know, since you once loved each other, and she was the main reason you asked me to keep your promise to Annika.

As for Anni, she is everything you describe and more, Uncle Charley, even though she just turned fifteen. If Schnuki was anything like her, I know how she captured your heart.

By the end of the final set, Ben and I met Anni's father Richard and her sister Katerina. We had so much fun, and Ben and I danced with both girls several times. I wish you had been there, but, at least, Ben captured it on video.

Since then, Anni and I have been texting, calling, and emailing. When her mom returns home, I've promised to visit. She lives near Pontiac. You expressed reservations over trying to locate Schnuki, but I promised Anni to email a photo of you. She plans to send them to Schnuki when she recovers. Anni also mentioned her grandfather died years ago. He was an architect. Schnuki is retired from the Faculty at Goethe University. She's a linguist.

Who knows? Maybe this will turn into something more serious. And for you too, Uncle Charley. For both our sakes, I hope so. I really do.

We'll post the video on YouTube.

Anni says hello and hopes you're better soon.

Larry

❃   ❃   ❃

Epilogue

At this point, the chain of emails ends. In seeking permission to have it published, I asked the relative who called me a few questions. I was curious whether Charley ever reunited with Angelika.

"No, they never did. She's in an elder living facility in Germany."

"What did Charley think of the video? Was he happy that, in some small measure, he kept his promise?"

"Well, the morning after Larry sent the email, Charley's secretary Doris came into work and found him sprawled on the floor, his new crutches next to him. She said when she left the previous evening, he was in the office, working. After his amputation, he was trying to catch up. The computer was on, and he had been checking his emails. His health was horrible—he was a heavy drinker—and must have suffered a heart attack. She called an ambulance, but there was no hope. Doris said she didn't know if he looked at Larry's message."

"What about Larry and Anni Schneider—are they still seeing each other?"

"Yes, they have struck up quite a match. He visits her almost every weekend, and he's taking her to her high school prom. The two of them and her family often go dancing at polka clubs around the northern suburbs of Detroit."

Made in the USA
Columbia, SC
06 June 2021

38999426R00134